BLACK SUN

A NOVEL
BY ANDREI LIVADNY

*Thank you FOR your support
and inspiration!
They mean so much to me,
Andrei Livadny.*

PHANTOM SERVER
BOOK#3

MAGIC DOME BOOKS

Black Sun
Phantom Server, Book # 3
Second Edition
Published by Magic Dome Books, 2017
Copyright © A. Livadny 2016
Cover Art © V. Manyukhin 2016
English translation © Irene Woodhead & Neil P. Mayhew 2016
All Rights Reserved
ISBN: 978-80-88231-10-3

This book is entirely a work of fiction.
Any correlation with real people or events is
coincidental.

TABLE OF CONTENTS:

CHAPTER ONE

DARG SYSTEM. THE ASTEROID BELT
ON BOARD THE FOUNDERS' FRIGATE

SPECKS OF LIGHT flickered in Liori's eyes.
Her personal module was awash with soft shadows. Candles burned on the little table next to the figurine of the dancing Drow. Droplets of wax thickened in mid-air, piling up fancy ripples of our memories — the memories of amazing universes where we'd faced danger only too eagerly. Carefree, we'd plunged into the thick of events, finding strength in the promise of a safe respawn, knowing that nothing irreversibly fatal could ever happen to us.

Our real-world lives had flashed past — miserable lives bound with wires, lives that still wriggled, doubled-up, inside in-mode capsules.

We'd felt young and strong regardless of our age. We seriously believed this would last forever. We had no idea that we'd already trespassed reality.

A dull jolt disrupted my thoughts. The bulkheads around me echoed with vibration. External view screens sprang to life, revealing the panorama of the Milky Way overflowing with fiery starlight. Slowly it began to shift as our ship was giving all its subsystems one final check in preparation for combat.

Liori's fathomless eyes glowed with fear and hope. You wouldn't think she'd long been dead. This was only her identity matrix, remembered and replicated by the nanites that were connected to my mind expander.

We'd been absolutely sure that we were testing a "game of the future" featuring exceptional authenticity levels. Daring and fearless we'd faced peril, innocent of the fact that our every step could have become our last. We'd had no idea that our new skills and discoveries were in fact the source of real-life knowledge which our neuroimplants had reported diligently back to Earth.

Crumbs of knowledge are akin to burning embers. They don't illuminate your way, only burn your mind.

"Zander," with a swipe of her eyes, Liori removed the icy starscape from the screens. The candlelight flared up, momentarily warm, then expired. "It's time."

Direct neurosensory contact mode disabled

The system message wiped away the mirage of Liori's room, dissolving her outline into thin air. I was standing by a low railing in cold crimson twilight.

Far within the depths of the launch deck, a

plasma torch exploded in a firework of sparks and tracers, sending long shadows dashing across the bulkheads. To my right, oval slits of power-shielded vacuum docks oozed darkness. One level below lay the delicately chiseled structures of docking pods housing fighter ships where the Haash techs hastily prepared our two Condors for a sortie.

The gravity elevator shaft popped open behind my back. I turned to the sound just in time to see Charon's lanky figure being extruded onto the platform.

A Haash. Sentient Xenomorph. Level 57. Pilot.

He was clad in an armored suit without a helmet. Short cable sleeves ran down his three-digit hands, ending in glistening connectors that Haash pilots used to tap into their *yrobs'* (fighter ships') systems.

"Zander?" the giant sentient lizard wheezed, tilting his head out of habit. "Zander, *wo'rhoom*?"

I didn't know that word. Before, I used to treat our communication difficulties as part of the game's setting. But now I knew for sure: whoever stood behind the avatars of "sentient xenomorphs" were no human beings in any shape or form.

Charon stood silent waiting for me to answer, his gaze keen. The pupils of his reptilian eyes narrowed. Hot wheezy breath escaped his half-open jaws.

Finally my semantic processor managed to translate the new word. Apparently, *wo'rhoom* meant someone who was about to "cross the line". Or, alternatively, someone who was "on edge".

Hah! You could say that! The Haash mentality had no provision for white lies. They're blunt and straightforward which is probably why they sometimes create this impression of being merciless.

Another popping sound echoed through the gallery, accompanied by a vectored current of air. "Oops, sorry! Wrong deck!"

"Max? Come over here, please," I crouched and asked in my best stern voice, "Who gave you permission to wander about the ship?"

The boy smiled shyly. "I'm looking for Liori. She promised to come and play with us. It's so funny when she appears out of the little floaty bits!"

Charon touched my shoulder, attracting my attention, then forwarded me the alarming image of the boy's Physical Energy indicator. It was flashing orange.

Mine by now was barely glowing, deep in the red. Ralph had taken to bed. Jurgen and Frieda were still on their feet. Arbido felt better than the rest of us which made sense: he'd logged in to Phantom Server much later than any of us.

Max was only five years old. He couldn't grasp the entire monstrosity of what was happening.

"Listen, Max," I said, "would you please go back to the other guys now? I'd like you all to take your seats and buckle up."

"Okay. But what if the girls don't listen?"

"Tell them I've made you group leader."

"No! For real?"

"Of course. Come on, off you go!"

Overjoyed, Max hopped and skipped toward the elevator.

Charon's gaze followed him, alarmed and

compassionate. Gray spots appeared on his rugged hide: a sign of extreme discomposure.

"We must hurry!" he barked. "You're all dying, all of you!"

* * *

THE FORCE ESCALATOR took us down to the docking pads.

We literally moved through time as we floated past numerous machines and devices whose purpose we had as yet failed to discern. Evidence of ancient battles kept drifting into my view: the many traces of fire exposure and the huge ragged patches tacked over the holes in the ship's hull. After the fall of Argus station, the Founders' frigate had become our new home — and its depths preserved the memory of its travels through space and of the ancient battles that we might never come to know of.

Only a few days ago, I'd have paid no heed to any of this. Some fire damage and traces of numerous repairs, so what! It was only a well-conceived game setting... or was it?

Now I knew that reality was much more complex than that. Our identities had been sent here via hyperspace, then integrated into an alien technosphere. We were capable of interacting with real-world objects, manipulating them even. That was exactly how the Founders had pioneered the Universe. Their technologies were way beyond our understanding, their principles lying in fields yet unknown to humanity. And still they worked.

Basically, the Darg system was just one insignificant location of the ancient interstellar network. It preserved a dozen derelict space stations ridden by darkness and clusters of debris drifting through space: evidence of bygone battles.

Our real-world controllers had been using us blindly. The technosphere of the long-gone civilization had suffered a lot of damage. It had remained static until we'd awoken it by collecting the remaining fragments and trying to manipulate them, often crudely and clumsily. Guided by the idea that we were part of a game world whose plot was based on this Founders myth, we hadn't asked unwanted questions. We'd raided the stations' perilous depths in search for the ancient AI modules; we'd implanted ourselves with what we'd believed to be cyber upgrades that choked us to death by the impossible authenticity of our experience.

The outlines of our two Condors and three of the Haash' *yrobs* bled through the mist: aerospace fighter ships frozen in the grip of delicate service towers. The flickering of their navigation lights cast a meager glow over their dented cargonite hulls.

Danezerath and Maurugael — or Danny and Mark as I called them these days, for Haash names were quite a mouthful — waited for us at the launch pad.

"The Daugoth Clan cargo ship is in position," Jurgen's voice echoed in the comm. "Foggs reports his assault groups ready for action."

"How's the Relic's energy levels?"

"I brought the reactors up to 12%. That should be enough for three minutes of power shield activation at full combat capacity."

"Acknowledged. We'll try not to allow it to come to that."

I turned to the Haash. Themselves ace pilots, today they had to play second fiddle. Storming of the Outlaws' abandoned base which was now controlled by ancient AIs called for some very special skills which only Liori and I had.

The situation was lethally simple.

Thousands of light years away from here, in the fading silence of deserted megalopolises back on Earth, the tinted plastic of our in-mode capsules flickered with the scarlet blinking of emergency lights inside. Our life support systems had been depleted, our body resources drained. Everything seemed abandoned. No one would visit us to replace life support cartridges. Humans had mysteriously disappeared. I couldn't offer a rational explanation to this, apart from suggesting that human civilization might have been flooded by a torrent of alien technologies.

It didn't matter anymore.

We only had one survival scenario. We had to go digital, just like the Founders had done. We had to sever the last remaining threads connecting us to Earth where the failure of our in-modes meant certain death for us all. It could now happen at any moment.

"Zander," Charon walked over to me and added softly, trying hard to find the right words to express his idea. "You need to use your old skills."

"You mean as if it's still a game?"

He nodded energetically, then headed for his *yrob*.

* * *

THE COCKPIT of my Condor was dark. The long curved shell of the empty pilot's seat was secured in the grip of its shock absorbers. The onboard life support was off. Traces of recent repairs were everywhere. Many of the screens were still covered in a gossamer web of cracks: we hadn't yet had time to replace them.

I lingered.

Zander, don't drag it out. Please.

I picked the tiny fleshfoam lid with my fingernail, revealing a mind expander connector and the dull glimmer of a cybermodule underneath.

In one practiced movement, I ejected it: the wafer-thin plate covered in neurochips. It felt like ripping a part of my soul out. Liori's voice faded. The mental sensation of our minds touching had disappeared.

The external neuronet has been disconnected.
-5 to your Mnemotechnics skill.

An instrument panel drive squeaked voraciously as a jury-rigged adapter clasped the offered cybermodule and sucked it into the ship's electronic innards.

Gray mist filled the air as nanites left my armored suit and streamed toward the pilot's seat, forming Liori's outline. The vague contour of her body began filling out: I could already make out her face and details of her gear.

"It feels so empty without you," her whisper scorched my heart. "Empty and cold."

No idea how she must have felt. If the ship were shot down now, all that would be left of her would be a handful of chips floating amid the debris. Liori knew this perfectly well. Still, there were no other options. We had to split. The Haash had no Mnemotechnics skill — and on my own I wouldn't be able to cover the target with Steel Mist. Neither would I be able to blanket their space defense sensors.

Instinctively I glanced at the translucent icons of my gaming interface. Charon had been right. Nothing had changed there. My char's levels, skills, abilities — everything functioned normally.

By learning the truth about ourselves, we had overstepped the boundaries of the game world. The question remained: who kept all the gaming attributes up and running? And why?

"Zander," Jurgen's voice in the speakers exploded the silence, "We're ready. Where the heck are you?"

"Go," Liori whispered. "I'm not saying goodbye."

Her image blurred as part of the nanites headed toward the ship's devices to form the heart of the fighter's cyber systems.

THE DOCKING POD slid out of the frigate's body and swung round. Launch deck structures flashed across the observation screens.

An oxygen mist rose, then dissipated slowly as the pod was being pumped free of atmosphere. Just beyond the force field I could make out the outlines of enormous rocks rotating slowly.

Acceleration threw me back into my seat.

Glittering with ice, asteroids swarmed toward me. I gave a correctional burst of the thrusters. The asteroids parted, speeding past, revealing a panorama of outer space.

The brownish sphere of Wearong, the system's gas giant, lit up the starboard screens. Far-off Darg the size of a pea glistened to my left.

Switching between view modes, my gaze lingered on the Relic. The Founders' frigate was shaped as a devilfish, the smooth curves of its six-hundred-foot body ripped by a random pattern of impacts. The ship was leaking radiation: the reactor blocks kept malfunctioning.

The Relic's power shields were barely glowing. The system kept streaming me its on-board systems status. Eleven of its electromagnetic coilguns (or ECGs as we called them) were ready for action, as well as one of the directional plasma generators.

The frigate was covered with wounds and badly patched up.

Two Wearongs accompanied it: amazing creatures indigenous to the planet of the same name. Capable of sentient actions, they were helping us of their own accord. Their giant translucent bodies glowed weakly as they banked into fiery spirals tracing the frigate's body, ready to shield it at any moment.

I came on course.

Liori's Condor steered a confident path next to mine. The Haash *yrobs* followed about fifteen hundred miles in our wake. The Relic's signature faded as the frigate lagged behind, maneuvering at a respectful distance from the targets. It would only join battle in the case of an emergency.

Having accelerated, I killed the engines. We now coasted, skirting a thin cloud of gas and dust.

Data kept pouring into my mind expander. There it was, the asteroid. About three miles long, it looked like a potato riddled with craters. One of the Outlaws' deserted bases, it had now been taken over by the Founders' AIs.

The unclear schematic picture gained brightness and detail. I could see the structures built around an ancient mine shaft: two oblong vacuum docks, locked and powdered with a fine layer of dust. Between them, the delicate openwork of a loading line glistened silver. The sloping bulk of a cargo ship loomed above the mine, adapted for defensive purposes.

Jurgen's intel proved correct. The Outlaws had used the space defense system developed by the Technologists clan. They'd concealed the controls deep within the ancient mine and set up their firing points on the asteroid's satellites: the large chunks of rock orbiting our main target. Together they formed the so-called "asteroid family" — a group of minor celestial bodies that shared the same orbit and speed as they traveled through space.

I was met by a surge of radiation. When your nervous system is at one with a ship's cyber modules, it feels like a gust of hot wind searing your skin, leaving behind the prickling sensation of a sore itch.

Our Condors' diaphragm hatches opened up, disgorging nanite colonies. Dispersing immediately, they formed a level-10 Steel Mist which concealed us from enemy sensors. Thus camouflaged, Liori and I began scanning our main target.

The asteroid's depths were threaded with a complex tunnel network that formed five underground levels.

"Zander? This looks like the right signature!"

A green marker lit up about five hundred feet below the asteroid's surface.

I began studying the object's power imprint, comparing it with the existing databases.

This was the Founders' artifact, no doubt about that. The only identity-copying hyperspace module, the last one in the Darg system!

This was our only chance to survive, the promise of a new life.

We closed in on the target. So far, everything was going to plan. Liori and I had to use our mnemonic abilities to paralyze the enemy's defenses, turning them into static targets for the Haash *yrobs*.

New details kept flooding in, filling out the picture.

But what the hell was that?

A cluster of bright red markers appeared out of nowhere within one light second from our position. Three cargo ships, about a hundred drones and... was that really a man-made object?

I banked away from the attacking course, then adjusted my speed to that of the nearest rock, camouflaging myself behind it. Liori mirrored my maneuver. The *yrobs* slowed down too, taking cover amid the asteroids.

My Condor's sensors kept collecting data non-stop until a picture of an enormous man-made space body formed in my mental view. It resembled a bundle of tumbleweed glistening with steel. My mind expander added detail. Now I could make out a gossamer exterior structure holding the body of a behemoth spaceship in the process of construction, several times larger than our frigate!

Was this a shipyard?

In the meantime, the three alien cargo ships had changed course and had opened their hatches, releasing hundreds of tons of cargonite ore into space.

The drones headed for the cloud of ore and began harvesting it with their power fields, delivering it to large energy bubbles. I saw the ore being melted within them, dissolving into clouds of Molecular Mist.

These were ancient technologies at their finest.

"Zander, what do you think you're doing?" Jurgen's voice rang out. Impatient, he'd used the laser beam communications. "Why aren't you attacking it?"

I streamed him the sensors' data. "I want you to kill the Relic's engines and activate the shields until further notice. We need some time to sort this out."

"That's not an option! I'm not changing course!" the Technologist snapped. I could detect desperate notes in his bravado.

Any delay could mean death for all of us. Literally. Still, a goliath technogenic object just next to our main target screwed up our plans. I refused to believe that the Outlaws could have built something like this "shipyard" themselves. It must have been created by the ancient AIs. They were the only ones who could manipulate industrial quantities of Molecular Mist.

I released a probe to form a general laser communication channel. "Liori? What d'you think?"

"The ship building process is being controlled by an AI," she replied. "But I don't think it has anything to do with the Outlaws' base. It's too far. Besides, I don't detect any activity in the area of the old mine."

Frieda sniffed in disbelief. "So you think they might ignore us as long as we don't approach the shipyard or attack it?"

"Don't you remember how maintenance robots behave?" Liori answered calmly. "They're always busy following their routines. They don't get distracted even if there's a combat going on just next to them."

"Weak reasoning," Charon snapped in his usual straightforward manner. "Our storming of the Outlaws base is bound to draw the AI's attention!"

This unexpected delay when we'd had our objective already in our sights was preying on our nerves.

"We can't go back!" Arbido's voice broke. "You know very well we have no choice!"

"I'm not aborting the attack. Danny," I addressed Danezerath whose *yrob* was equipped with an advanced tracking station, "do you register any data exchange between the shipyard and our target?"

"*Nowr*," he snapped in the negative.

Our radars were pockmarked with hundreds of bright red dots. I clenched my teeth without even realizing as I watched them. The clusters of markers were all heading for the shipyard. The cargo ships seemed to be leaving to bring another batch of cargonite ore. Soon their signatures faded, disappearing from sight.

The Founders' drones de-energized the power bubbles, spilling their contents into space. Molecular mist rose about the shipyard, forming an incandescent veil of gas that shielded it from our scanners.

We kept watching. Just as Liori had suggested, the Founders' drones minded their own business. They changed their formation, breaking into several groups, then commenced the next production stage, creating electromagnetic fields that compacted the incandescent substance.

This process was followed by a series of dull flashes.

The drones had just used the Object Replication command to create armor plates! I could clearly see the diamond-shaped segments drift through space, oozing heat, until they fused into small formations.

I had to agree with Charon. Our storming of the mine was bound to attract the shipyard's AI's attention. But what did it have to offer against our Relic? There were no large ships around. All of Avatroid's forces were now tied up chasing whatever was left of the Eurasia Colonial Fleet.

"I've got an idea!" Jurgen exclaimed.

"Go ahead."

"Relic's tractor beams! I can use them to grab the asteroid and tow it to the edge of the system. And whoever's holed up inside, we can sort them out nice and quiet later, without attracting the AI's attention!"

"That's logical," Charon agreed.

"Good. That's what we'll do, then," I had no time to mull over alternatives. "Take your positions! Don't aggro the drones! And stay away from the shipyard!"

* * *

I HAD THE FIRST of the asteroid's satellites in my sights.

The oversized boulder kept growing rapidly, its depths concealing a compact reactor. Scanners reported laser and electromagnetic guns outside.

My heart palpitated but I couldn't help it.

The ancient alien drones were buzzing around just one light second away. They scurried amid the clouds of Molecular Mist, collecting the slowly cooling armor segments and transporting them toward the vessel under construction.

My Condor's systems kept scanning communication frequencies but detected no data exchange between the shipyard and the old mine.

The communication scanner clicked, switching between frequencies. A distant voice broke through, distorted by interference,

"This is Eurasia Station! Mayday! We're under attack from an unidentified enemy! Our shields are failing! We're losing atmosphere! Mayday!"

New quest alert: Eurasia Rescue!

Find a way to stop Avatroid. Reward: your relationship with the Colonial Fleet command will improve considerably. You will be able to trade with the station and use its equipment to repair your ships.

"Liori? Did you hear that?"

"I did! I also got a quest!"

We zeroed in on our target. Our Condors circled it rapidly, intersecting each other's orbits. Our guns were silent. We attacked the space defense unit using nanites alone, controlling them with our Mnemotechnics skill. The microscopic robots penetrated the defense installations, blinding their sensors and disrupting their data exchange, paralyzing their kinematics. The enemy batteries began sporting tags which read,

System Failure
Critical Damage
Equipment Failure

This one was done for! We changed course, bringing the next satellite into our crosshairs. The faint signature of the Relic reappeared just within my scanners' range. The frigate was heading toward our main target.

The Haash *yrobs* stormed the paralyzed defense unit. They had two minutes to scorch its gun nests.

Liori and I repeated our attack.

System Failure
Critical Damage
Equipment Failure

The second satellite had been deactivated. Now that we'd made a dent in the enemy's defenses, we headed for the ancient mine shaft. Our Condors were still concealed by Steel Mist. I wish I could say the same about the Haash *yrobs* which now came under long-range fire. True, the enemy's firing arcs were awkward but still it was hardly pleasant.

We didn't meet with much resistance. No one had expected us to attack. At the moment, everything was going to plan, but still the proximity of the shipyard made me uneasy.

The Relic kept accelerating, its signature glowing brighter with every moment. It was closely followed by the bright dot of a cargo ship transporting the assault groups of the Daugoth clan. The moment the frigate grabbed the asteroid with its tractor beams, Vandal and Foggs were to take their men inside.

I was a bit worried about the old spaceship that the Outlaws had turned into a permanent fire position. I marked it as target. Unfortunately, we didn't have enough nanites so we were forced to continue orbiting the asteroid looking for a structure rich in cargonite suitable for utilizing.

Finally, we found one. The small crater lit up with a series of flashes as we began the nanite replication process. A system message appeared in my mental view,

Your nanite stocks have been refilled

I focused on the entrance to the mine and sent the nanites in to disable the gun control module and prevent it from coordinating the satellites' operation.

Now the old spaceship. We dashed to attack it — apparently, just in time. Our sensors detected two batteries of plasma generators. Their signatures glowed brighter with every second as the weapons accumulated enough energy for a volley.

Our coil guns ripped through the ship's hull, then breached the shields of its power module. It took but a split second. An explosion gutted the old vessel, ejecting the hatches and gun ports out into open space. The ship's docking nodes failed. With a jolt, they released its mangled body, sending it into an uncontrollable drift.

I took my bearings.

The Haash had done their job too, littering space with clouds of debris. No casualties.

Four minutes till the Relic's arrival.

* * *

"GOOD JOB!" Liori's Condor floated up to my side, taking up the position of a wingman.

I switched to autopilot, unsealed my helmet and used the back of my gloved hand to wipe the perspiration from my forehead.

My fingertips twitched. I'd never noticed this before.

A couple more minutes, then everything would be over. Our new life, what was it going to be like? In a moment, the Relic would engage the asteroid with her tractor beams and drag it to the star system's edge. There we'd mop up the old mine and get to the Founders' device discovered by the Outlaws. We would then use it to digitize our identities. Basically, we were about to conquer death in emulation of the ancient alien race.

"Scanners report an unidentified signature!"

Danezerath's report brought me back to reality. My visor's drives squeaked, sealing the helmet. Both my mind expander and metabolic implant went into overdrive.

Just next to the shipyard, the cloud of diamond-shaped armor segments revealed large clots of swirling matter. The Founders' drones stopped whatever they'd been doing and surrounded these new formations, pumping them up with energy.

I did a quick evaluation of their power imprints and flinched. "They're Phantom Raiders!"

I'd been the only one "lucky" enough to witness the alien ships' materialization just before they had attacked Argus. You just couldn't mistake it for anything else.

"Give me one minute!" Jurgen's voice pleaded in the earphones. "I've already activated the tractor beams!"

"Foggs," I snapped, "dock your ship in the Relic! Charon, I want you to cover Liori and myself!"

Flash!

My Condor's optical multipliers streamed the frightful scene into my mind as a fighter ship complete with an AI module loomed out of the incandescent cloud, fire scales still flaking off its armor. Its 10-megawatt shields glowed, betraying their presence; its hull bristled with gun ports, its bow reflected the phantom light of its antimatter engines. The Raider began to accelerate.

I double-checked its course. It was heading for the Relic!

"Just one more moment!" interference drowned out Jurgen's voice. "I'm busy with the asteroid!"

The vicinity of the shipyard was lit up with yet more arrivals. A volley from a giant laser system missed the Relic by a hair's breadth, hitting the chaotically rotating asteroid instead.

The enormous rock, already deorbited by the frigate's tractor beams, spewed flaming slag into space.

186,000 miles was a perfect effective fire range for a weapon firing at the speed of light!

"Jurgen, try to maneuver out of their arc of fire! Take cover behind the asteroids!"

Too late.

A fresh volley hit the frigate. In order to activate the tractor beams, Jurgen had to transfer part of the energy from the shields. The frigate's power fields surged, then extinguished, unable to absorb all the damage. The laser beam sliced through the frigate's hull. Luckily, it wasn't fatal: the impact zone was one of the ship's already-damaged depressurized areas which luckily prevented an explosion. The ship's hull was peppered with about a dozen fire-polished breach holes, not large caliber even, but at least it stayed in one piece.

The two Wearongs headed forward, blocking the danger zone and taking the next volley onto themselves.

"Jurgen, get the ship out, now!"

The Relic's bow glowed with the activated plasma engines. The ship accelerated smoothly, heading toward Argus. This must have been the best decision. For a while at least, they could use the destroyed space station as cover.

The Wearongs (who now resembled two gigantic medusas, their translucent bodies permeated by red-hot veins throbbing with electricity) blocked another volley, then began to fade away. Their glow was rapidly losing its intensity.

The Relic spat back from her main calibers, obliterating the nearest asteroids in a cloud of rock debris which shielded her from the enemy, forcing the Raiders to abort the firefight in order to close in.

Unexpectedly, the Raiders split. Five of them continued their assault while the rest turned back toward the shipyard. Why would they do that?

Their signatures gave the answer. They looked pale and distorted. Did that mean that the shipyard's AI had failed to build fully-fledged combat ships with whatever Molecular Mist it had available for armor plate replication?

"The Raiders' antimatter engines are at 30%!" Liori confirmed my suspicions. "They don't have enough antiprotons!"

"Attack!"

* * *

WE'D BEEN just one step away from a new life, and what now?

Five Phantom Raiders were coming for us head-on. The rest had been swallowed up by the clouds of Molecular Mist swirling around the shipyard. They'd left in search of more nanites but they were bound to be back!

Even despite their replication faults, the enemy's combat characteristics were way out of our league. Both Liori and myself had already encountered them in battle and knew well what they were capable of. Still, we'd come on a lot since then. We'd done some decent leveling and acquired new abilities. If only we could prevent the Phantom Raiders from getting to the Relic!

Slowly the frigate accelerated, heading for Argus. Tethered by tractor beams, the asteroid obediently followed in her wake.

I squeezed every ounce of power out of the

engines. We needed to smoke the Raiders ASAP! Liori by my side held a confident course while the Haash *yrobs* intentionally lagged behind, maneuvering non-stop. Our Haash friends hadn't wavered under fire: they were diverting the enemy's attention to themselves, allowing us to regroup for a surprise attack.

The Raiders continued to close in. Still, their scanners couldn't see us yet, their sensors powerless against the Steel Mist.

Ten thousand miles. Seven... six.

I nudged my thrusters into a strafe. My Condor was still closing with the enemy while shifting to one side. I kept a bead on the Raiders, waiting for the right firing angle that could allow me to attack them all at once.

Got it. Their outlines began to superimpose. I opened fire from all four coil guns.

We were exposed. Spewing fire, my ship strafed to one side, leaving a large plasma arc fading in her wake.

The Raiders' shields weakened sharply, absorbing damage. Liori's Condor was strafing in the opposite direction.

The Raiders' AIs didn't like our three-dimensional crossfire! They became nervous and left the Haash alone, reacting instantly by switching their targets.

Liori and I were reversing toward the shipyard, picking the targets off one by one.

The AIs hadn't dared leave us in their rear. They about-faced. Their shields were virtually dead, barely glowing at one megawatt and unable to restore. They'd channeled all their power to their weapons, hoping to wipe us out in one fell swoop.

The Haash jumped at their chance and opened up rapid bursts of laser fire. The already-compromised power shields of two of the Raiders flashed and went out. Crimson scars covered the ships' hulls; then they exploded in a shower of debris.

Their antimatter engines blew up, blinding my sensors momentarily.

The two leaders were toast! The remaining three were left without shields. I sliced through one with my ECGs. Liori shot down another one. Only one last Raider managed to escape: maneuvering dangerously, it ducked into the safety of the Molecular Mist.

* * *

THE AMMO LOADING INDICATOR kept blinking.

Sweat trickled down my spine. My light onboard suit was soaked.

Switching your mind expander to overdrive always costs you. The seconds of combat burn your body's resources, followed by acute bouts of sickness when reality seems to lag. Still, it doesn't last long.

We'd shot down four of the Phantom Raiders. My Condor had gotten away with minimum damage: weakened shields, a couple of red-hot scars still glowing crimson on her hull plus the scorched sensors which had already been replaced by the backups.

I killed the speed and surveyed the scene. The shipyard was a meager seven thousand miles away. Thin clouds of slowly cooling Molecular Mist were camouflaging me from the enemy but it was a mixed blessing as my scanning range had been decimated. Liori's Condor was nowhere to be seen. Gremlins prevented my communications with the Haash.

One thing I could detect very well was the Relic's power imprint. Which was bad news. The ship was still within the asteroid belt and leaving it wasn't going to be easy.

An unread message icon persistently blinked within my interactive visor. Mechanically I opened it,

You've received a new level!
You've received +1 to the following skills:
Piloting of Small Spacecraft, 11 (+0.93)
Combat Maneuvering, 13 (+0,74)
Your Navigation skill is at 15 (+0,3)

So the in-game interface was still functioning. Apparently, we'd have to learn to live with it. "Liori?"

No answer. Where was she now?

I maneuvered my Condor along the edge of the artificial cloud enveloping the shipyard, looking for a gap in the incandescent molecular mist large enough to take stock of the situation. No Raiders in sight. Plenty of drones scurrying around though, plus occasional clusters of armor plates that they'd failed to deliver to the ship under construction.

The location where our asteroid had just been was now aglow with silent explosions as its absence had affected other asteroids' orbits, causing them to collide and crumble into red-hot boulders.

Finally, the Relic was within my line of sight, allowing me to employ laser communications. "Jurgen, report!"

"We've got about a dozen breach holes but we'll

live," he replied instantly. "The tractor beams survived!"

"What's with the asteroid?"

"Unstable energy emissions. An intense heat imprint. I think that the impact followed by the acceleration might have caused damage to some equipment. The artifact it still there but I really couldn't tell you whether it's still operable. Foggs and Vandal are itching to find out."

"Tell them to wait. You can't send assault groups down the mine yet. It's not safe. Can you contact the Haash?"

"I can indeed."

"Tell Charon I want them to cover the Relic. Whatever it takes. What's with the Wearongs?"

"Dead."

"You sure?"

What a shame. Such amazing mysterious creatures.

"Frieda has lost mnemonic contact with them. Our sensors detected two disintegrating signatures. I just hope they have a respawn point back on Wearong somewhere," he didn't sound too sure.

"Has Liori contacted you?"

"No," he sounded surprised and anxious. "Isn't she with you?"

"She was. We lost each other. She must have chased after a Raider. I'll go and look for her. I might check what happened to the other Raiders while I'm at it."

"Zander, be careful!"

He didn't need to tell me. I just hoped that today Lady Luck had sided up with us for a change.

I approached the shipyard.

The gossamer structure I'd noticed earlier turned out to be part of a much larger installation that counted dozens of shipyards. An entire fleet was currently being built there.

The sheer scope of it humbled you. The Outlaws had resurrected Avatroid without pausing to consider the consequences of their daring experiment. And when they finally had, it had been too late.

I scanned the ships' bodies. To my surprise, I detected neither sign of bustling activity inside nor the presence of complex equipment.

What could that mean? Could Avatroid lack all the necessary knowledge? Does that imply that he too had to study the Founders' technological legacy to fill in the gaps, just like we had?

"Zander!" Liori's Condor slipped out of the crimson cloud just in front of me. "I've found them! Eleven Raiders! They're heading for the Relic!"

THE FOUNDERS' FIGHTER SHIPS sliced through the dark. Liori was right: they were heading for the frigate. They moved fast, concealed within the plumes of Molecular Mist.

Although our Mnemotechnics skill put us at a slight advantage, our enemy was better armed and protected with their 10-megawatt shields. They'd managed to find the necessary source material and replenish their active matter stocks for the ships' antimatter units.

Two against eleven? A chill ran down my spine.

What was it Charon had said? *You need to use*

your old skills. His words pierced my mind. "Liori, we should attack them with nanites, then retreat toward the shipyard."

"We can't do it! Nanites can't penetrate their force fields!"

"I know! We're going to use Molecular Mist," I forwarded her my mind expander data.

"You're crazy..."

We banked in synch, approaching the Raiders. Still safely camouflaged, we breezed through their formations without opening fire, leaving their AIs dumb with amazement.

Replication!
Replication!
Replication!

A trail of newborn nanites followed in our wake. The molecular cloud created by the drones made perfect material for nanite replication.

We accelerated sharply, breaking off and heading toward the nearest building dock.

"Liori, max out the shields! Full energy to the stern hemisphere!"

I activated Plasma Blast.

A blinding sheet of fire cut through the Raiders' formation, predictably followed by a powerful explosion as the nearest clouds of Molecular Mist detonated with the impact.

The drones' markers blinked and expired. Swirling jets of plasma spewed into the shipyard, cutting through the unfinished ships and melting the gossamer structures of the docks.

Our own shields were hovering dangerously

close to zero. I struggled to stay on course. Debris whirled past, tumbling uncontrollably. The translucent windows of my interface flashed a constant flow of messages.

The Raiders, where were they?

I hurried to employ thrusters, steering my Condor into a narrow gap between two white-hot crossbeams which suddenly spattered a hail of molten steel, hit by heavy laser guns.

We zipped through the open-work structures and swung round, scanning the area non-stop.

Two of the Raiders were down. The others had survived the Plasma Blast but lost their shields and received minor damage in the process. They didn't chase after us. Instead, they restored their shields and went for the frigate again!

Dammit! My plan had failed to stop them!

Quest alert: Eurasia Rescue. Quest completed!

By destroying the shipyard's control module, you've diverted Avatroid's attention to yourself, forcing him to abort his attack on the dying Eurasia station. It now has a chance to-

I didn't read any further. "Charon, nine Raiders are heading toward the Relic!"

"Roger that," the Haash pilot's voice barely cut through the interference. The area was at the mercy of a magnetic storm.

The space around us was chock full of cargonite debris.

"Commence nanite replication!"

In two brief flashes, our ships were safely blanketed within a new layer of Steel Mist.

"There's no way Avatroid's fleet can get here soon!" Liori's voice rang with victory. "It'll take them three hours at least! And now that we've destroyed the shipyard's AI, it can't make more Phantom Raiders! We've smoked over a hundred drones. I've done four levels!"

"I've done five."

"Zander, you need to invest in Disintegration. We really need it now!"

Good advice. We had very few ECG projectiles left and mid-range lasers were no good against our enemy's shields.

There was no time to think it over. We headed off to intercept them. The Phantom Raiders' antimatter engines were way superior to our weaker plasma units, but the sheer amount of junk littering space didn't allow them to attain their full capacity.

We closed in.

Our emotions faded. The tension was palpable. The distance between us continued to shrink. The Haash wing couldn't tackle nine lethal fighters. We had to split the enemy, destroying or at the very least engaging some of them, preventing them from reaching the Relic.

Liori tuned into my idea and began lagging behind, our mnemonic channel offering us a silent means of communication.

A small asteroid came into my crosshairs, complete with a few Raiders skirting it.

Disintegration!

I banked behind a pre-chosen rock, and still my shields dropped all the way down to zero.

The asteroid was reduced to atoms.

My ship's hull was red-hot. Sensors kept beeping anxiously. I activated the emergency decompression. One less thing to worry about.

The enemy shields were down. Liori charged.

Her Condor traced a complex path through space as she fired non-stop, not letting the Raiders' AIs restore their shields.

One of the Raiders dissolved in a flash; another's hull was ripped open by tracers. A weak glow escaped the structural damage — she'd hit the power unit!

The remaining Raiders turned around. Four of them came for me, three went for Liori.

Maneuvering desperately, I broke through their formation, hurrying to her rescue. I got one of the Raiders with my ECGs, showered another one with lasers and sent nanites to attack the third one. I didn't even try to finish them off but banked into a steep turn — I still had four more AIs tailing me!

We were closing head-on. I focused on their leader, bringing him into my crosshairs.

Disintegration!

Simultaneously two heavy lasers sliced through my Condor. Control panels began exploding all around the cockpit. Navigation equipment and engine controls were down. Spinning uncontrollably, my ship began drifting away from the scene.

I managed to swipe my eyes across the remains of the downed Raider, sending a quick succession of mnemonic commands,

Replication
Emergency Repairs

The latter was an ability I'd acquired when I'd perused the Technologists Clan's databases.

Immediately nanites set to work with damage control.

I was drifting.

Four of the Raiders had been destroyed but the surviving ones accelerated again and closed on the Relic. They didn't bother chasing after us to finish us off. We were neither worth their time nor their power resources.

"Zander?" Liori's voice rang with anxiety.

"I'm fine. You? Any damage?"

"I've burned my reverse thrusters. The ship looks like a sieve. But it's nothing critical. Engines are still working."

There, I found her! Her reactor was in overload, leaking radiation. Her injuries were much worse than I'd thought. "I want you to try to get to the Relic's docking pods," I said. "I'll catch up with you. My controls are almost restored. Don't engage anymore. The Haash can finish them off without us now."

"Zander, I-"

"Just do it! Please!"

We both knew this was a touch-and-go situation. If her reactor failed, there'd be no respawn for her.

"All right... Promise you won't be long... Make sure you follow me... You promised..."

Her voice distanced, consumed by the crackling of interference.

CHAPTER TWO

ALL I COULD DO during the ten minutes it had taken to fix the ship was watch helplessly as the Raiders went for the Relic. More drones and three cargo ships appeared from the shipyard and headed for the frigate: reinforcements!

The Relic's heavy ECGs spewed fire three times in a row, downing the cargo ships, then fell silent. They didn't have enough energy. The tractor beams were consuming most of it.

Space was rife with battle as the Haash confronted both the Raiders and the drones. Still, they were outnumbered badly. I put my foot down. Hold on, guys! Steady just a bit more!

"I can't see them! Where are they? Where are they-" an animal growl rose to a scream of agony.

They'd downed Danezerath! The remains of his *yrob* sped past me.

I entered the dogfight head-on, attacking the nearest Raider and planting the remaining ammo into the skirt of its cockpit. Molten metal splattered everywhere. The Raider's AI attempted to change course — too late. His deadly ship kept accelerating, strafing haphazardly, until it rammed one of the drifting cargo ships and disappeared in a splash of flames.

The laser pulses of three Phantom Raiders continued to rake the Relic's hull. The frigate shuddered with a number of internal explosions. Her armor burst in places, gutted by decompression. Ugly long gaps in the hull spewed tornadoes of murky discharge and clusters of technogenic debris.

Jurgen wasn't replying. The frigate's signature was crimson and deformed.

Her shields were down. The Relic drifted on, her engines dead, as she sacrificed her last remaining watts of energy to the towing beams. The three-mile asteroid obediently followed in the frigate's wake. Still, its path was littered with debris which continuously collided with the asteroid's surface, demolishing the last remaining structures of the ancient mine shaft.

My ECGs choked and shut up. I only had one charged accumulator left complete with two localizer lasers connected to it. The rest of my weapons were out of commission.

We were one step away from immortality and a hair's breadth away from death.

Still, there were only three Raiders left.

I accelerated. I'd managed to burn my shock absorbers so now every maneuver pinned my body to the seat. The Raiders noticed me and scattered. You didn't have to be a mind reader to second-guess their actions. Two of them would try to attack me while the third one would wait for an opportunity to finish me off.

I steered my ship within inches of the Relic, aligning myself with her as I pierced the murky clouds of debris.

"Someone, cover me!" I wheezed. "I'm engaging!"

I shot up vertically. My vision darkened. The mangled ship's outline on the screens keeled over and began to distance itself. I had one Raider on a collision course while another one was trying to intercept me as I maneuvered. His laser beams traced past, barely missing my engines.

An *yrob* flashed past, hacked into several pieces, its frayed remains of fiber optic cables sparking. The scorched stump of the pilot's seat trailed behind, tethered by a cable.

I passed the Raider head-on, just managing to get in a burst from my lasers. The two others flanked me from behind. They weren't firing yet, trying to save power. Very soon they'd be able to shoot me at point blank.

Take that, you bastards!

I lingered, waiting for the right moment. Just as the Raiders were about to fire, I released a cloud of nanites and sent them a mental image.

Object Replication!

Space exploded.

My mind went blank. One Raider less. Still speeding, he'd rammed the swarm of cargonite pellets head-on. The second one had managed to swerve, avoiding an inevitable collision.

The Relic's signature was dying away as the frigate had reached the edge of the asteroid belt heading for Argus. But was there anyone still alive on board?

"Jurgen... Arbido... Frieda... anyone! Talk to me!"

Immediately the frigate's tractor beams croaked. The three-mile rock tumbled and collided with a few smaller boulders. The collisions threw it off course. Slowly the asteroid began to drift away from the collision site, heading back into the asteroid belt.

The two Phantom Raiders were still following me. Space around me seethed with countless collisions. The stars in my screens faded, obscured by clouds of debris. I had no nanites left nor could I replicate them: the suspended mixture of fine rock dust and incandescent gas was not good for nanite replication.

I killed speed, forcing my ship to dive under the chaotically spinning body of a cargo ship.

The Raiders whizzed past, unable to react in time, then swung round, looking for their evasive target.

They didn't have it easy, either. Their power field emitters were also down, their hulls planished with impacts. Expert warriors, the Haash had put up a good fight. Pale light seeped through numerous breaches in the Raiders' armor. Their antimatter units had had it. They were destabilizing.

I was going to kill them, then catch up with the asteroid and see if I couldn't get to the artifact. There was no other option.

The Raiders had located me and followed my radiation trail, the two of them. My reactor was damaged, about to explode at any moment, but I wasn't even considering ejecting it. I had to make it last as long as I could. The alternative was a long slow death drifting through space.

I skirted the cargo ship and went into a spin, preventing the Raiders from opening fire. I then ducked into a huge hole in its hull and swung round, reducing speed with a few calculated pulses.

The enemy kept tailing me but my radiation trail wasn't a reliable target — rather more a guideline.

The Raiders' signatures kept approaching. I spent my last nanites on activating Piercing Vision. My ship's sensors had been scorched dead, the cockpit depressurized. Many of the control panels had melted.

There they were.

They were still keeping together. The leader turned toward the cargo ship as if sensing the danger coming from within its breach holes, trying to second-guess my actions.

The other Raider's guns were down but its shield emitters still worked. It was now trying to stretch its sickly power field to cover its leader.

I shouldn't let this happen! My lasers couldn't breach their shield.

Thanks to Piercing Vision, my mind expander could "see" the targets well. The nanites kept streaming information but their quantities were dwindling. The Raiders couldn't see me: my radiation trail created a shapeless blind spot.

I had but a split second to come to a decision.

My thrusters cast a fiery glow onto the ship's hull. Slowly I turned my Condor round. Her portside was now facing the breach. A powerful side thrust pushed my ship out to face the enemy.

Fire!

Molten metal spewed everywhere. Deep scars

started to glow on the Raider's hull, breathing heat, like the scores left by a clawed gauntlet.

My last accumulator was dead. My ship strafed to one side: mangled and defenseless, stripped of her technogenic power. The overheated reactor gushed radiation everywhere.

I didn't expect another explosion. The apprehension of my own doom had tricked me into desperation. But I'd smoked the last Raider, after all!

Both of us dissolved in a circle of fire. A torrent of debris shot past. Some of it hit me, sending my Condor into an uncontrollable spin.

The accumulator indicators glowed weakly. I tasted blood in my mouth. I didn't feel as if I'd won. I felt empty inside. I could barely move. Communications were dead. I had almost no thruster fuel left.

THE ASTEROID that used to be the Outlaws' base continued to drift through the asteroid belt. I navigated my disfigured ship past countless rocks and blocks of ice of every shape and size, catching up with it slowly but surely.

I released the last remaining probe. The spherical device headed toward the structure's vacuum dock gates. They'd been gutted. Deep cracks had ripped through the ancient mine's framework.

In expectation of the probe's report, I plotted the trajectories of the nearest asteroids when I detected a Condor drifting nearby.

"Liori!"

Her ship was dead, its reactor block ejected.

Most armor plates had been destroyed, the grid of her Condor's support beams resembling a skeleton's ribcage.

While the probe was busy studying the ancient mine, I swung my ship around and closed with the drifting ship.

"Hold on, sweetheart... just hold on, my love," I mouthed non-stop. *Sweetheart, darling, my love* — and I used to think that these words were hopelessly dated and meaningless!

The automatic docking system kicked in, connecting the two crippled ships with a short pressurized hose.

Her cockpit was pitch-black. All the control panels were fused solid. Her empty pilot's seat had been sliced in two by a laser beam. Tiny droplets of hydraulic liquid floated around it in zero gravity, having escaped the emergency anti-G system.

I received no feedback from the nanites that used to make up Liori's avatar. She had used them all up when she'd run out of both ammo and power.

I refused to believe this was the end of her. A lump in my throat prevented me from breathing. I felt like screaming. Still, I clenched my teeth and perched on the seat's edge, scanning the jury-rigged adapter.

Her cyber module was deformed. Its neurochips sported fire damage. Right here and now it was pretty impossible to tell whether Liori's identity matrix had survived the predicament.

I used a laser from my repair kit to cut out a fragment of the control panel with her cyber module still in it, then placed it gingerly into my inventory. I cast one last look at the silent cockpit and began retracing my steps back on board my own ship.

During the last few days, I kept getting these moments of absolute confusion. My life in other game worlds had been exciting and simple: trouble-free. Words like *grief, desperation* or *loss* had never entered my vocabulary. They'd had no meaning. Now that they'd revealed their true sense, my heart struggled to accept them.

The world had changed forever. Your past was dead; your future wasn't born yet. All you had was this now-moment and the fire-polished fragments of a cybermodule in your inventory. Plus the faint hope that you could still recover the bytes containing the digitized soul of the woman you loved.

* * *

I WAS CLOSING IN on the asteroid. I suppressed all irrelevant thoughts. First I had to get to the Founders' artifact, then take it back to the Relic and restore the cybermodule containing Liori's identity. Together we'd be able to work out what was going on, then find our way around our new environment.

The target loomed ever closer. The data collected by the probe seemed positive. The ancient artifact was still functioning. The numerous impacts had damaged the asteroid, creating a plethora of deep cracks in its surface which considerably simplified my task. Basically, the asteroid was only held together by the mine's powerful superstructure made of cargonite alloy.

I was really pressed for time. The asteroid belt was growing denser. Hundreds of rocks of every shape and size crowded the asteroid, most of them capable of dealing the final blow which could disintegrate the ancient facility.

The reactor had stabilized at 30%. I forwarded all of its power to the shields. Manipulating the maneuvering thrusters, I steered the ship into a dark crevice and began threading my way through the web of distorted and degraded support structures.

My speed kept dropping. I couldn't help that. My path grew more littered with my every turn. Fractured walls revealed glimpses of mangled rooms — once embedded into the rock and now ripped to pieces. My mind expander greedily absorbed all available data. This was where the Outlaws had built Avatroid!

There must have been loads of precious data still left in the ruins of their cybernetic laboratories, like nanite activation codes which could open new areas of nanite technologies yet unknown to me.

The sensors kept beeping anxiously. The walls of the crevice kept shrinking ever closer — but I now was a mere hundred feet away from my target!

I engaged reverse thrusters, then stopped. The ship couldn't go any further. I had to get out.

The rock walls quivered treacherously as new cracks traced across them. In places, they dissolved in soundless rockfalls filling the narrow space with sharp fragments of stone that floated in the void, endlessly colliding.

My armored suit wasn't going to take it. I had to find a different way. I activated navigation lasers and cleared the shortest path with a series of pulses. With a circular motion of my guns, I cut an opening in the nearest mangled bulkhead that offered access to the surviving premises.

The docking hose hissed, expanding. The plasma torches snapped into action.

I touched a sensor, disabling my suit's security harness. I was just about to get up when a premonition of impending danger assaulted my nerves.

The signal had come from the probe still left outside. One of the many asteroids was on a direct collision course!

It crashed.

The walls of the crevice began to close around my ship. The force field throbbed. I heard a screeching sound as the ship's stabilizers were being compressed into its hull.

My mind writhed in agony under the direct neurosensory contact with the ship's systems as if it was my own flesh being crushed.

My mind crashed. Mercifully, it expired.

GRADUALLY I came round.

The data I received from my implants was sparse. The area around me was saturated with radiation. My mangled Condor drifted amid the rocky remains of the destroyed asteroid. Not a single active power implant within the scanners range, meaning that the Founders' device was no more. We'd lost it for good.

My mind expander kept piecing data together, connecting the ship's surviving modules. I managed to stabilize the reactor at 10%. One of the force field generators offered all of 0.3 megawatts. This was all the protection I currently could offer against radiation and any further impacts.

I wasn't going to give up so easily.

I set the communications automatic repeat to *Call Relic* and switched to manual controls. I had to get out of this cesspit. Then I'd have to scan each and every one of the asteroid's fragments while I still had time. Very soon Avatroid's fleet would be here. You never know, the Founders' artifact might have simply been deactivated with the impact.

I steered the ship slowly and gingerly past the larger fragments until I entered a safe orbit around the swirling mass of debris.

Liori's Condor drifted nearby. I sent some nanites on board her de-energized ship with a dozen micro nuclear batteries I'd robbed from the survival kit. They were going to activate the on-board scanners. With two sets of scanners, I could finish the job much quicker.

An incoming call, finally! I had the frigate on the line. Judging by the signal's bearings, the Relic was still heading for Argus!

"Zander? Where are you?" Jurgen's hoarse voice sounded first, followed by a murky image. He looked even more gaunt and weary than normal.

"I'm at the asteroid. It's been destroyed."

"So it's the end of us, then?" he asked bluntly.

"I'm just trying to scan it. I'll stay here for as long as it takes. How's everything?"

"The Haash have respawned. They've lost their *yrobs*. The Wearongs are dead. The children are all right. Their room was well protected. What do you want us to do now?"

"Just don't lose hope."

"Is Liori with you?"

"She is. Her cybermodule's been damaged. She's incommunicado at the moment."

"Zander? I think the artifact is ruined."

This wasn't an easy conversation. "If I don't find it, we might try to contact the Oasis."

"The hybrid? You think he might help?" Jurgen's voice perked up. "Do you want me to go there and speak to him?"

"No. I'll give him a call from here. I have Oasis within my direct line of vision. You take care of the Relic. Do whatever repairs are necessary and check the life support. Give Charon a ship: let him go collect the fragments of their *yrobs*. I'll take care of Liori's Condor. Tell Charon that I'd also appreciate his bringing any fragments of the Raiders he can find. We need to study them."

"Just what are you hoping for? Tell me!"

He'd lost all optimism. I could read it in his stare.

"If the artifact's destroyed, we'll have to build something similar," I added a note of confidence to my voice. "Between my Mnemotechnics and your Technologist skill, we might come up with something."

Jurgen sat up. "Then you should come back! No good wasting time taking stupid risks!"

"There're loads of fragments of various devices here. I've never heard about most of them. I'll keep searching for the artifact while leveling up my skills. Creating artificial neuronets will demand a very high Mnemotechnics level."

"Avatroid's fleet is coming," Jurgen reminded me.

"I know. Which is why I'm asking you to take

care of the frigate. I want you to dock her to the station and camouflage her signature. Tell Vandal and Foggs to check the Technologists Clan's quarters and search the debris for any data storage devices they might find. The Founders' technologies are the key. When I'm back, I'll need any information that might help me to level my skills and abilities."

"Zander, all this rushed leveling will kill you."

"It might," I snapped. "Then Liori will have to finish it for me, won't she? Enough of this, Jurgen. We're losing time. Let's each of us do his own job."

"Very well. As you say," he sounded anxious. "I'll keep communications open just in case."

"Just please don't bother me with the basics. You can take care of them yourself."

* * *

AS WE SPOKE, the nanites had finished patching up Liori's Condor. I sent it the instructions to join in the scanning of the asteroid fragments.

The mnemonic load indicator surged into the orange as my mind began receiving data from two combat scanning systems.

Translucent schemes of various devices drifting in space flashed before my eyes: some floating on their own, others bejeweling angular slabs of rock.

I switched data collection to background mode and opened the abilities tab. In all honesty, we stood very little chance of ever locating the artifact. But apart from that, the Outlaws' base had been literally stuffed with equipment. Most of the already-discovered devices belonged to the Founders' technosphere. I'd never studied them before. In just a few brief minutes of data collection, my Alien Technologies skill had already grown two points.

This was a good start. Still, too early to celebrate. I kept replicating nanites over and over again, then sending them deep into the mangled mines toward the surviving rooms of the ancient installation. Soon they would begin streaming more data; in the meantime I could finally take a breather.

I injected myself with a dose of combat metabolites. My mind cleared somewhat. The mnemonic load indicator reluctantly crawled into the yellow zone.

I switched on the long-distance communications. The far-off spark of the Oasis station glimmered on its grid. Obeying my mental command, the optical multiplier kicked in. The image zoomed in, gaining detail.

The hybrid was neither our friend nor foe. He was a synthetic identity, an AI pieced together by the Corporation out of the dead players' neurograms. He was, intrinsically, the result of a chilling otherworldly experiment that brewed fear and resentment.

When we'd last met, he publicly declared himself the opposite of Avatroid, announcing his intention to restore Oasis to its original glory.

Still, it looked as if it hadn't come to anything. The skeleton of the ancient station was still dark and gloomy — not a sign of any repairs in sight. There was one other thing I couldn't understand: why hadn't the hybrid even attempted to help the Eurasia? I knew from experience that his technological skill at least equaled that of Avatroid. He could have thwarted the Phantom Raiders' attack — and still he hadn't lifted a finger to save the defeated Colonial Fleet.

I activated the communications with Oasis. The only things that the hybrid seemed to have restored were the locator tower and the transport beam control devices associated with it. He'd apparently used those ancient alien systems in order to spy on the Eurasia fleet and listen in to their command frequencies; he'd even managed to beam me up to the Eurasia station with the orders to bring him Genesis: an ancient planet-forming device safely stashed away on Darg.

Never mind. This wasn't the right time to rake up recent developments.

A green indicator lit up on the control panel. I had a connection with Argus; still, no one seemed in a hurry to answer me.

Whatever had happened to the hybrid? Why wouldn't he speak to me?

When my Darg mission had been over, I couldn't help wondering why he hadn't claimed Genesis' scanner files that I'd made. Those were indispensable for him to restore the station. Why hadn't he tried to buy them off me or even take them by force?

Now I understood: he'd had nowhere to hurry to. He knew about his own true nature — and certainly about our desperate situation. In case of my death, the neurograms of my disintegrating identity would return to the Corporation's server where he'd immediately be granted access to them.

He wasn't our friend. Oh, no.

"Zander... what is it?" I could barely recognize his voice through the interference. "What do you... want?"

That was weird. There were no obstacles in the

laser transmitter's path capable of distorting or diffusing its signal. Could it be the hybrid? He seemed to have blocked the video channel. His speech was slurred and faltering.

"I need you," I said. "I know that you need the Genesis files in order to restore Oasis. I'll give them to you. In return, you must teach me to build artificial neuronets."

"Not interested," he said, wheezing as if his every word was a physical struggle.

"Why? Tell us!" Jurgen butted in. "Don't you understand we have children on board?" his desperate voice rose to a scream.

"I... don't... care. I... won't help... anyone. I have... my own... problems..."

The communications indicator blinked and went out.

I sat there, gasping. "Did you hear that?"

"I did," Jurgen echoed. "What a piece of shit!"

"Never mind. Forget him. It wasn't meant to happen. I'm sure we'll know everything when the time is right."

"Zander?" Frieda chimed in. "Any news? What did the scan show?"

"I haven't found the artifact yet if that's what you mean. My levels keep growing but not as fast as I thought they would. The scanners keep bringing lots of interesting stuff but nothing we can use at the moment."

"Arbido seems to have an idea," Jurgen joined in.

You've received a new level!
Your Mnemotechnics skill has grown 1 pt.!

Your Alien Technologies skill has grown 3 pt.!

You have 2 new nanite activation codes available!

"Sorry, Jurgen, can it wait until I'm back? I'm a bit busy right now."

"Very well. You do what you can."

* * *

I OPENED my character's characteristics.

The rapid developments of the last few hours had forced me to ignore system messages. My mind barely registered them, dismissing their contents.

Within that time, I'd destroyed the shipyard, smoked about a hundred drones, downed five Raiders and was constantly busy with nanites.

No wonder I'd grown 12 levels.

My Robot Technician skill which I'd received way back on Argus and which had grown 3 pt. during my memorable fight with Dargian pythons, had now risen another 50%.

The question remained, was this information worth anything anymore?

The ambiguity of the situation was quite unsettling. On one hand, once I'd learned the truth I'd stopped paying the same attention to the char's characteristics as before. On the other, I was contradicting my own logic still putting my faith into the abilities I knew I had.

The truth had to lie somewhere in between. I wouldn't be surprised to discover some real-life skills integrated into the game interface.

At the moment, all I was interested in were nanite activation codes. They were definitely real. I knew that from experience!

> *Mnemotechnics Skill*
> *Current level: 25*
> *Abilities available:*
> *Replication, 15*
> *Steel Mist, 5*
> *Object Replication, 4*
> *Piercing Vision, 3*
> *Integration, 2*
> *Breakdown, 5*
> *Plasma Blast, 5*
> *Differential Nanite Control, 3*
> *Disintegration, 10*
> *System Failure, 5*
> *Advanced integration, 2*
> *The Call, 1*
> *Self-Sacrifice, 1*
> *Plasma Lash, 2 (requires a generator built by Object Replication)*
> *You have 2 new nanite activation codes!*
> *You have 19 characteristic, skill and ability points available!*

On Liori's advice, I'd boosted Disintegration already during our battle with the Raiders. As a close-range weapon, it was truly lethal — but as it had turned out, using it required a powerful ship with excellent shields.

We couldn't even fathom the true potential of these ancient alien technologies. Even at my current level of Disintegration, we could have deterred the

Raiders' attack had I been on board the Relic and had it had enough energy to power the shields. I was beginning to understand that Founders' ships didn't really need any cumbersome weapon systems which were a pain to operate. All they needed was a well-trained crew with advanced nanite control skills. The range of nanite application was so broad one couldn't even imagine all the possibilities it offered.

In which case, who had equipped the Relic with all those coil guns, laser beams and plasma batteries? We had to examine the ship again and try to envision it the way it had been when it had first been conceived.

But I digress.

My mind was in turmoil. The sheer thought of all the mysteries contained within the Founders' technosphere was overwhelming. As my combat with the Raiders had just shown, I could select a target by focusing on it and then decide whether I wanted to disable it or disintegrate it on the spot.

Let's see what the activation codes would offer.

I entered them in a special box, one after another.

New ability available: Global Net. You can now receive status reports from devices located in other star systems. Requires 70 Mnemotechnics and a functioning hyperspace communications module.

New Ability available: Active Shield. From now on, the nanites you create will automatically react to any threat by forming a protective cover. Requires 30 Mnemotechnics, 20 Replication, 10 Differential Nanite Control and an implanted artificial neuronet module to recognize any potential threat and control nanite groups automatically.

The new abilities' icons were gray. Blocked. What a shame.

The nanites busy exploring the asteroid fragments kept streaming data to two scanning devices which relayed it to my mind expander. I felt increasingly unwell. Once I received another level, my XP bar began to slow down.

Alien Technologies, 30. Finally! Now I'd be able to examine neurochips.

Actually, I already had two artificial neuronets available for study. One was the AI module implanted into my nervous system (yes, the one that used to belong to the monster who'd attempted to take control over me when our assault group had been about to land on Darg). Plus I had Liori's identity matrix confined within the cybermodule that the hybrid had made for me.

I glanced at the sensors. The asteroid belt seemed calm. Still, I knew this was a lull before the storm. Avatroid was obliged to send drones to investigate the wreckage of the base which had been his birthplace.

Which meant I shouldn't waste time. Let nanites keep collecting data. I had other things to do.

* * *

A SLIM PLATE bespangled with neurochips floated in mid-air in front of me.

I'd removed the silvery cover. A light cloud of

nanites surrounded the object, awaiting my command.

I was taking my time. I had no margin for error. The neurochips were oxidized but not destroyed. The cover had taken the worst of the heat exposure. Restoring it wasn't a problem.

I began scanning the neurochips, trying to locate the damage.

Gradually a 3D model began forming in my mental view. I watched the layers of artificial nervous tissue grow, immersing myself into this yet unfamiliar world of neurons and their complex interwoven structures which resembled three-dimensional cobwebs. Some of its threads were broken, unable to transmit electric impulses.

My breathing was fast and deep. I had to remain calm. I was to locate one undamaged neurochip, then copy its structure.

I didn't notice the time fly. My tension was such that reality had faded.

The object's matrix has been created and downloaded to your mind expander

Finally, the data processing stopped. I channeled all available resources into copying a simple neuronet module built by the hybrid. They were the building blocks of every AI. If I managed to build it, then-

That was irrelevant. The nanites were ready.

The replication matrix accepted.
The mental image recognized.
Warning! The object cannot be replicated.

Creating it requires 100 Mnemotechnics.

Dammit!

Trying not to disrupt my concentration, I pulled the Founders' glove out of my inventory and slipped it on.

You have activated an item: Modulator.
Class: rare, indestructible.
Permanent effect:
+1 to Intellect
+1 to Learning Skills
+2 to Alien Technologies
+1 to Mnemotechnics

Let's do it again.
Object replication. Come on, now!

The object cannot be replicated. Your skill level is too low.

Dark circles swirled before my eyes. I was shaking with tension. As I tried to catch my breath and concentrate, the Founders' glove blurred, enveloped by an aura. Threadlike charges of energy reached out for the broken cybermodule, touching its chips and branching off as if exploring them.

Not enough data to commence automatic repairs. Please connect specialized databases to continue.

The system message brought me back to reality. Did that mean that by the Founders' standards, an artificial neuronet was a rather ordinary device?

I checked my interface again. Apparently, this glove — part of an ancient gear kit I'd come across back on Argus — had a number of built-in functions. Until now, their controls had been disabled but now that I'd gone up through the levels, I discovered a new entry in the Repairs tab:

Damaged Equipment Repairs
Requires: a Founders' glove (a Modulator gear version), 30 Alien Technologies and 30 Mnemotechnics.

I could do that!

I selected the freshly-scanned model of the functioning neurochip and uploaded it to the Modulator.

The replication matrix accepted. Please select the object requiring repairs.

I focused on the cybermodule's damaged elements, selecting them one by one.

Task accepted. Now attempting to restore the neuronet units using the sample provided.

I watched closely as the threadlike charges of energy enveloped the damaged plate. Nanites obediently joined in as the Modulator used them as raw materials. A separate bar appeared in my interface to report on the repairs' status.

An emergency signal entered my mind, disrupting my thoughts. Several weak notches appeared just within the scanners' range. Avatroid's fleet!

I called off the nanites still busy studying the asteroid's destroyed laboratories. They'd failed to locate neither the artifact itself nor its fragments. Still, there was nothing I could do about it. We had to make ourselves scarce.

Both The Call and Object Replication worked like a dream. The recalled nanites formed two strong cables, towing Liori's ship safely in my Condor's wake.

I headed toward Argus. Considering my engines' feeble output, it would probably take me six hours to get there, give or take.

I checked the auto pilot. It worked fine. I double-checked the repairs bar. It was barely moving even though the nanobots kept toiling away.

I could barely keep my eyes open. I hadn't slept for over twenty-four hours. I needed some rest. Or rather, my mortal body needed it, left on far-off Earth.

Trying to fight off fatigue wasn't a good idea. I was beyond exhaustion.

* * *

I AWOKE to a quaint long-forgotten feeling, warm and peaceful. The way I used to wake up when I'd been very, very young.

I opened my eyes. Was this the same old cockpit? Dozens of holographic tablets exuded a soft light, scrolling data interspersed with schemes of strange devices. The dead fire-damaged control consoles towered further away. Overhead, breach holes leaked darkness.

The cockpit was at the mercy of the infinite

vacuum. Half-turned toward me, Liori sat cross-legged, leaning comfortably in a seat formed by nanites.

She wasn't wearing a pressure suit. Still, the resemblance was striking. Sensing my stare, she turned round.

What was technology doing to us?

Our minds touched, then merged in an acute, desperate bout of gentleness.

The cold melted away. The darkness shrank back. Warm sunrays lit up our faces. A breeze ruffled my hair. The gray outlines of sea cliffs acquired shape and depth. The roots of squat pine trees clung to the cracked rock. Flat waves shimmied along the pebble beach.

An uncontrollable surge of emotion surged through us, burning our minds, distorting reality and wiping away the panorama of deep space. We failed to keep our balance on the edge.

Darkness embraced us.

Connection error. The external neuronet is not connected to your mind expander. Direct contact is not possible.

"Zander? Can we ever be together?" Liori's voice brought me back into the Condor's savaged cockpit.

The dull glow of screens assaulted my eyes. Once again the veil of nanites formed her image. This was enough to drive anyone crazy. Still, I resisted insanity.

"We'll manage," I answered with a quiet confidence. "There must be a solution."

Liori returned to her seat and zoomed in the

repairs status bar.

99%

"You've repaired me. *Repaired.* Do you understand? I'm a machine now. A cyber system that can be fixed or rebooted. And what if we don't find a solution? Does that mean I'll stay here all alone?"

Cruel but true.

Liori cut herself short, as if regretting her hasty outburst. "I'm sorry. I didn't mean it."

Both of us were crushed by this spontaneous mind contact which had ended as abruptly as it had started.

How did I want to bring it back! Then again, why not? The module containing Liori's identity was within my reach. Problem was, I couldn't unseal my helmet in the surrounding vacuum.

Still, this was something I could solve.

I activated Nanite Replication. Starboard echoed with a dull thumping sound as I sacrificed a few of the ship's armor plates. I had no other source of cargonite available.

Liori cast me a quizzical look. "Are you increasing the Steel Mist? Why?"

"Just in case."

The nanites had already commenced emergency sealing procedures. They might need several minutes to repair all the numerous points of damage to the ship's hull. In the meantime, I motioned to the screens, trying to assuage her anxiety, "What have you been doing?"

"Just fooling around. I tried to look into the game's interface and see which of our abilities were part of the Founders' technosphere and which were just figments of game developers' fantasy. Here, take a look."

Four holographic tablets moved closer to me.

Each one revealed a first-person view.

My interface was the one on the right. I immediately recognized its translucent ability icons crowding the quick access slots — and below them, Life and Physical Energy bars. Danger sensors of all kinds waited drowsily in their gray boxes. The fine inconspicuous lines of the scanning grid covered my entire field of vision. The gravitech and life support power levels glowed green; the outlines of life support cartridges that might need changing were highlighted in yellow. A flat micro nuclear battery unit was hatched in red.

The second screenshot was definitely Charon's. It showed a fragment of the Market Desk back on Argus. The Haash' eyesight is different from ours in that they can see the objects at the periphery of their eyesight, as well as objects' thermal imprints. For that reason, the three-dimensional image on the screen looked unusual as every object was outlined in greens of every shade and degree of intensity.

"Take a look at the icons' design and positioning," Liori said softly.

I took a second look — and was astounded. You'd think that a Haash interface would be utterly alien to the point of being unidentifiable. Still, his interface was a carbon copy of mine!

I turned to the third tablet. This was the screenshot I'd received from the Disciples' leader back on Darg. When we'd been battling our way through the ancient biological laboratories, Roakhmar had forwarded me this snapshot in an attempt to help me focus on the target. A hydra-like monster was careening at us head-on through a long succession of rooms. Its abominable shape was overlain with elements of the Dargian interface. The resemblance was striking: the picture was virtually identical to mine!

The fourth screen showed my ship's cockpit in real time, streamed by Liori.

"As you can see, my interface is identical to the other three," she said. "Even though it in fact belongs to an ancient AI."

This revelation was mind-blowing. The only difference in the four layouts created by four unrelated space civilizations was in their languages: the tongues of the Haash, the Dargians and humans respectively. All the rest, down to the relative positioning of the development branches and their effects was identical!

"Does that mean that the interface was built by the Founders?" after having seen it with my own eyes, this was the logical conclusion.

"Absolutely. The way I see it, the military back on Earth discovered some artifact — a neuroimplant, most likely. They must have studied it and used it as a prototype to build more of them. Then they used us to test them. I'm pretty sure the Haash and the Dargians followed the same route. Plus dozens of other civilizations we know yet nothing about," Liori turned to me, hope in her gaze. "Do you understand? None of our abilities are made-up! The Founders built this interface to use it themselves in order to travel through the Universe. Even if I'm the only one who survives," tears glistened in her eyes, "I'll level up

Mnemotechnics and bring you all back to life, I promise! I'll piece your identities together neurogram by neurogram and byte by byte!"

By then, the nanites were done sealing the ship. I sent a mental command, assigning part of the ship's power to atmosphere regeneration. Then I removed my helmet, unbuckled and rose, reaching out my hand.

"Zander? What do you think you're doing?"

The thin plate covered with neurochips clicked shut in its dedicated mind expander slot.

External neuronet connected.
+5 to your Mnemotechnics skill.
Direct neurosensory contact established.

The gloom of deep space faded away.

Sunrays began to fall on our faces. A breeze tousled Liori's hair.

"Zander," she returned my kiss, nestling up to me.

Red sand crunched underfoot. A purple surf broke over the boundless coastline awash with orange light. No idea where my subconscious had unearthed these images from. For Liori and myself, they'd forever remain the epitome of happiness.

CHAPTER THREE

THE DARG SYSTEM

THE RELIC'S DARK OUTLINE was barely discernible against the backdrop of the gutted station.

The frigate lay low, safely concealed by the veil of her force shields.

I began closing in, Liori's fighter following in my wake. The area around was littered with pieces of mauled framework and other debris left from the battle for Argus.

"Docking pod 10 activated," Jurgen reported. "I'm sending you a plotted course."

Having received it, I steered my Condor into a narrow crevice between two of the station's hull structures. Soon I was tucked away safely within the Relic's shields.

The docking pod's position lights flickered into view. The frigate's body was rapidly approaching.

"Second docking pod ready," Jurgen reported. "Forced docking protocol initiated. Berthing generators ready."

The nanites forming the towing cables dissolved into a fine mist. The frigate's force beams grappled Liori's ship and dragged it toward its docking pod.

I slowed up and turned my ship's aft toward the Relic. My engines flashed one last time and died. The docking pod's robotic arms clamped onto my Condor's hull.

Liori, here we are!

Zander? Mind sorting it out on your own for a while? I'm a bit busy here.

Liori had already snuggled up in my mind expander, creating a workspace for herself, and was busy poring over the Founders' interface. We maintained uninterrupted neurosensory contact. The sensation of our minds touching filled me with warmth. Funnily enough, my Mnemotechnics skill had continued to grow which was a welcome surprise.

The docking mechanisms clanked as they sucked my ship into the pod. A force field swelled up around it. Jets of whitish liquid sprayed the inside of the pod, restoring the atmosphere.

Charon, Jurgen and Foggs were already waiting outside.

Without saying a word, Charon scooped me up in a bear hug, expressing his pleasure at seeing me. In recent days, he'd picked up quite a few human habits and mannerisms, doing his best to behave appropriately around us (whatever his idea of "appropriately" was).

Foggs gave me a friendly slap on the shoulder. "Good to see you back in one piece. Where's Liori?"

"She's here."

"Well, show her to us, then! I'd like to thank her personally. You did a nice job on those Raiders."

"Plenty of time for you to thank her. How's it going?"

"We're finding our way about," Foggs replied. "Although we've already crossed swords with the Manticore."

I immediately remembered this fabled clan whose members I'd met on board the Eurasia. So they hadn't taken part in the storming of Darg, after all. They must have "gone their own way", just as they'd planned. "What was the problem?"

"We took hold of the old warehouses in the Exo sector. And just as we'd finished sealing two hangars, they arrived and read us the riot act: like, they were the first to land there so they were the legal proprietors of Argus and everything that was on it. They gave us an hour to piss off before taking action. Vandal's now busy setting up defenses."

I didn't like this latest development at all. "This isn't the right moment to wage a clan war. Was there anything in the Exo worth your while?"

"Some metabolites. Novitsky's now busy itemizing them."

"I'd like you to call the Daugoths off. Tell them to return to the Relic."

Foggs didn't seem to like that at all. "We shouldn't show any weakness!"

I wasn't going to comply. "For the moment, the

Daugoths need to take a step back. Their only safe respawn point is on board the Relic, anyway. Jurgen, do we still have some respawn marker paste?"

"We do."

"I'd like you to bind the Daugoths to our mobile respawn point. I'll sort this thing out with the Manticore myself."

"They won't talk to you. They really think they're something."

"I have a few things up my sleeve that just might convince them. Actually, where are Arbido, Ralph and Frieda?"

"Arbido's in the conference room," Jurgen replied. "Ralph's not in a good way. His in-mode must have packed up. I don't think he's gonna last. Frieda's with the kids now. Danezerath and the rest of the Haash have gone to pick up their *yrobs*, just as you ordered. They'll be away for a couple of hours, I think."

"Right. Let's do it this way. I want to listen to what Arbido has to say first. I also have some important information that concerns everyone. Foggs, I'd like you to get your men off Argus, then join us in ten minutes. Agreed?"

The Daugoth Clan leader nodded, reluctant to accept the fact that I was right. There was plenty of space on board the Relic to accommodate everyone. This was a safe well-protected location where his men could finally take a break from their Dargian tribulations.

* * *

"THIS WILL BE YOUR ROOM," Jurgen pointed to the

entrance of a living module, then forwarded me its access code. "Sorry, but it's the best we could do. Part of the personnel deck is still depressurized."

The room was nothing to write home about but at least I could finally remove my suit. A lot of petty details I'd never noticed before had become vital due to the 100% authenticity.

I removed my heavy gear, peeled off my clothes and headed for the shower. I needed to freshen myself up a bit before the meeting. I had a feeling that it wasn't going to be an easy conversation. No idea what Arbido had come up with, but one thing I knew for sure: the only route to survival was by studying the Founders' technologies combined with my own rushed leveling. Once I'd brought my Mnemotechnics up to 100, I could start building neurochips all on my own.

"How would you do that?" Liori's form materialized out of millions of nanites.

I put on some new clothes. You had to give the Founders their dues: they valued creature comforts and knew how to create them. Their Object Replication command could be applied to most everyday situations. I'd already noticed that I sent certain orders to nanites mechanically without even realizing it.

"We'll have to work as a team," I replied. "We'll need some volunteers. Some of Foggs' men might agree to help me."

"Are you going to activate their Mnemotechnics skill for them?"

"I am. I want to explain the situation to them and offer to open a unique development branch. I'll need at least fifty people. We'll make a group which will keep scanning the Founders' devices and manipulate nanites, and I'll be getting their XP for the time being."

Liori did some calculations. "Sorry. It's not gonna work."

"Why?" I asked as we walked out into the corridor and headed toward the module that Jurgen had converted into a conference room.

"A level 1 or 2 Mnemotech can only study the most primitive of objects. It serves no purpose. Neither you nor them would be able to grow your skill properly. It would be much better if you and I continued to level up on our own."

"We're pressed for time and you know it."

She paused, thinking. "We don't even need to look too far. The Relic is one giant artifact in its own right. Take the mobile respawn point: it's never been studied before. We can ask Jurgen and Danezerath to join us. A top Technologist and an expert Mechanic will be much more use to us than a hundred inexperienced volunteers. We all need to level up as fast as we can. We don't even have the artifact itself, only bits of scanner files. Which means we'd have to build our own machine capable of digitizing our identities."

I opened my interface and forwarded its image to Liori. "You've already proved that the entire leveling scheme was developed by the Founders. I need to understand what it was that the military added to it. Which particular skills and abilities will still work? Considering I've just done a bit of leveling, I need to know how to distribute my XP points wisely. I'd hate to waste them on something that won't work."

"Let's have a look," she agreed. "We'll think logically. Everything to do with nanites and neuroimplants would remain functional. Some of the characteristics might fall by the wayside but even that isn't a certainty. We still don't know how exactly our minds interact with the real world, do we?"

Zander. A Human. Level 91. Pilot

Main Characteristics:

Intellect, 23 *pt.* (+1 Semantic Processor bonus)
Strength, 22
Willpower, 29
Agility, 15 (+2 Reflex Enhancer bonus)
Perception, 17 (+2 Semantic Processor bonus)
Stamina 30 (+5 Metabolic Corrector bonus)
Learning Skills, 15
Charisma, 5

Skills:

Piloting of Small Spacecraft, 27
Piloting of Medium and Large Spacecraft, 15
Combat Maneuvering, 30
Navigation, 20

Mechanic, 4:
Repairs, 4
Equipment Building, 2

Science, 59:
Creation of scanner files

Reading of power imprints

Equipment modification

Creation of replication matrices using existing models (requires Mnemotechnics skill)

Alien Technologies, 30:

Enables the study of alien equipment

Mnemotechnics, 39:

Enables the use of Mnemotechnic abilities and the reception of nanite control codes

Technologist, 5:

Enables Technology databases connection.

Combat abilities, 15 (0,0):

Light weapons, 10

Heavy weapons, 15

Energy weapons, 9

Accuracy, 12

Critical hits, 5 (+5% to the possibility of dealing critical damage to the enemy)

Defense, 10 (lowers all incoming damage 10%)

Mnemotechnic abilities:

Replication, 15 (on your command, a small group of nanites uses a selected source material to self-reproduce until the total number of nanites reaches 100,000)

Steel Mist, 10 (protects you from enemy scanners)

Active Shield (requires a Founders' neuronet module). Requires activation

The Call, 5 (brings available nanite groups under your control, including small numbers of enemy nanites)

Differential Nanite Control (requires a Founders' neuronet module)

Object Replication, 10 (allows the use of available nanites and power to build working copies of various devices)

Piercing Vision, 5 (allows the dispatch of nanite groups on reconnaissance missions with further reception of data from them in real time)

Global network (allows the scanning of star systems using the hyperspace network). Requires activation

Disintegration, 10 (destroys molecular bonds in a selected object)

Plasma Blast, 5 (allows a selected nanite group to self-destruct, forming a cloud of ionized gas)

Plasma Lash, 2 (requires a generator built by Object Replication)

Self-Sacrifice, 4 (allows your nanites to self-destruct in order to exterminate enemy nanites)

Integration, 2 (allows you to upgrade your weapons and gear)

Advanced Integration, 2 (allows you to upgrade complex equipment, including spaceships' subsystems)

System failure, 5 (temporarily disables cybernetic parts of a selected device)

Breakdown, 5 (temporarily disables moving parts of a selected device)

Critical Damage, 5 (permanently disables moving parts of a selected device)

"In my opinion, Strength, Willpower, Learning

Skills and Charisma are the biggest suspects," I summed up. "They are the ones most likely to have been forced on us by the military geeks. All the other skills have a confirmed history of being used in implants, databases and nanite control codes."

"We should tell all the others about this," Liori agreed. "I'll forward them the files to study while they still have time."

"Excellent. Now let's go and see what Arbido has come up with."

* * *

THE CONFERENCE ROOM was quiet: the same room where I'd stood yesterday showing the others how the Founders' hyperspace navigator worked by connecting it to my Earth-bound in-mode capsule.

Arbido kept silent, brooding and fidgeting in his seat which was too large for his current build.

The door hissed open, letting in Novitsky and Foggs. I hadn't seen Novitsky since Darg. Now, as I shook his hand, I was surprised to notice his tag,

Level 29. Exobiologist.

He'd done some nice leveling in the meantime! He stood tall and proud. I could barely recognize the Colonial fleet lieutenant who had once sat sobbing on the edge of that fetid alien swamp.

"Hi, man," I said. "Great to see you. You haven't wasted your time."

"The Exobiologists sector on Argus only looks looted," he added, openly pleased with the effect.

"There's actually a lot of interesting stuff still left over there."

"Everyone ready?" Arbido interrupted us. Same old, same old. He was too used to bossing everyone around to drop the habit overnight.

"No point in waiting for Frieda," Jurgen fidgeted with the wedding ring on his finger. "She's with the kids. Why did you want to see us? Just keep it short. We have too many things to do."

"They can wait," Arbido grumbled. He scrambled down his seat and began pacing the room. What an unfortunate avatar, being stuck in the body of a puny goblin. Not that he'd had much say in the matter.

Unexpectedly for everyone, Charon rose, grabbed Arbido with his long scaly arms and lifted him in the air, perching the old man on the back of a seat. "Now we can see you well," he barked. "Speak up."

Arbido paused, gathering his wits. "I know many of you won't like it but I'm absolutely sure the game developers are still fucking us around!" he blurted out.

I watched the others' reactions.

Foggs listened closely. Ralph waved Arbido's suggestion away. Jurgen got predictably angry,

"Didn't Zander prove to us all last night that our identities have been transported via the interstellar network while our physical bodies are about to croak in the in-mode capsules back on Earth?

"I don't believe it," my ex-employer snapped. "There are no Founders. There is no interstellar network. They keep using us as guinea pigs, as simple as that! And Earth must be thriving!"

Jurgen rose from his seat. "Novitsky, have you got any downers? He obviously could use some. Let's go, Zander. We're wasting our time."

"Jurgen, wait," I said. "Let Arbido speak."

Unlike the others, I knew the old man well. He could always offer a realistic view of any situation, however peculiar it might seem at first.

"Just let him keep to the point," Jurgen fumed. "Did he gather us here to whine? *He doesn't believe it!* What a drama queen!"

"I've spent my entire life in the real world!" Arbido snapped. "Trust me: the biggest gaming corporation on Earth couldn't have just gone bankrupt overnight! It's bullshit! Whatever Zander saw there — all those deserted cities and such — I doubt! They could have shown him whatever they wanted!"

Arbido pointed a gnarly finger at Charon. "So you think he's a *'Sentient Xenomorph'*? And who am I, then?"

"Nothing human, by the looks of it," Ralph chuckled.

"Exactly! They made me whatever they wanted me to be! So what makes you think that Charon is an alien? What's the difference between him and myself? And what have the Founders technologies got to do with it?"

"Good question," Foggs suddenly agreed. "Listen, guys, he might be right. All those who logged in via the Second Colonial Fleet, their in-modes seem to be fine. They're perfectly healthy. Their Physical Energy is in the green. How do you explain this? What if the admins are indeed applying pressure to you?

What if they're busy creating the world's history and testing new technologies? Liori's avatar is made of nanites. Arbido is stuck within this fantasy char...”

“So how do the dying children fit into this picture?” Jurgen turned pale with fury. “It's all theory! And we need solutions!”

“That's exactly what I'm about to offer,” Arbido scowled. “For those who don't know, I used to have a gaming business. I spent my entire life building it. I used to rush chars. I had my employees planted in all sorts of worlds. I supplied some very special artifacts. I had a whole shedful of top programmers working for me. Just to give you the idea, I could supply firearms to fantasy worlds, provided the price was right,” he cast me an evil eye. “Let Zander be my witness. He knows.”

“So how did you end up here?” Foggs asked.

Arbido frowned. “I was caught where I shouldn't have been.”

“Which was where?” Jurgen demanded.

“I take it, you've all been to the Crystal Sphere? Apart from Charon, of course,” Arbido added sarcastically. “This was,” he sounded businesslike again, “a young world with great potential. I had some very interesting goings-on developing there. I did it my usual way: I collected intel before going big. I bought some insider information from players, I studied hidden locations and their potential access routes. I looked into unique plot lines. The moment I'd found out that the Corporation was about to make neuroimplants obligatory for all players, I had one installed too.”

“So how did you get burned?” Ralph asked.

“Curiosity killed the cat, so they say. I decided

to check out Phantom Server. I was wondering why players kept going missing. The corporate bosses didn't like it, apparently," he shuddered. The memories of endlessly going through the Gehenna respawn purgatory must have still been vivid.

"Are you going to get to the point?" Jurgen asked, losing patience.

"That's what I'm talking about!" Arbido fidgeted, stooping — he didn't feel comfortable being the center of attention. He wasn't used to it. "When I collected the intel on the Crystal Sphere, I was tipped off about one very interesting location. Apparently, there was a secret path that started in the newb zone. No one knew where it would take you. I sent my man to investigate — and it turned out that the path came out directly at the Corporation testing grounds!"

"Into the real world, you mean?" Jurgen sounded puzzled.

"Exactly. Only I never used it. I don't shit on my own doorstep."

"So!" Foggs grinned. "That gets interesting!"

"How can we access these service locations?" Liori asked.

"The access is at the low-level starting zone," Arbido replied. "The one in the European sector."

I got angry. "Why didn't you tell me before?"

"When was I supposed to tell you?" Arbido snapped again. "You're constantly busy, either rescuing Liori or fucking off to Darg on the hybrid's quests or whatever!"

I stood up. "I beg your pardon!"

"It doesn't matter," Arbido added appeasingly. "Until last night, this information was purely academic."

"You mean until I overrode the logout ban?"

"You got it. But I can't do much while my body's stuck in the capsule. The Corporation must have blocked all communications. If only I could get into the Crystal Sphere! You understand, don't you, that we have nothing left to lose. We have no other options. But I, I still have connections in the real world. They'll get us out of here, trust me, and no one will ever bother us again."

Frowning, Jurgen glared at Arbido. "But what if the Founders' network does exist? What if what Zander saw was true?"

"Then we'll find out what exactly happened back on Earth and try to recharge our in-modes," Arbido replied.

"But why the Crystal Sphere?" Jurgen asked. Sarcasm had now left his voice.

"Because I know how to log in inconspicuously. We'll check it and if we see that it's functioning normally, I'll be able to pull a few strings. And if things are indeed so bad, at least we can get to the service location. I have some very interesting software that I bought by chance from a Corporate worker."

Jurgen frowned. "You want to say that you managed to memorize megabytes of code?"

"Of course I didn't. You're dead right there. I need to get to my in-mode first. But as far as I understand, it's not a problem anymore, is it?"

Mechanically I touched the artifact hanging on a thin chain around my neck.

This was a truly mind-blowing development. Still, Arbido's arguments made sense. We needed time: both to level up our skills and to build our own identity-digitization device. If we managed to replace our in-modes' life support cartridges, we would have it.

"There's never a dull moment with you!" Foggs exclaimed in excitement. "Count me in! Actually, I have two questions."

"Spit them out."

"If indeed shit has hit the fan back on Earth, wouldn't that bring game worlds down too?"

"The Crystal Sphere would work no matter what," Arbido replied confidently. "The Corporation has its equipment located in special bunkers. It has several disaster-proof backups which are powered by independent supply sources. You couldn't have found a better way to access our planet's cyberspace if you tried. That's why we need to log in to it," he repeated.

It looked like the old man was right. There was also another argument in favor of our using the Crystal Sphere. None of us seemed to question the fact that it had been the testing ground of the first neuroimplants. Which meant that the Crystal Sphere's engine had been adapted to their use. For us, it was a huge advantage.

Oh, yes. A lot of things had finally revealed themselves to us in their true light. I could have sworn that the three Dargians I'd met in the Crystal Sphere as well as the Mechanic in a slave collar were nothing but NPCs: a well-calculated setup aiming to draw my attention to Phantom Server.

"Jurgen?" I turned to him. "What do you think?"

"It might work," he answered without hesitation.

"But how about the technical side of it? You think we can pull it off?"

"We might if we managed to activate the Relic's hyperspace module," he said. "Do you remember me telling you about Argus' central respawn point?"

"I think so. Didn't you use the station's locator tower to redirect the respawning pilots to Founders Square?"

"Exactly. You can call it the first case of mass identity transfer. So I have some experience in this field. We'll have to fine-tune a thing or two, of course. I'm pretty sure the Founders used to travel in groups too. We'll try and automate the entire process but it would be safer if each of you who goes to Earth has his or her own navigator. You think you can make a few more?"

"I can help," Liori offered. "Together we can do it. But how do you want us to decrypt these icons?" she pointed at the symbols covering the outer ring of the device. "This seems to be an input panel but I've never seen most of the signs!"

"Danezerath knows!" Charon growled. "He'll help you! The programs controlling our *yrobs* are written in the Founders' language. I want to go with you too," he added, curt as usual.

"Very well. We'll start small," I glanced at Arbido. "Are you ready?"

He turned pale. "Already? Just like that? Don't you want to make any preparations first?"

"You're the one who asked for it. No point dragging it out. The artifact has been tested. All you need to do is connect to your in-mode while Jurgen downloads the data."

"Wait a sec," Jurgen motioned me to stop. "I'd rather we wait till Danezerath comes back. That'll also give me some time to get some equipment ready. I'd like to copy the navigator's settings. That might help me work out the Relic's communications module."

"All right. It's up to you. When will the Haash be back?"

"They still have about an hour's journey back."

"In that case, Liori and I will start making the artifacts. Foggs, I want you to billet your men in the meantime. Don't meet Manticore representatives quite yet. Let them stew in their own juice."

"And I? What do you want me to do?" Novitsky asked, apparently impressed with the proceedings. The decisions we've just made seemed to have left the young player in some awe.

A simultaneous hyper jump of several digitized identities was indeed a risky step born of our desperation. Still, the chance to service our in-modes and find out whatever had happened back on Earth was worth it.

"I have a special task for you," I said. "Have you ever used street vending machines?"

I was already beginning to plan our future course of action in case of our success. Arbido shouldn't hold his breath. I hadn't dreamed up all those deserted cities and decomposing bodies.

"Sure. They're everywhere, aren't they?"

"Then you know, don't you, that they use the principle of molecular replication?"

"Yeah, why?"

"I'd like you to write down the formulas of the most potent metabolites you know. Then check the Exo Clan's databases and make a list of chemicals required to replicate them. Think you can do that?"

"I'll try. Can I come with you?"

"I don't think so. It's a trip for those who have

nothing to lose."

"Yeah, right. How about Charon, then?"

"That's his decision. Please don't argue. At the moment, you're the only exobiologist on board the Relic. We need you here. Understood?"

"All right," he grudgingly agreed. "But what if you don't come back?" he blurted out.

This question got me thinking.

Liori? Need to talk.

* * *

ON BOARD THE RELIC
FIVE HOURS LATER

BREAKING THE FRAGILE ICE from its edges, the hatch between decks clanked open.

We were in zero gravity. Stars twinkled through the breach holes. Strange objects floated around. My mind expander enveloped them in an emerald shimmer, highlighting them, while trying in vain to identify them against the Technologist Clan database.

No human had ever set foot here. At least I didn't think so.

Liori materialized next to the nearest entrance and cast a studying glance around. "Power's down," she said. "I can't locate the interstellar communications module."

"It's about a hundred feet further up the corridor," Jurgen's voice replied as he controlled our progress online. "Watch out. I'm powering everything up."

Stars distorted in the haze of the force field blocking the breach holes in the hull. Flailing cables began to spark. Invisible exhausts spewed out little jets of oxygen snow as the automatic life support system attempted to restore atmosphere.

Once again I heard the sound of the ancient machinery start up behind my back. This time it was Arbido. He clambered out onto the service deck and chuckled with satisfaction, noticing the abundance of artifacts. Without hesitation, he began collecting them, simultaneously taking stock of his finds and streaming their data into the group's local network.

"Zander, everyone, wait for me!" Foggs had fallen behind us all. He'd used this opportunity to deactivate his gravitech and was traveling in zero gravity, practicing this new mode of movement. His floating cargonite-clad figure scrambled out of the hatch.

"You haven't wasted your time, have you?" he teased Arbido who was busy stuffing his finds into three containers at once. "Why won't you use the inventory?" miscalculating his movements, Foggs bashed his head against the ceiling and grabbed at a broken piece of pipework in the wall.

"Inventories are for personal possessions only," Arbido grumbled. "Loot belongs to everyone. Waste not, want not. You'll all be grateful. Did you see the size of those breach holes? You did. Good. Once Jurgen switches off the shields, half of these goodies will be ejected into open space."

"Leave him," I told Foggs. "And please switch your gravitech back on. This isn't the right time to practice."

My body tensed like a coiled spring. I couldn't

explain this sudden sense of foreboding. This part of the Relic had never been explored. The Dargians hadn't attempted to restore it, either. The surrounding rooms had been at the mercy of both vacuum and cosmic cold for thousands of years.

My interface pinged. The tactics subsystem operative window revealed a handful of scarlet markers. A few of them blinked and then expired.

"They're mobs!" Liori shouted a warning. "They're not in the database!" her outline disintegrated, returning to me in a swarm of battle-ready nanites.

"Arbido, step back! Foggs, you cover him! Keep behind me, both of you! Charon, where the hell are you?"

"I'll outflank them," Charon replied. "There're some breached bulkheads here."

Foggs switched on his gravitech, preparing for battle. He pushed Arbido toward the wall, controlling the service hatches above his head, gutted by some ancient blast of decompression. There were plenty of them around and they might prove too inviting for *serves*. These local maintenance robots-turned-mobs were smart enough to use them, especially when attacking in a network-connected pack.

But why? There shouldn't be any aggressive mobs here. Immediately my imagination offered me the gruesome shape of Avatroid. After everything we'd gone through on Darg, I knew only too well what a hostile AI was capable of.

A segment of the force shield flashed weakly, snapping me out of the haze of my confusion. I stepped forward, covering the others. Luckily, the corridor was quite narrow and the threat was still a long way away.

I read their signatures. Liori had been right. There was nothing like them in our databases. Were they some unknown type of on-board cyborg?

The number of scarlet dots continued to dwindle. There were only five of them left now. For mobs, their behavior was weird. They were supposed to attack us, fiercely and blindly. Instead, they kept retreating. I zoomed in on a scale model of the deck. They were retreating toward some unidentified structure, taking shortcuts through demolished rooms and breach holes.

"No idea where they came from!" Jurgen commented tensely.

"Check the logs. Could the power activation have triggered some of the deck's machines?"

"I've done that! The only things that came on were the emergency shields and the life support!"

"It's all right. We'll see in a moment."

My mind expander kept showing five targets. They'd now clustered about fifty feet away from us, next to a strange-looking disk-shaped structure that differed dramatically from all the others.

Slowly we advanced amid floating debris that consisted increasingly of more and more lumps of molten cargonite. Darkness lurked within the breach holes. Rooms to both sides of the corridor were completely ravaged. There must have been one hell of a battle here at some point in the past.

I should have got used to it, really. Wherever we turned, the echo of mysterious ancient developments followed us everywhere: on board spaceships and stations, in the asteroid belt, on Wearong's satellites and even on the system's only habitable planet.

Outlined in yellow, a large object appeared in our way. Unlike all the others, it wasn't floating but lying on the floor. Its signature was easy to read: this was the typical aura produced by discharged power units.

"Foggs, cover me!"

The leader of the Daugoths clan, Foggs was an experienced player. He realized the ambiguity of our situation perfectly well — and still he wasn't going to trade his gamer mentality in for questions without answers. Now too he acted without hesitation. In a few well-rehearsed moves, he shone laser beams into the nearest breach holes, pointed Arbido at a small niche formed by two bulges in some deformed bulkheads, then nodded back to me: *Go to it!*

* * *

THE YELLOW AURA enveloped a creature lying on the floor.

It wasn't humanoid. It lay sprawled, extending its thick tentacle limbs like a starfish.

What a strange mob. I crouched next to it and ran my right hand over its body.

The Founder's Glove switched to scanner mode. The creature's body was covered with a rough hide, crackled and bulging. Within it lay power cells.

A cyborg!

Confirming my initial idea, more technogenic details began forming in my mind's eye: the creature's core, the servomotors, the cargonite tubing of its artificial skeleton entwined by dry mummified muscles.

You have studied a cyborg. Origin: unknown.
You've received +3 to your Alien Technologies skill.
Your Exobiologist skill isn't active yet. You cannot level it up.

"Zander? What have you got there?" Foggs asked impatiently.

"It's a cyborg. Judging by its state, its organic flesh has been dead ever since this deck was decompressed."

"Has it been lying here for thousands of years?" Arbido asked in disbelief.

"They were in energy saving mode," Jurgen explained with calm expertise while receiving the data in real time. "These mobs have been lying there until conditions have become favorable for their activation. Now I understand why most of their markers went out. Their internal power supplies are completely depleted. When I activated the deck's power, they came out of their hibernation hoping to charge up."

"It doesn't look as if they succeeded. Their markers first faded, then expired completely. It didn't even come to a fight."

"I've found an alien ship!" Charon's voice echoed in the earphones. "It's small. It's fused with the hull. I've never seen this kinds of creatures before."

"Novitsky," I called out. "I want you to sort it out. Get Danezerath and a few men to cover you. Liori will meet you there."

"Got it!"

We continued on our way. We didn't stay to investigate. Exploring an alien ship was an important and interesting thing indeed but at the moment, we had totally different objectives.

Charon scrambled out of a breach hole. "All clear," he reported. "All the mobs have been deactivated, whatever they are."

The Relic was bursting with mysteries. We were yet to learn the story of her space travels which she guarded so closely. I was pretty sure the Founders hadn't been her only crew. The frigate must have engaged in battles and performed hyperspace jumps long after her original creators had exited this stage of history.

"Here's the communications module!" one of the rooms on the deck floor plan began to glow, highlighted. "It doesn't look as if it has power though."

"Little wonder," I walked in and took a look around. "We might have to attach all the cables by hand. This is probably the work of cyborgs. Charon, can you help me?"

I grabbed at a bunch of cables hovering in a fancy loop in mid-air and studied the connectors. They seemed all right. No sign of fire damage.

"Please don't rush it," Jurgen told me. "I need to study the diagram, then I'll tell you exactly what to do."

We paused, waiting. Charon held the cables. Arbido looked around him, taking in the scene. Foggs took up position at the room's entrance, controlling the corridor just in case.

Liori and I stepped aside.

Her cybermodule was surrounded by a thick cloud of nanites forming her image. She looked me in the eye, anxiety in her stare. "Zander, it's probably better I come with you."

This was a hard decision. Still, we had to part ways. Someone had to stay behind in case the ancient device malfunctioned and sent our identities to some God-forsaken part of its network. Or just tore our neurograms apart and scattered their fragments over hundreds of star systems. The device had been out of use for several millennia, after all.

"Don't worry," I said. "I'll be back."

Charon began connecting the cables. The ancient control panels lit up with a complex pattern of indicator lights.

"All done," Charon growled.

Liori and I stood there silent, looking into each other's eyes.

A makeshift adapter fashioned by Jurgen clicked its jury-rigged clamps. The sound fell flat in the stale rarefied atmosphere. Five ports glowed on the adapter's surface: the number of navigator artifacts about to be connected.

"Excellent," Jurgen commented. "The communication module works. Now I want each of you to connect your navigator to an available slot."

Nanites touched my lips. "I'll be waiting," Liori whispered.

Click.

My navigator was connected. Charon was the next to use the module, followed by Arbido and Foggs. We'd brought Jurgen's navigator with us and activated the last slot.

The light flickered and went out. Three intersecting circles of energy lit up at the center of the room.

"Excellent," Jurgen said. "Everything's working. I'll connect myself from here via the onboard network."

"And what do you want us to do? Should we stand in a circle and hold hands?" Foggs joked clumsily.

"No need for stupid rituals. Either the device accepts your settings and kicks in, or it doesn't, becau-"

A surge of interference swallowed the rest of his phrase, distorting his voice. A pale glow filled the room.

Reality blurred and flickered, then expired.

Chapter Four

An unidentified location in space

WATER WARBLED NEARBY. My visor was broken. The odor of decaying leaves mingled with the aroma of flowering grasses.

My vision came back slowly. At first, reality was akin to a blurred pencil sketch.

Gradually the world began gaining detail, glitching occasionally as it grew in color. I could already see a large mossy boulder half-buried in the ground; a green meadow edged with fluffy seed balls; and further on, the swaying branches of brambles heavy with tiny red fruit.

The icons of my interface were gray: inactive.

A rabbit sneaked past. A large lizard froze in a small rocky crevice.

A breeze ruffled the trees, bringing the faint disturbing odor of decomposition.

A scattering of red indicator lights on the inside of my visor blinked, then went out. I couldn't move.

My armored suit hindered my movements, digging into my body as if deformed.

Communications were down. My mind expander didn't respond.

Right! No good lying around! I leaned against one arm and tried to heave myself up. My suit's servodrives screeched.

My heart was pounding. I was short of breath. Where on earth had this fabled Founders' network sent me?

I struggled to catch my breath, then took a look around. A greenwood forest towered nearby, looking rather worse for wear. Its branches were broken as if ravaged by a tornado. A siege tower lay overturned on the ground at the forest's edge. Its sharpened pales, dark with time, pointed every which way.

This was the Crystal Sphere!

I could barely recognize my stomping ground. This newb location had suffered some drastic metamorphosis. Once bustling with life, it was now uneasily quiet. The village where a few years ago I'd completed my first quest had been reduced to a few houses, and even those stood roofless.

I could see a range of low hills to my left, their slopes peppered with craters and scorch marks. This looked very much like the aftermath of a mass use of top-level spells which was unacceptable in a newb zone.

There were some marshes not far from here, inhabited by an old friend of mine. I might need to ask him whatever had happened here.

My companions were nowhere to be seen which worried me quite a bit. I wasn't used to having so little information about my surroundings.

Never mind. The main thing was, we'd made it! Even though this good old fantasy world wasn't our ultimate port of call, still I found it encouraging. Our identities had just traveled through an ocean of light years and ended up in a predetermined location of Earth's cyberspace!

As I took my bearings, my armor had completed its transformation. Instead of the cargonite suit I'd been used to, I was now wearing a pair of statless canvas pants and a matching shirt.

So the Crystal Sphere's engine had apparently accepted me, stripping me of any technological advantage. The only thing still reminding me of Phantom Server was the Founders' navigator device which had suffered no transformation.

"Zander!" a desperate scream made me swing round. This was Arbido's voice!

A narrow river flowed behind some shrubs to my right. I could distinctly hear the warbling and splashing of water.

"Help!" the scream was coming from the river bank, accompanied by the clashing of steel.

A wide trail led off in that direction. It was still quite fresh, the leaves on the hacked-off branches of the surrounding bushes still rigid.

"Help, someone! They're killing me!"

I ran as fast as I could.

The trail ducked into a small ravine, then brought me out to the bank.

Wow! What was that? A battle must have unfolded here, and very recently too!

Decaying bodies in muddy bloodied armor lay everywhere, pillaged by groups of looters.

I saw Arbido. He stood with his back to a

blackened piece of driftwood, clumsily brandishing a *naginata* with a broken shaft. Three ragged skinny bandits (definitely NPCs, judging by their vile expressions) stood there in sullen determination, waiting for him to run out of steam. They didn't want to take any risks but they apparently weren't going to let him go alive, either.

Their gear was all mismatched, their dented armor bloodied and pierced in places.

I picked up a sword as I ran: its blade jagged, its tip broken off.

I knew the Crystal Sphere like the palm of my hand. I used to play as Paladin, and I still had all my skills at knee-jerk level. No idea how the game engine had gone about adjusting my current levels, but it should at least be good enough to smoke a few robbers!

Arbido noticed me and stopped yelling. He perked up a little. His helmet was gone, his Dargian suit (the only one that could fit his goblin build) still surging with charges of energy. That's why the NPCs hadn't dared to attack him yet. They must have thought he was bewitched!

I had about a dozen paces between him and myself left when the looters turned around and took off.

Further upstream the bank was ripped apart, forming wide ravines. One of them parted, revealing Charon, also without a helmet: all covered in mud, angry and disoriented. He held an uprooted young tree in one hand and clenched a rabbit by its ears in the other.

"Phew," Arbido crouched, gasping. "I nearly had a heart attack. I thought that was the end of me."

Noticing us, Charon growled a greeting. In a flash, the bank emptied. The looters disappeared very promptly.

"Did you see Jurgen and Foggs?" I asked.

"*Nowr*!" Charon cast a curious look around. "Is this your world?"

"Not quite. This is a made-up reality. Will you let go of the rabbit, please?"

Charon released his fingers. The harmless NPC scampered away.

"What do you mean by a made-up reality?" Charon asked. "I can see no traces of civilized life here! Why are the local technologies so primitive?"

"I'll explain to you later. Now I'd like you to remove your suit. Arbido, that applies to you too."

"Why?" the old man wasn't in a hurry to comply. "What have you done with your own suit?"

"The Crystal Sphere's engine has utilized it. But before that happened, the wretched suit very nearly broke every bone in my body. So you'd better get out of yours pretty quick. We'll get some new gear here."

"What, take it off corpses?" Arbido cringed.

"Just do it!"

While they were busy removing their suits, I tried to explain to Charon the meaning of a "game world".

"I still don't get it," he finally admitted. "Who killed them?" he pointed his improvised club to the river bank strewn with bodies.

"No idea," I admitted. "The rules forbid any serious fighting here at all."

The two neat piles of cargonite armor began to quiver, losing shape. Soon both suits had totally dematerialized.

Arbido shivered. All he had left on was a pair of knee-long pants.

Charon's light onboard suit wasn't affected.

"Am I supposed to freeze to death?" Arbido began to moan.

"Just wait a little. I'll get some gear from somewhere. Weren't you going to contact someone?" I reminded him.

"To do that, I need to get to the nearest tavern! It's not very far from here, don't worry. We'll get there in no time at all."

"I don't think so. You can forget your tavern. The village has been reduced to ruins."

He looked flabbergasted. "What do you mean?"

"Can't you see what's going on?" I stared at the dead bodies. The memory of my arrival in Phantom Server sprang to mind. This was exactly what I'd encountered in the alternative start location on Oasis when I'd first arrived there. Some of the avatars there wouldn't disappear after the character's virtual death. Which meant that the player had died in both worlds, crumbling under the realism of the experience provided by his or her neuroimplant.

Thousands of players had died here as they tried to hold the river bank. Who could have attacked them? The broken weapons, the pools of blood, pierced armor and shattered shields — all this pointed at a fierce struggle, but at least half of the gruesome picture seemed to be missing. Whoever had created this battle painting was a very, very strange artist.

I could see hoofmarks in the sand. A lost horseshoe. A broken piece of a spear with a very unusual tip. A scaly glove lay by the water edge. I picked it up. It must have been hacked off with the bearer's hand still in it. Still, it was empty inside.

Did that mean that the attackers, whoever they were, had successfully respawned?

"Zander!" Arbido scurried toward me. "There's something I need to tell you! I have a cache here somewhere!"

"All right," I agreed. "Let's see if we can find it. What have you got in it?"

"Just some gear I stashed away for my mercs. You know very well that these start-up locations are a dream to work in. Newbs can be too impatient, too hungry for adventure. So my guys did their bit by offering them a free ride through the local dungeons. It's not much in terms of gear, really, because my guys didn't want to stand out too much in the crowd. Still, it's better than robbing corpses."

"I wouldn't say so. They have all sorts of gear all the way up to level 50. It looks as if the entire area came here in order to deter the invaders or die."

"Whatever. It's up to you."

"It's okay. We'll open this stash of yours, that's for sure. What did those looters want with you? I saw them talking between themselves. They didn't seem in a hurry to get a taste of your naginata."

Arbido shrugged. "They were weird. They could kill me in their own sweet time. At first I couldn't even move. One of them stumbled over me and saw that I was alive. You can't imagine how pleased he was! That grin of his! He said to the others, "We need to bind this one! We can carry him to the old well and throw him down. Once the Reapers have him, we can count on a reward!"

"What did you say? The Reapers? Never heard about them."

"Neither had I," Arbido headed toward a small ravine, then pointed at two flat rocks on the ground. "That's my stash, down there."

* * *

ARBIDO'S STASH proved untouched. I moved the rocks aside and scooped the sand out until I discovered three large chests.

Arbido opened them and quickly equipped himself in some leather armor and a short sword. I was more interested in the scrolls he kept in a separate box.

Arbido proved a foresightful type. Actually, why would his business acumen surprise me?

We couldn't find anything that would fit Charon though. Never mind. We would think of something, that's for sure.

The scrolls proved extremely handy. They were nothing special, just a bunch of regular spells, but you didn't have to be a wizard to use a scroll. All you had to do was break the seal. I took all of them. I also found a slotted belt and moved the Wall of Fire and the Hand of Earth to quick access slots.

My interface was still dead, the icons of my mnemonic abilities inactive. But once I'd handled the scrolls' yellowed parchment, two of the Founders' icons suddenly appeared in my mental view. Both were related to high-temperature exposure.

"Step aside, guys!" I focused on the bottom of one of the ravines and activated a Wall of Fire.

It worked nicely! The shrubs exploded in flames, the heat searing my face. The local critters scattered in all directions.

"Why did you have to waste it?" Arbido demanded.

"Because we'd better check it now than be stuck with a dead scroll in the heat of battle. You should have stashed away more of them, man. We could use them, that's for sure."

"That's a bit of wishful thinking now, isn't it?" he grumbled.

While Arbido and I sorted through his stash, Charon waited on the bank, looking pensive. He paid no heed to the stench of the dead bodies; instead, he watched the waves rolling onto the sand shallows and frothing around the rocks.

"A long time ago there were rivers in my world too," he half-growled with a sad gasp.

"Why, what happened? Why did they disappear?"

"We entered the era of the Black Sun," the Haash announced sadly.

"Did that have something to do with the Founders?" I suggested.

He nodded gloomily.

"Can you tell us?"

"Not now," he growled. "It's a long story. Zander, when are we going to get to your planet?"

"I'm afraid it's not going to be easy now," I glanced at Arbido but he preserved a broody silence. "First we need to find Foggs and Jurgen. Then we'll go for a walk. I have an old friend living nearby. He might be able to tell us more about all this."

Charon shook his head. "You just said this is a

made-up world. Does it really matter what happened here?"

His words made me think. The idea of a game was alien to him. The Haash viewed their lives as the only possible reality.

"Listen, Charon, why didn't you ask me to send you to your own star system?" I asked. "Don't you want to go back home and see how things are going there?"

"*Nowr.*"

"But why?"

"I haven't done my duty yet. I can't go back. Let's change the subject."

"All right. I'm not forcing you. But one day you'll have to tell us."

Charon lowered his head. "Where are we going now?" he gasped hotly.

"There's a ford across the river nearby and a village next to it," Arbido said. "We need to check it. You never know, there might be survivors there. Besides, Foggs and Jurgen know this area so they're sure to head for the ford. You just can't miss it."

THE BATTLE had been impressive. When we turned a bend in the river, we saw row after row of sharpened stakes set into the shallows, their tips facing the water. I just didn't understand anything anymore. It looked like the mysterious riders had attacked the village at full tilt, otherwise how does one explain the dead horses still impaled on the stakes? Did that mean the riders could gallop on water?

The little village by the ford had been burned down. The ford, too, was gone, replaced by a fast torrent, deep and dark. Someone must have used some very powerful spells here in order to deepen the river bed. The local defenders had spared neither lives nor effort in stopping the yet-unknown danger that had descended on them from the opposite bank.

Arbido looked completely lost. The sight of the burned-down village seemed to have disheartened him.

"Zander!" Charon growled. "Look!"

Two people walked along the bank. They were still too far for us to make out their faces.

"That's Jurgen and Foggs," Charon said confidently.

Soon I recognized them too. They looked tired. Their clothes and gear were mismatched.

"This machine has quite some range," Jurgen wiped the sweat from his forehead. The day was hot and virtually windless. "We'd walked a couple of miles at least," he perched himself on a hillock. "It's the same everywhere. Vultures and dead bodies. It looks as if a whole army came through here from the other bank. They forded the river in full stride. Lots of dead horses are lying around. Over there," he pointed, "they met with some resistance put up by archers and wizards. But the wizards were no good. All they did was burn all the undergrowth."

"Have you seen any of the attackers' bodies?" I asked.

Jurgen shook his head. "No. Those who defended the river bank were regular players, no doubt about that. A rather motley bunch, very badly organized. But who on earth could have attacked them, I've no idea."

"NPCs, who do you think," Foggs said confidently. "I just don't understand why they kept coming from the opposite bank. There's nothing there, only the forest and some cliffs. That's where the location ends."

"And that's where the Corporation testing grounds start," Arbido added. "The trail I told you about, it starts among the cliffs."

That was a surprise. Could this mean that the source of the invasion lay within the testing grounds?

The river was wide. I couldn't see much on its far bank. It was shrouded in a gray mist that crept toward the water's edge.

"We shouldn't go there blindly," I said. "First we should try to find out what happened."

"There's nobody around!" Arbido said. "Who do you want to ask? Even the looters legged it the moment they saw our Charon."

"I have an idea. Come with me."

* * *

I NOTICED MY OLD FRIEND from afar. Forrest the Forest Sprite was busy skirting a deep crater that had formed on the site of an evaporated marsh. He looked bewildered and distraught.

"Those bastards!" he groaned as he walked. "Why would you destroy something this good?"

By *good* he meant the tangle of old gnarly driftwood covered with moss which used to be his home. Forrest — which was the name we'd given to this grumbling but rather harmless NPC — used to hide here from some of the more forward players that craved a quick bit of leveling. The game developers had messed up his settings somehow, allowing newb players to smoke him three times, every time receiving a nice (for a start-up location) bit of XP for his trouble.

"A talking plant?" Charon looked puzzled.

"Who are you calling a talking plant?" Forrest snapped. He had excellent hearing. "That's a bit rich, coming from a talking lizard! Quit staring! Even better, go your own way! I have things to do. Or... do you think you could help me? Listen, Lizard, think you could bring me a few broken branches from the woods?" Forrest wearily perched himself on a hillock on the opposite side of the crater, casting wary glances at Charon. "You could also bring some water from the river to fill this in," he added. "What, so you're not interested in doing social work, are you? How typical. Everybody's happy to smoke an old man. But once he needs a bit of help, there's never anyone around!"

Completely confused, Charon shook his head, then forwarded me a screenshot of his interface. "Zander, please translate this. I don't understand it."

No wonder. Why would the Haash know our language? The Dargian semantic processor wasn't much help here.

Curious, I hurried to read.

Quest alert! New quest available: Help the Forest Sprite

The marsh which used to be Forrest's habitat has dried out as a result of the battle. Bring some gnarly branches from the forest and fetch some water from the river to rebuild his home.

Reward: 100 pt. Experience and a Rusty Sword.

PS. Personally from Forrest:

If you fill the crater one-third or more, I'll share with you my Happy Days neurogram.

Neurogram description: the scent of swamp mud, the aroma of the woods, the taste of stagnant water and a touch of warm sunshine.

PPS. If you manage to fetch thirty gnarly branches, I'll throw in some mushroom smells and a neurogram of peace and tranquility.

My blood ran cold. Arbido, Jurgen and Foggs froze too as they read the quest specifications.

A low-level Crystal Sphere NPC dealing in neurograms on the side?

"And?" Forrest creaked his gnarly joints to look more miserable. "Will you do it, son?"

Charon sniffed in confusion.

Forrest kept casting wary glances at me filled with hungry anticipation. I didn't like it. He was apparently sizing me up as a potential opponent.

"Hi Forrest," I said, trying to defuse the atmosphere. "Don't you recognize me?"

"Do I have to? There're too many of you coming here, and you all look the same. Everybody's happy to smoke old Forrest. But when it comes to fetching a bit of water-"

"Hey, come on, quit creaking. Better tell us what happened here."

"Yeah right. As if you don't know! Or... have you come from afar? I don't recognize the gear your lizard is wearing," he cast another wary glance at Charon in his onboard suit, then backed off a little just in case.

His speech sounded strange. He seemed to have picked up some gaming slang somewhere. Also, he was sort of jittery. We really should put the heat on him and question him properly. Or... wouldn't it be easier to just fetch him some branches?

I motioned Foggs and Jurgen to flank the old man. I just didn't like the whole situation.

"So that's how it is, then?" Forrest yelled, noticing the danger. Immediately the earth parted, sending up new shoots which tried to entangle our feet. Still, the debuff didn't work.

"Forrest, wait! All I need is to talk! No one's going to touch you, I promise! Just tell us what happened here, then we'll part ways."

The creature cast an evil look around. "So it's five against one, is it?"

"We're not touching you!"

"I see. You want the neurograms?" he assumed a combat stance.

"No! We need to talk, that's all!"

The thorny shoots managed to ensnare my leg, the thorns sinking deep into my skin. It hurt. I had to use one of the scrolls as a warning. The clingy growth crumbled to dust.

Forrest panicked. "All right, all right, ask me already!"

He'd always been afraid of fire. Newb wizards loved nothing better than use him for fire practice, forcing him more than once to duck into his swamp to put out smoldering flakes of his bark-like skin.

"Who was fighting here and with whom?"

"Yeah right! As if you don't know! The Neuros were defending their lands here, is that clear enough?

Only how did they want to overcome the Reapers? It was so scary! So scary! Flames rose high in the sky! The river turned to ice! Riders galloping right across as if it were firm ground! Those cack-handed wizards, they fired a sky stone right into my swamp! It was so, so scary," he whimpered. "The Warbler, our sweet river, boiled in places and froze in others!"

"Slow down," Foggs interrupted him, puzzled. Who are the Neuros?"

"Quit playing dumb," Forrest twisted his creaky torso and pointed his gnarly arm at me. "Look at him, isn't he a Neuro?"

"By Neuros he probably means players," Arbido suggested.

"Looks like it," I agreed.

"Those Neuros, are they the ones with neurograms?" Jurgen specified.

"That's right!" Forrest nodded enthusiastically. "The Reapers didn't kill them at once. First they sucked out their neurograms. The screams — my blood still curdles when I remember!"

"And you, where did you get those neurograms from?" Arbido asked matter-of-factly.

"Don't you know? We had a Holy Update! It affected everyone who wasn't a Neuro."

"When did that happen?" Arbido kept pressing him.

"A couple of days before the battle!" Forrest kept casting glances my way. "I received those smells. And the tranquility. And the taste of swamp water."

"And those Reapers, did they come from afar?" I asked. This story and the looters' conversation we'd overheard earlier suggested that this might have been a glitch at the testing grounds.

"From the other bank," Forrest confirmed my suspicion. "No idea how far. I'm too scared to go there. They might take the neurograms away from me. I need them. I really need them. I can't survive without warmth and sunshine!"

"The weather seems okay," Foggs tried to reassure him. "Why are you scared of cold in the middle of summer?"

"You *are* stupid, aren't you?" Forrest snapped back. "You may be a Neuro but you aren't that bright! The Reapers said clearly: we are entering the era of the Black Sun!" he stopped short, noticing Charon startle.

"Say it again!" Charon bellowed, so that even I jumped.

"Black... Black Sun," Forrest shrank. "That's what they said. There'll be no sunshine anymore. Cold and darkness will rule for eternity. But those who collect enough neurograms might be able to occasionally remember the old times and warm themselves with the memory. What times are we living in! Will this place really freeze over? If I could only get some branches and fetch a bit of water... while the sun's still shining... I have to do it... I have to make it..."

"Was it the Reapers who told you that?" Jurgen asked. "Who the hell are they?"

"I've no idea who they are or where they came from. They kill Neuros where they see them. But they don't touch us locals yet."

My head span with his confused explanations. A recent update? Which had apparently granted NPCs the ability of sensory perception? Then some monsters had arrived from the Corporation's testing grounds and started slaying players?

"They told us to catch whatever Neuros we could find and throw them down the wells. For doing this, they promised us a reward: neurograms. They said, whatever neurograms we managed to stock up on now, would have to last us for eternity. That's something I don't understand. It's something new. And scary."

He began to ramble, mumbling and creaking, as we stepped aside for a talk.

Charon was shaking.

"Charon, you sure you're all right?" Arbido asked, anxious.

"The Black Sun!" he finally uttered. "Your world will die as did ours!"

His eyes filled with desperate fear. I tried to make him tell us more about it but he didn't make sense. He hunched up and fell silent.

"Leave him alone," Jurgen came to his defense. "Let him calm down a bit, then he'll tell us," he paused, then announced, "We need to go to the testing grounds. The answers are there."

"I agree," Foggs said.

"Should we maybe try and find out more about these Reapers?" Arbido offered tentatively. "I'm pretty sure those looters are still hiding somewhere around."

"We'll only waste time," Jurgen said. "I suggest we cross over and see for ourselves."

I nodded. But when I glanced at Charon and Forrest who'd perched himself next to him I realized we needed a breather. It's not that we were going to waste much time. We could always make up for it later.

"Don't you worry so, poor soul," the old NPC

creaked in an attempt to comfort Charon. "The sun's still out, isn't it? No need to get so pale. They might be telling us fibs, the lying bastards. I know, I know that you lizards need to stay warm to survive."

We were within a stone's throw of the woods. "Foggs," I looked around until I saw an old pile of broken branches overgrown with moss. "Let's go fetch him a few bits of wood. It's not as if it'll cost us anything."

"Why do you think we came here? To complete some stupid community-work quests or to rescue our in-modes?"

"One doesn't affect the other," I snapped.

* * *

THE CRYSTAL SPHERE

THE OLD FOREST SPRITE got all emotional. We'd refused to take his neurograms and his rusty sword, so he accompanied us all the way back to the river bank.

"There're no boats left," he said ruefully. "Those cack-handed wizards burned everything in sight. You'll have to swim, I'm afraid. We should have taken a few floaty branches with us," he said with regret.

"Leave it," I said. "We'll manage. You'd better tell us: have they killed all the Neuros? Has no one survived at all?"

"No idea! From what I heard, a few castles are still holding," his outstretched hand pointed at the wisps of mist floating over the water. "Beware of the gray mist. Our village men said if you die from it, you'll never respawn again. What do you need in the land of the Reapers?"

"We need to get a few friends out," I said in all honesty.

"You'd better take this, then," Forrest offered me a scroll. "Only break the seal when there's no other way."

"Thanks."

While we were talking, Foggs had decided to set an example and had begun swimming across.

"Your turn," I nudged Arbido to the water edge.

He cast a fearful glance at the rippling waters, took a deep breath and stepped in. Immediately he lost his footing and sank shoulder-deep.

He panicked. "Zander, I can't swim!"

"We should have found him a horse," Forrest creaked, "only there're none left, are there?"

Arbido struggled, splashing about right next to the bank. I was forced to get in the water too. The steep sides of the bank plunged into a clay bottom. "Grab at my belt! Stop freaking out!"

With a splash, Charon jumped in the water. After about half a minute, his head finally resurfaced. He had a very peculiar way of swimming, his arms pressed to his body, his legs kicking. He looked perfectly at home in the water.

By now, Foggs was already halfway to the other bank, struggling with the current.

"Zander, don't leave me!" Arbido kept flapping his arms around, preventing me from saving him.

"Stop it! No one's gonna drown!"

"Water is getting inside my armor!"

I kept swimming, trying to pace myself. You

had to be really down on your luck to drown in a digital river located in a virtual world. Still, I couldn't help the realism of the experience. Before those neuroimplants came about, I'd had no problem whatsoever swimming in full knight's armor.

My Physical Energy indicator began to fade. My vision blurred, my arms refused to move. I was drowning.

Charon hurried to my aid. He supported me with one hand and grabbed Arbido with the other, all the while battling the current. He dragged us out onto the shallow bank and went back to get an equally exhausted Jurgen.

We sat on the bank, gasping. Water poured from under our armor. Wet clothes clung to our shuddering bodies.

It was taking us too long to restore our strength. Which was bad news: apparently, our in-game abilities couldn't help us much. When I'd picked up the scrolls though, a new tab containing a few simple spells had appeared in my interface. I tried Healing and Vigor but neither worked. Our lives continued to dwindle.

Groaning, Jurgen collapsed onto the wet sand next to me. He lay sprawled there for a while, staring at the sky. Then he propped himself up on an elbow.

"It's only going to get worse," he said. "We don't even know how far we have to walk. What if we have to fight?"

I kept thinking about that too. Whoever it was, they weren't likely to let us through without a struggle. "Can't we block the data coming from our in-mods?"

"Too risky, isn't it? At these authenticity

levels... The in-mode feedback prevents us from overexerting ourselves. Feeling sick is basically a fuse. If we switch it off, our bodies might burn out, it's as simple as that."

"So you'd rather drown in a virtual river, would you?" Arbido snapped.

Foggs walked over to us. "It's all frozen over there," he pointed in the direction where we were about to head.

"Jurgen, I'd like you to disconnect my in-mode's sensors," I wrote access codes for him in the sand. "Don't touch yours for the moment. Three of us is enough."

Foggs nodded his approval. His Physical Energy levels were fine, and so were Charon's. We still had to find out why.

"If you wish," Jurgen grudgingly complied. "Just remember that-"

"It's my decision. Here, take my navigator."

* * *

THE ENERGY SURGE was incredible. It felt as if someone had breathed life back into me.

While Jurgen was busy with my hyperspace navigator disabling some of my in-mode functions, Foggs did a quick recon of the area. I couldn't agree more with Forrest: the defenders' wizards had done a very sloppy job. Then again, how much could they see in this weird mist? The whole bank was pockmarked with deep craters; it was singed in some places and frozen in others. The wizards must have used blanket attacks wasting inordinate amounts of mana with virtually nothing to show for it.

"Are you two done?" Foggs sat down next to me.

"We are," I replied. "I feel much better now."

"Then you'd better come with me. I want to show you something."

He took me to a very unusual group of statues. Three goblins, a couple of orcs and five armed peasants had been caught in a Frost spell. The mist enveloping the shore had conserved its effect.

"Could these be the Reapers?" I asked.

"I don't think so," Foggs replied. "More like their cannon fodder."

We walked on. Soon we emerged into a large burned-out glade strewn with the bodies of mobs disfigured by fire.

"Could this mist block their respawning?" Foggs wondered.

"I think so. Forrest told us so, didn't he?

I noticed a dead ogre. A direct hit from a ballista had pinned him to the log wall of a squat hastily built fortification. A spiked club had fallen from the giant's stiff fingers. It might actually make a nice weapon for Charon. The magic oak it was made of was as strong as steel.

"Heavy!" Foggs struggled to lift it. "Let's go give it to Charon to cheer him up a bit."

Indeed, Charon was sitting all hunched up on the river bank.

"Here, take this. It's for you. Perfect, don't you think?"

Charon cast a disinterested glance over the weapon.

"Hey, man, whassup?" Foggs crouched next to

him. "You shouldn't get so worked up. Forrest loves telling stories just to scare people. You believed him, didn't you?"

My mnemonic chat icon suddenly blinked. Things were definitely different on this bank. My interface seemed to be waking up. It must have had something to do with the proximity of the Corporation's testing grounds.

Arbido startled and swung round. The door of a fisherman's hut creaked open, letting out Jurgen. He was holding a harpoon and an expired torch.

"Mnemonic communications are back up," he squinted at the light. "Who activated them?"

"I did," Charon said.

"Why, what did you want? Why did you call me?"

"Zander asked me about my world," Charon gasped hotly. "I couldn't explain it with words. I want you to see for yourselves! This is what happened a thousand years ago," he closed his eyes and froze, wheezing.

The mental images he forwarded to us felt like a very old faded memory. They transported me to an alien setting. Glaciers rose all around. I could see craters encircled by ice ridges and an occasional cliff — the lifeless landscape of an ice-bound planet devoid of any atmosphere. I could just make out the dark skyline of a city lying far ahead. Its architecture was dominated by oblong shapes; most buildings looked like the yet unopened buds of some fantastical flowers encrusted with frost, immobilized by an abrupt ice age.

The picture shifted as if Charon had raised his head to look up at the sky.

Deep space gaped overhead, studded with bright clusters of unblinking stars. In one place their pattern seemed to be overlapped by an invisible spherical object. I couldn't make out any details: I could at best compare it to a blob of darkness against a backdrop of gloom. But as I've mentioned already, the Haash are capable of seeing part of the infrared spectrum so the longer he looked, the clearer the various shades of temperature appeared.

There was a source of energy lurking within the mysterious dark celestial body!

"Our star," Charon wheezed.

Their sun had gone out? Was that how their planet had lost its atmosphere?

No, that couldn't be right. A dead star looked totally different. Its surface was obliged to emit a weak reddish light. The agony of a star normally lasts billions of years, but Charon had just mentioned a millennium.

The picture blurred, moving, as it returned to the sad panorama of the glaciers as cold and gloomy as the morning twilight.

A narrow staircase cut in ice spiraled down a crater's side. I could see a few cliff ledges and some kind of buildings below.

The picture blurred, then came back into focus.

I saw a frosted-over airlock gate. It was ajar. Behind it a tunnel descended under the surface, deep into the depths of the planet's crust where its magma core still preserved a semblance of warmth, allowing the remnants of the Haash civilization to survive.

The descent seemed to be never-ending. The enormous artificial spherical caves were all deserted. I came across occasional structures that looked like underground shipyards. I recognized the familiar outlines of *yrobs* decaying in the grip of their service towers.

The local civilization kept retreating. Step by step, year after year the Haash continued to lose their battle against the cold. Forced to abandon their underground dwellings and workshops, they continued to dig, deeper and deeper, in order to start afresh, losing time, energy and knowledge. One doomed generation after another kept going down in history until one day a discovery was made at an underground building site. A mysterious fragment of an alien spaceship had been found on the shore of a gigantic underground lake whose leaden waters rippled deep below.

Charon opened his eyes. He shrugged as if trying to shake off his frozen stupor. Mental contact didn't come naturally to him. His concentration disrupted, he was forced to switch to a more familiar communication mode.

"That discovery gave us hope," he said hoarsely. "The hope to be able to jump to another star system and find a new home there."

"How did you manage to fly your ship through hyperspace? Tell me!" Jurgen demanded.

"I don't know. I can only fly *yrobs*. I wasn't privy to the sacred mystery. Only the chosen ones knew how the jump worked: those who built and controlled our starship."

"The jump, was it instant?" I asked.

"It was," Charon lowered his head in sorrow. "We failed to find a new home. We met Dargians instead. They attacked us straight away. No negotiations, nothing. The battle was brief. Only two wings of *yrobs* managed to escape. One retreated toward Argus. Humans killed them all. My wing attempted to take cover on the destroyed station. Rash took us prisoner. The rest you know."

"And what had happened to your star? Tell us!"

"Alien machines did that. They built," Charon faltered, searching for the right word, "they built a *shell*."

"So your sun didn't go out completely, then?" Arbido sounded surprised.

"*Nowr.* It turned black. There was no warmth coming from it anymore. It happened many generations ago."

"We call it a Dyson sphere," Jurgen said. "It's an artificial structure that captures a star's entire energy output. The creatures that built it must have been incredibly advanced technologically — and desperate for energy."

"Not creatures. Machines," Charon repeated. "Our ancestors tried to rid themselves of them but failed. Now it's happening to you. I'm very sorry."

"Oh please!" Foggs exclaimed in indignation. "Who are you listening to? This Forrest will tell you everything you want to hear just to get you to fetch him some old branches!"

I sat next to Charon. "How many of you are left?"

"A few hundred. They're building another ship. A big one. One that allows them to spend countless years flying to the stars. Not everybody trusts alien technologies."

"Where do they want to go?"

"Our objective was to find a habitable planet

and communicate its system's coordinates back to the rest of us."

"So that other ship, is it equipped with the Founders' communications too?"

"Exactly."

"Don't despair," I gave him a friendly slap on the shoulder. "I'm sure we'll find a way to help them."

* * *

"ZANDER," Arbido walked over to me. "I've no idea where to go! It's this mist everywhere!" he sounded lost.

"Do you think you can find the place where the trail begins? Are there any reference points?"

He nodded. "There was that tree over there, you can't confuse it with anything. We probably need to keep to the right of the ford."

"So? You see! Okay, guys, time to move it. We're only a stone's throw from the location's edge. Through the forest, then across some wastelands, directly toward the cliffs. We can't miss it. How're your interfaces, anything new?"

"Nothing," Jurgen said. "I can't even get the map working. I have question marks for my level. My race is marked as Human. All other characteristics are gray."

"Likewise," Foggs said.

"That's weird. I've got the spell tab working," I checked it again just in case. "The spells are no good but at least we have the scrolls. If we come across some mobs, Charon, you'll do the tanking. If we can't tackle them, we'll try to lose them. Jurgen, Arbido, you try to keep out of it."

"Got it," Foggs answered for everyone. "We should have taken Forrest with us. He could've controlled any mobs."

"Yeah right, dream on. He never ventures too far from his little lake. Our Forrest is a stay-at-home guy. He hates adventures."

So we kept talking as we delved into the woods.

We had barely taken a hundred paces when the terrain began to change. We kept coming across areas of tree stumps until finally we were confronted by a wide swathe of felled trees.

No mobs yet. The beaten track was taking us toward the location's edge. A hollow silence surrounded us. Gray mist enveloped everything around.

The gloom grew deeper, trees more sparse. Soon we'd clear the woodland and see the impassable cliff range...

"Charon! Wait!"

The Haash froze, listening in, casting wary glances around.

"Zander, what is it?" Foggs readied for a fight.

A clatter of hooves was dying in the distance. It sounded as if the invisible riders were traveling along a paved road.

"Easy now. Advance slowly. Keep quiet."

The mist began to disperse. We left the trees behind. I could make out layers of crimson that glowed far ahead.

After a few more steps, the gray fog parted.

We faced a gigantic shallow crater. The location's edge didn't exist anymore. We'd crossed it without even noticing.

The world of the Crystal Sphere had spilled out into the Earth's cyberspace.

Chapter Five

The Infosystems Corporation testing grounds

ARBIDO GASPED. "We must have gotten sidetracked."

"Not at all," Jurgen pointed at the fire-polished remnants of the cliffs which once marked the location's edge. In the crevices between them, gray dust rose swirling in the wind. The earth underfoot had fused into what resembled bubbly glass. Fat bundles of cables snaked beneath it.

Jurgen curiously studied the technological underbelly of the testing grounds.

Foggs crouched next to him. "This is still the virtual world, isn't it? What's with all the power cables and data lines? They're just part of the setting, surely?"

"No, they're not. This is how our minds visualize data," Jurgen replied, his face clouded. He kept casting looks around as if trying to recognize the area.

Foggs lit up a torch and brought it close to the uneven fire-swept surface. "If we find something to break the glass with, do you think we could tap into it?"

"Possible," Jurgen found a crackled section of the surface and kneeled, peering down into the vitrified mass of frozen bubbles.

"All you'll do is attract attention!" Arbido warned us, anxious. "They're sure to notice the fire!"

Jurgen sighed. "Wish we had a diamond drill," he sank his dagger into one of the cracks. The tip of the dagger broke.

"Let me try," Charon took a swing with his ogre club.

The hardiness of this glassy substance was impressive. Charon's club bounced off. A few of its spikes broke off in a cascade of sparks.

"We can't do it here," Jurgen concluded. "We'll have to keep going. The lines are protected. This glassy stuff is in fact an access-restricting program."

"What's there at the testing grounds that might help us?" Foggs asked.

"They were created to quickly and efficiently interact with new locations and facilities," Jurgen explained. "This is the latest-generation working environment. I used to know some Corporation workers that stayed online for months, making it their new home from home."

"Is your memory finally coming back? Who exactly do you mean?"

"I'm talking about Frieda and myself."

"Did you work for Infosystems? You're one of

them?" Arbido recoiled.

"I am," Jurgen answered calmly. "Used to be, rather. Back to the point," he cut any potential questions short, "the grounds consist of three types of locations. Some imitate the real world; others are off-limits while yet others considerably facilitate shared data processing. I'm not sure whether they're still intact, though. We need to go and look."

"Does that mean this used to be your workplace?" Arbido kept on grilling him.

"So what?" Jurgen rose from his knees and brushed the ashes off his pants. "Didn't you do the same when you met your clients online? Lots of people prefer going virtual. The possibilities are boundless compared to the real world."

"What exactly are we looking for? And who might we meet here?" Foggs was more interested in the practical side of the matter.

"We'll either be looking for certain locations or for special programs granting restricted access. Usually they look like a piece of gear. Once you put it on, you get access to lots of devices."

"So easy?" I couldn't conceal my surprise.

"In case you're interested, Frieda and I were involved in the development and testing of the Crystal Sphere. Not anyone can get access to the testing grounds. But once you're here, you get to do lots of things. Just don't hold your breath," he glanced ahead of himself, "things are different now. The two worlds have fused together. It's difficult to say what or whom we might encounter here. Pay special attention to any instances of transparent purple glow. It's not too bright or easy to notice. It's usually shaped as a dome and spreads over large areas. Those are the zones offering shared access to data and processor power."

"And this crater, does it also have a purpose?" asked Charon who'd been hanging on Jurgen's every word.

"I don't think so. Most likely it's the result of the activation of the grounds' defense programs."

* * *

A TRAIL SNAKED DOWN through the fire-polished cliffs.

A dull light seeped from the sky. Every step was a struggle. All our movements were forced as if walking underwater.

Foggs staggered and barely stayed on his feet. "Watch out! There's some sort of boundary here!"

I took one step over the invisible barrier. Freezing cold breathed into our faces.

This was a familiar phenomenon and one that did not bode well. Gusts of frigid wind hit us, whipping swirls of ash into the air.

The Crystal Sphere developers had created a special warning system to alert players of any potential danger by using abrupt unmotivated weather changes or illogical natural phenomena which contradicted the known laws of physics.

Jurgen stopped. The freezing wind ruffled his cropped gray hair. Withered yellow leaves fell, whirling slowly in the gloom. There was nowhere they could have come from. Unyielding to the gusts of the rising hurricane, they didn't seem to be part of it.

Normally, a player received a much more delicate albeit persistent warning. For instance, you'd walk through the forest unsuspicious of a robbers' den — or a ghouls' lair nearby which was still way out of your league. And as you walked, you'd suddenly feel a touch of chilling cold or the freezing breath of a wintry mist which would pass as quickly as it had started. Had you chosen to ignore the warning, you might have gotten another system alert of a similar kind. And if you disregarded that one too — oh well, then you were too stubborn for your own good and master of your own undoing.

An experienced player could always tell the magnitude of the impending danger just by the intensity of this phenomenon, deciding whether the risk was worth it.

"The location's defense programs are trying to stop someone!" Jurgen exclaimed.

"Wonder who that might be?" Foggs croaked. "Couldn't it be us, by any chance?"

Charon shook his head in bewilderment. His still damp pilot's suit was already covered with ice.

"Jurgen, we need to do something!" Arbido panicked. "We'll freeze to death here!"

"We need to keep going," Jurgen snapped. "Move on!"

He was right. There was nothing else we could do.

After a dozen more paces, the wind calmed. The surrounding rocks crackled with frost. Gray ash swirled in the air, hindering all visibility. The insidious rustle of leaves grated on my nerves. The leaves disappeared the moment they touched the ground.

I heard the clatter of hooves and the exhausted snorting of horses. The air carried the sounds far, the riders' approach preempted by a new wave of freezing cold.

"Reapers!" Jurgen peered hard at the new danger but the visibility was still poor.

"How do you know?" Arbido wheezed, chattering his teeth with cold.

"The warning's intensity! It's them the defense programs are trying to block! They wouldn't have bothered to waste so much power on us!"

His reasoning was rather faulty. We had no idea who was in control of the virtual world now. It would be nice to think that the location's software was on our side but... it looked as if this phenomenon wasn't selective: it was global.

The unbearable cold and paralyzing fear was taking over my body and mind.

A rider on a white horse charged out of the fog and galloped past. Then he reined in his stallion which reared up, its hooves striking sparks from the rocks.

He was followed by a squad of Reapers. A thunderous tsunami wave of frosted flesh, glittering steel and fiery runes charged us.

"Neeeeuuuros!" their blood-curdling scream froze in the deafening silence.

"Form a circle! Back to back!"

Arbido shrank and crouched, covering his head. Foggs stood next to me, his face distorted, a ray of light snaking down the blade of his two-handed sword. Charon's wheezy breathing escaped his jaws in clouds of mist. Jurgen was whispering something in singsong — the words I couldn't quite make out.

They were coming closer.

Terror sank its teeth into my mind.

My fingers didn't bend. The rough parchment of the scroll was powdered with frost. The seal had frozen solid, refusing to obey my clumsy fingers.

The tips of their spears glowed in the dark. Their ranks arched, outflanking us. The riders reined in their horses, awaiting command.

The frosty mist wasn't going to stop them. The location's defense programs couldn't do much against them, either, The Reapers' faces were concealed by their helmets, but no breath escaped their slotted visors.

"Neeeeuuuros!"

They charged. Faster and faster, dashing at us from every direction.

Arbido broke down, dissolving in a desperate scream.

With unbending fingers I broke the seals on the scrolls one by one.

The air breathed heat into our faces as a Hand of Earth surrounded us with a moatful of thick magma. The vitrified ground crackled, fissuring. Fire escaped its depths, followed by an instant growth of uncoiling vines that whooshed into the air, tripping the horses and beheading their riders.

Still, the spells didn't last.

The assaulting vines crumbled to dust. The Wall of Fire expired. Only the Hand of Earth was still glowing crimson as the magma bubbled, quickly forming a crust of slag.

The swift shadows charged at us. The cooling moat couldn't stop them any longer.

A club swung through the air. A horse snorted; a sword blade arced through the air, splitting the unhorsed rider in half. His frozen flesh exploded.

Shards of bloodied ice glistened in the flames before dissolving in a crimson-colored spray.

Foggs and I fought back to back. Two more Reapers collapsed, unmounted. Hot blood trickled down my slashed cheek.

A furious Charon looked around himself, searching for more enemy, but... it was already over.

Twilight hurried to envelop us. The torch in Jurgen's hand struggled to dispel the thickening gloom.

The clatter of hooves died in the distance.

Sheets of shimmering greenish mist floated around us.

Otherworldly whispers came from everywhere as the Reapers' bodies began to fade and lose shape. Scorched earth stank of roasted flesh.

You've received a new level!

Warning! The skill and ability calculator is temporarily unavailable. The XP points you receive will keep accumulating and will be available for distribution once the interface is fully functional.

Recommendation: in order to prevent the levels you received earlier from being blocked, you need to leave the incompatible cyberspace ASAP.

* * *

"IT'S GETTING WARM! Did you notice?" Foggs wiped his sword clean with a spare piece of cloth.

Arbido didn't say anything. He cast wary glances around, still in disbelief that the danger was over. Charon looked shaken. He'd suffered a metabolite overdose. He froze, his every muscle tense like a taut spring, his glare searching for his next victim.

"You told me this was a made-up world!" he growled.

"It is, but it's been perfected to look 100% authentic," Jurgen was pale and calm. "You do have a neuroimplant installed, don't you?"

"That little device over there?" the Haash touched the back of his head. "I do."

"Why do you think they fitted you with it?"

This wasn't curiosity. The Haash civilization was on the brink of extinction. An idle adrenaline rush was the last thing their pilots needed on their quest for a new celestial home.

"You can't jump without an implant! That's what we were told!"

"And your ships, were they controlled by automatics?" Jurgen decided to dig deeper.

"*Nowr!*"

You'd think that the recent battle would have us worrying about a totally different set of problems. Still, this subject — albeit fleetingly mentioned — contained grains of vitally important intel.

"I got the impression that only living beings are capable of using the Founders' network," Jurgen said pensively. "That might explain a lot of things."

"Like what?"

"Like the arrival of the hybrid at Oasis," Jurgen replied. "I kept thinking: why would the military have chosen such unreliable — pardon me — methods of exploring the Darg system? Why would they plant players' minds into an alien technosphere? What prompted them to build an identity pieced together from hundreds of neurograms? You have to agree it's a huge risk. It would have been so much easier to just use cybernetics."

"What are you driving at?"

"I think there must be a certain restriction in place. Some kind of security filter. As far as I know, even the Founders' AIs don't enjoy the right to travel. Which was why I didn't find any signs of automatic flight controls back on the Relic."

"Could it have something to do with the nature of hyperspace travel?"

He shrugged. "Possible. But personally, I think the Founders were simply aware of the danger of machine expansion."

"Enough, please!" Arbido poked at the solidified lava with the point of his sword to make sure that the Hand of Earth had already expired. "We've very nearly been killed, all of us! That's what we should be thinking of! Zander, do you still have scrolls left?"

"Nothing too powerful, unfortunately."

"So how do you want us to keep going? Did you see those monsters?"

"Keep your voice down. We're protected by the location's defense programs."

"As if they did much to help us!"

"At least we have a very clear warning system in place," Foggs said. "It's the cold. The location tries to freeze the Reapers out."

"With zero results!"

"I don't have time to argue with you on this one," Jurgen said. "We need to keep going. We need to find some kind of access to the servers. The cold is as good a warning as any. We should steer clear of any life-threatening weather phenomena."

* * *

THE SLOPES of the enormous crater were devoid of any signs of life. The area looked like a post-apocalyptic wasteland setting. The visibility was just as bad. Sheets of dull green shimmer heaved in the sky — the only source of light we now had left. The cracks in the ground spewed an occasional jet of ash. Our feet kept sliding: the vitrified surface powdered with ash considerably hindered our progress.

Charon stopped and raised a warning hand.

"Are we taking a break?" Arbido asked, hopeful.

"*Nowr!* I can see some buildings," Charon pointed at something far ahead, slightly to the left of our path.

I peered in that direction, barely discerning the dark outlines of some cliffs. They reigned over the crater's edge like an island exposed by a parting sea. I couldn't see any buildings.

In the absence of my mind expander, I felt awkward. Amazing how quickly man gets used to creature comforts. The world of high technologies had become part of our mental build, to the point where normal human perception seemed substandard.

"Take us there," I said, knowing that the Haash could read the objects' thermal imprints. We could hear the occasional clatter of hooves in the distance: the Reapers were on the prowl. Still, until now Charon's natural ability had allowed us to avoid new encounters.

I walked, leaning on my sword, digging its point into cracks in the vitrified earth in order to keep my balance on the slippery surface so treacherously powdered with ash. Foggs did the same. Jurgen and

Arbido lagged considerably behind. We had to make frequent stops waiting for them to catch up.

Soon the precipitous outlines of the cliffs loomed up out of the dull green shimmer. Now I could make out a few modern buildings high above, perching on the edge of one of the cliff faces. Enveloped in the mist, they seemed to be hovering in mid-air, impregnable and unapproachable.

"That's where we need to go," Jurgen motioned us to keep slightly to the left. He seemed to be getting his memory back, reclaiming the experiences he'd once lost under the constant pressure from his neuroimplant back in deep space.

The mist parted, revealing a crooked fence of planking. Soon we arrived at a neat row of cottages. They'd been ravaged by a recent fire, their roofs collapsed, their windows gaping black. Their neat front gardens had been ploughed up by horses' hooves.

"Over there! It looks like there's a road tunnel," Foggs pointed at a cracked stretch of tarmac disappearing inside the cliffs. The entrance to the tunnel was marked with rampant stumps of rusty building steel and gray mounds of concrete debris.

"Wouldn't it be better to give it a miss?" Arbido asked cautiously. "Do we have to go there?"

"That's the only way," Jurgen replied. "This is the oldest part of the testing grounds. One of its first locations, in fact."

"Take five," I ordered. We needed a breather. God only knew what lay ahead.

"How weird," Foggs studied the burned-out car carcasses, the broken fences and trampled flowerbeds. "Jurgen? Why did they have to build all this?"

His question was quite logical. I too used to imagine the testing grounds as somewhat different.

"The testing locations are slightly higher up in the mountains," Jurgen looked around with sadness. "Frieda and I used to live in one of those," he added, meeting incomprehension in our stares. He shrugged. "You don't understand me, do you?"

"What's wrong with just telling us? Why would they need all these roads, houses and cars? Wouldn't it be easier to simply log in directly to your work place?"

"And where are we supposed to live, then?" Jurgen took offence. "You had it all nice and easy, didn't you, traveling virtual worlds to your heart's content! But how about us? What kind of life is that, living between your workplace and a capsule hotel? You have any idea what a couple of months of this life can do to you? They can turn a man into a monster!"

"All right, all right, don't get your knickers in a twist!"

"At least here I could walk out of my own house in the morning, take a breath of fresh air, get into my own car and *drive* to work, understand?"

Charon in front turned around, alarmed.

"It's all right," I told him.

"Are they arguing?"

"Not really."

Actually, Jurgen was absolutely right. In the last ten or fifteen years, virtually all of the Earth's population had moved into in-mode capsules. Working in cyber space was just so much more comfortable, the choice of occupations so much better and virtually no competition between humans and *serves* — the maintenance robots.

I grinned. Did we really differ that much from the Founders' then? Were our low-level technologies and the modest size of our planetary network our only drawback? Weren't our mentality and our so-called lifestyle basically the same?

Foggs left Jurgen alone and crouched next to me. "I keep thinking about what could have happened in the Crystal Sphere," he said. Since our encounter with the Reapers, he seemed constantly on his guard. Still, at the moment we were enveloped in a weird thick silence.

"Are you talking about the neurograms?" I asked.

"Of course. I used to know Forrest very well too. All our dialogues... I remember them almost by heart. He was just a regular NPC, but what is he now? I just can't see any logic behind that update he told us about. Why would the Corporation take such risks? Just to make the virtual world random and unpredictable?"

"That's true," I agreed. "NPCs are at the center of most plots. They're obliged to play by the book, otherwise the game would collapse. Do you think it's been hacked? Could someone have *infected* NPCs with neurograms?"

"I can't see how it could have happened any other way," Foggs replied. "Jurgen," he turned around, "come on man, don't get so worked up. You'd better tell us how far we still have to go."

Jurgen walked over and crouched next to us. "These wastelands point at the defense system's attempt at complete data destruction," he commented on the route we'd just taken. "This is a last resort measure that indeed suggests a hacking attack."

"An unsuccessful one, hopefully?" Arbido asked.

Jurgen grinned sadly. "I'm afraid that the boundaries of other virtual worlds have been wiped out, too. The testing grounds, the Crystal Sphere and dozens of other gaming worlds might have become a single cyberspace. The Corporation owns lots of virtual realities all of which use different modifications of the same engine and are physically located in the same server complex."

The picture he'd painted wasn't rosy.

Foggs pointed at the buildings at the cliffs' edge. "Can we get access to the city network from there?"

"Don't know. I'm not sure of anything anymore. We need to go and try."

"Excellent. Let's go, then," I stood up. "Pointless sitting here theorizing!"

* * *

THE CAR TUNNEL met us with a fetid gloom. Evidence of desperate battle were everywhere. Here, the defenders had used modern weapons.

Wheezing, Charon studied the remains of flybots peppered with bullets.

Arbido scurried after me, looking depressed.

Jurgen strode decisively, his head held high, a feverish gleam in his eyes.

Foggs stepped softly like a cat, his gaze keen and fearless.

Breathing was a struggle. We kept coming

across the avatars of dead Corporate workers. The location's engine continued to dutifully generate stomach-churning "special effects".

I caught up with Jurgen. "Why didn't they log out?"

"Out of habit?" he suggested. "Think about yourself: whenever did you log out at the sight of a mob?"

"Me, never! Wait a sec... Does that mean there're respawn points here too?"

"Well, what do you think? They test new worlds here. Accidents happen. All sorts of glitches and power misbalances. Sometimes mobs escape from their designated locations. Creating a new gaming world is a complex business; you can't think of everything at once. Accidents weren't an excuse to drop your work and disconnect," he slowed down, then stopped and crouched next to a dead avatar still dressed in the uniform of a Corporation security officer. He turned the man over onto his back.

"But whatever happened here," he said softly, "wasn't normal. What could have killed them?"

"Can't you see? Neuroimplants, that's what did it. Not everyone can survive death, no matter how virtual."

"You're wrong. Look, his gear is practically intact," he shone his torch for me to see.

The man's battle helmet wasn't damaged. His sturdy composite suit was covered in a series of shallow scratches and dents, left apparently by some bladed weapon. I also noticed a few traces of bullet impacts. Still, Jurgen was right: there was nothing life-threatening.

I peered through his transparent computerized

visor. The man's face was distorted by death throes. He had died in agony for no apparent reason.

The clattering of metal made me swing round.

Foggs had discovered something in the narrow gap between the wall and the burned-out skeleton of a flybot. "Charon, give me a hand."

Unhesitantly the Haash grabbed at the car's mauled door and yanked hard. With a loud screech, the car inched aside.

"That's enough!" Foggs bent down and picked up an automatic weapon covered by a fine layer of concrete dust. "Look at this! That's not a pulse gun. It has to be some really old system."

He unclasped the clip and pulled back the breech spring. The cartridge which was still in the breech clattered onto the floor and rolled away.

Arbido picked it up and turned it in his fingers. "Did you notice there aren't many weapons lying around here?" he handed the cartridge to Foggs. "Try and shoot it."

It worked. A thunderous echo rolled across the tunnel. The bullet went through the hood of a flybot.

"It'll do," Foggs slung the weapon behind his back. "You're right: someone's already been here and picked up all the loot. Which isn't good."

Charon kept peering into the dark. He'd noticed something as soon as the shot had been fired. I walked over to him.

"Do you see anyone?"

"A human. Not tall. Blond hair," he answered curtly. "He's gone now," he forwarded me a snapshot.

I couldn't make out his face — and still I startled, recognizing certain details of his gear.

"Zander, what have you got there?" Arbido

asked. "You look as if you've just seen a ghost!"

"It's probably a glitch. I'm just tired."

"The floor here is covered with ice!" Foggs' voice came from within the depths of the tunnel. "And the walls! It looks like the defense systems are kicking in again! The exit can't be far away and it's letting in the cold!"

"Is this the only way out?" Arbido asked anxiously, forgetting all about me.

"It is," Jurgen nodded. "We'll come out by the lake in a minute. There's a recreation zone just past it, followed by a junction. That's where we need to go."

* * *

AN EERIE LIGHT seeped over a small mountainous location.

A narrow beach framed an ice-bound lake. A few deck chairs still sat in the frozen sand. Further on to the right was a park, the trees' bare branches gripped by frost. Not a rustle of wind, not a sound anywhere.

The buildings' top stories faded in the thick fog, their window panes gleaming weakly. The ringing silence seemed about to explode.

Jurgen craned his neck, casting anxious glances around, his white-knuckled fingers almost fusing with his weapon. "The cyber labs are further up," he gulped. "If we turn left at the junction, we'll get to the bunker's entrance. Our in-modes are there — Frieda's and mine."

Charon turned round. "And the children's? Are they there too?" clouds of mist escaped his jaws.

"They might be," Jurgen didn't sound too sure. "I was with the first twenty, wasn't I? I've no idea what happened here after that."

The road skirted the lake. Snowflakes swirled in the silent gloom. I could sense something was coming but I couldn't quite put my finger on how I knew this.

The Reapers were here! Right here! Not two paces away!

I swung round.

In a silent flash of purple, a portal opened behind me, disgorging a rider. He appeared in a swirl of snowflakes, crushed ice flurrying from the horse's hooves. The rider's eyes glowed purple through the narrow slits of his lowered visor, his spear aiming at my heart. All this flashed through my mind in the milliseconds — beyond which lay the sticky darkness of death.

"Neeeeuuuro!"

A burst of automatic gunfire thundered above my shoulder, burning my cheek, dumbfounding me. I dropped down and rolled aside as the scared horse bolted, dragging its unmounted rider behind.

Another portal!

And another one!

And yet one more!

"Neeeeuuuros!"

A bizarre medley of realities gushed forward out of the gap between worlds. Each of the Reapers was surrounded by a pack of motley creatures. Fangs and claws, the frozen gleam of steel and the rusty armor of androids, the shabby futuristic gear of post-apocalyptic dwellers — imagine that all the boundaries between the gaming worlds had been torn down and their NPC inhabitants had received both purpose and absolute freedom in achieving it.

Charon reacted quickly. He didn't give a damn about the phenomenon's illusory nature. All he could see was a bunch of aggressive mobs. Unfazed, he didn't try to analyze their origins. In one shattering blow, his club struck sparks off the nearest serve's steel casing, crushing him and sending him flying a good thirty feet.

Foggs (it had been him shooting over my shoulder) had already spent what meager ammo he'd had. He dropped the gun and whipped out his sword, beheading the nearest mob, unable to see yet another portal open up behind his back.

Stumbling and falling, Arbido staggered toward the nearest building, desperate for cover.

Several riders attacked Jurgen, knocking him down. He wriggled in the snow, his face distorted with agony. Numerous shallow wounds seemed to appear strategically over his body. They didn't bleed: they just oozed a dull green haze.

"Zander! Help me!" he wheezed.

The dull haze enveloped him, thickening into phantom images. His wounds were leaking something deeply personal, hidden in the recesses of his heart. The haze formed Frieda's ghostly outline. She looked so young and happy...

Those were neurograms!

The Reapers were harvesting Jurgen's identity! They needed his memories, his feelings — any manifestations of human nature!

His personality was about to be ripped apart and absorbed by these raiders who would take its fragments away as precious trophies.

I too was circled by NPCs craving human experiences. No idea what kind of sick experiment this had been but its results were obvious. Now I knew what kind of agonizing death they'd all met: both the Corporation workers and the players trying to stop the Reapers on the river bank.

I desperately wielded my sword, fighting my way toward the kneeling Jurgen. He was clasping his head. Arbido hadn't made it to the nearest building: he lay motionless. Foggs was fighting off the creatures with his last ounce of strength. Time slowed down, growing more subjective, dragging out the nightmare until it became an eternity.

A bullet hit my shoulder and went right through my armor, sprinkling the melting ice with claret.

Blood?

Why not the ominous green haze?

Your neuromatrix has been stabilized

The brief system message didn't make it clearer but, gleaming like a ray of hope, breathed renewed strength into me.

Charon came into my field of view. The Reapers seemed to be giving him a wide berth. Apparently, a xenomorph's emotions weren't to their liking! Charon had managed to break his club in his rage but he wasn't giving up, going hand-to-hand with several *serves* at once.

I noticed a spear lying on the frozen ground, dropped by the rider who'd been gunned down by Foggs in the very first minutes of the melee. "Charon, cover me!"

This was some gizmo, I tell you! A complex energy-thirsty device, judging by the numerous power units embedded in its shaft and the microchips forming its tip.

The Reapers who'd attacked us in the wastelands hadn't been a patch on these. With their humble weapons and the absence of portals, they'd been quite easy to defeat. These were definitely top level ones, arrogant and experienced.

Clasping my wound with one hand, I dodged an attack, picked up the strange weapon, swung round and buried it in my adversary's chest.

The spear's microchipped tip lit up with a deadly glow. It pierced the swordsman's breastplate with ease, extracting a blood-curdling scream from his chest.

His bloodless wound coursed with pulses of emerald light. They surged toward me, snaking around the spear shaft. Microscopic charges of energy sank into my fingertips. A foreign memory woven of hundreds of mental fragments clouded my mind.

I'd never experienced anything that cold and dreary. Fragments of NPC's visual memory are an endless sequence of repeating images. The ground underfoot, slimy with blood; severed limbs; bodies split open. The everyday life of a swordsman, if you wish.

My mind choked on these images, their pain and stench eating through my brain while trying to become part of it. The cables of emerald energies entwined my arms and shoulders, sinking into my neck and piercing my temples.

"Nooo!"

The riders busy attacking Jurgen turned to my

hoarse screaming.

It all happened faster than words can tell. The portals were still open, their long shadows still glowing purple, staining the ice and blotting the snow. I couldn't feel my legs. My fingers closed around the spear. My face distorted. The world froze in eternity.

The riders' figures dripped with emerald auras. The mobs were calm as they awaited the outcome of the combat in the knowledge of their own absolute superiority. This was their territory and their rules. The location's defense programs were helpless against them. All they did was freeze everything solid without causing any harm to the Reapers. After the very first rounds, our firearms had stopped working. Foggs had managed to wrestle a gun from one of the low-level mobs but the bullets now flew right through the creatures surrounding him, helplessly hitting the snow or screeching as they ricocheted off steel.

The spear!

The thought scorched my mind, pulsing within its mauled constraints. My convulsing fingers closed around the spear, pulling it out. Its microchipped tip crunched as it left the mob's frozen flesh. The swordsman collapsed on his side. Neurograms gushed out of his wound, breaking down into flashes of pulsating light. Dozens of phantom silhouettes escaping their prison, unsure what to do with their freedom. They floated, circling in mid-air, until gradually losing all detail.

Some of the mobs rushed to trap the dissolving images. Frantic, they seemed to have forgotten everything; they left Foggs and Charon alone and squabbled among themselves trying to get hold of the precious neurograms.

I was shaking uncontrollably. The nightmare of the NPC's memories had released my mind, bringing back the agonizing pain.

One of the riders attacking Jurgen must have sensed something. He turned round, then nudged his horse unhurriedly in my direction. I staggered to my feet. The flaking sheets of dull green haze began to fade. The clatter of hooves grew closer. An ominous blood-curdling figure in frosted armor loomed out of the ghostly fog.

His purple eyes shone in the slits of his visor.

"Neuro, you're strong and stubborn," his dull voice paralyzed my will. "Give it to me!" he reached out for the spear in my hand.

"As you say," I obediently lowered my head. "Here you are!"

I aimed the spear upwards, piercing his throat. His horse reared up. Taught by experience, I released my fingers and recoiled just in time.

His deadly wound surged with light. His freezing scream deafened me with debuffs. I was thrown back a good thirty feet: I was lucky not to have broken my neck. My vision darkened: a darkness that squirmed with agonizing tentacles, its emerald gloom replaced by crimson, followed by an almighty explosion which shattered every pane of glass in the nearby buildings.

I could still hear the tinkling crystal of the crumbling windows. The darkness had been burned out.

The rider was gone. Dozens of phantom figures circled the deep crater where he'd just been. Unlike the swordsman's neurograms, fragmented and unstable, these coagulated identities used to belong to dead human beings.

They were doomed. Still, in these last moments of freedom, they craved revenge.

The Reapers recoiled, scattering. Too late. Flames enveloped them. Smoking, their frozen flesh hissed. Their armor melted. The portals collapsed.

Flashes of blinding energy hit them all one by one. Their frightened horses bolted and disappeared into the distance.

* * *

You've received a new level!

Warning! The skill and ability calculator is temporarily unavailable. The XP points you receive will keep accumulating and will be available for distribution once the interface is fully functional.

Recommendation: in order to prevent the levels you received earlier from being blocked, you need to leave the incompatible cyberspace ASAP.

"Zander? You okay? Help me, somebody!"

Someone lifted my head and wiped my face with a handful of melting snow.

Foggs. Arbido.

I sat up and looked around me. I didn't recognize the location. A cloud of thick fog hovered over the lake. The buildings gaped with broken blackened windows. The sky beyond the cliffs' ragged outline shimmered with ghostly aurorae.

"How's Jurgen? Where's Charon?"

"They're all right," Foggs helped me back to my feet.

I noticed Jurgen at a distance busy collecting something, trawling through the damp steamy sand.

From the direction of the buildings, I heard the rending of a door being forced, accompanied by Charon's impatient growling.

Arbido offered me a water flask.

Good idea. I was parched. "Thanks. How long have I been out?"

"Dunno," Foggs answered. "I've only just come round myself. That was one hell of a blast!"

"Ask Charon if there's anything in those buildings we can use. Better still, go and look for yourself. I'll go speak to Jurgen."

"What do you want me to do?" Arbido asked.

"You can check out the area for any loot," I gave him his flask back and hobbled toward the lake.

At the sound of my footsteps, Jurgen swung round. There was the stamp of madness upon his face. He was clutching another one of those weird weapons.

"May I? Where did you get it from?" I tried to sound calm as if nothing had happened. We had very little time. Yes, I knew he was scared. The Reapers had very nearly ripped his soul out. Those monsters seemed to crave one's deepest and most secret experiences, leaving their numerous retinue to feast, vulture-like, on the carrion of basic human emotions and ordinary memories.

Having had a taste of the disembodied swordsman's mental imagery, I still felt like I'd been covered with blood. "Keep your chin up, man."

Jurgen blinked a few times. His eyes were tearful. His fingers shook. "Here," he offered me one of his discoveries.

A *Short Sword of a Reaper*

Class: service artifact

Power units had been built into the item's hilt. A line of neurochips had been welded into the blade along the blood groove, each of them carrying the signs of the Founders' language.

I focused on the sword, trying to access its properties.

Wish I still had my mind expander! If only I could activate my technology scanner and access a couple of databases...

This wasn't just any old sword. I closed my hand around the hilt. Immediately it sprouted long threads of a metal which began to intertwine, some forming a lacy guard while others hugged my wrist and my clenched fingers.

I focused on them. Slowly a prompt came into view:

Servoids

The word said nothing to me.

The double-edged blade began to shimmer with intense light.

Plasma?

Could be. What else would you need these heavy-duty power units for? A blade like this could slice through any kind of armor with ease. Still, the presence of an artificial neuronet betrayed its true purpose: neurogram harvesting. Was it an AI sword? Hardly. Most likely, it contained an exchange buffer which trapped fragments of the victim's identity and forwarded them to the owner of the weapon.

I shared my thoughts with Jurgen.

He nodded moodily. "I'm going to alter a couple of things," he said. "Then we might be able to use it against the Reapers. You disembodied one of them by realizing you had to let go of the spear. A blow with a weapon like this disrupts the structure of a person's identity matrix. I need a bit of time, okay?"

I glanced at the collection of items he'd already amassed. "All these things contain the Founders' neurochips. Now where could mobs have gotten hold of them?"

"The neurocyber labs are not far from here. You might find all your answers there."

"Okay. Keep going," I released my fingers. Immediately the servoids slid back into the hilt. "We'll check the area while you're at it."

* * *

WE DIDN'T FIND anything useful inside the buildings. There was nothing left of them but their gutted frames.

Oh well. We walked back to the lake shore where Jurgen had already laid out his collection of weapons on a couple of scorched beach chairs. "Help yourselves."

Arbido wasn't in a hurry to touch them. "You sure they're safe?"

"I've disconnected the neurochips from the handles. Once full, the exchange buffer will simply release the harvested neurograms."

"Which will go where?" Foggs asked.

"Which will become part of cyberspace, I suppose," Jurgen pointed at the dull green mist enveloping the wastelands, filled with whispers both bitter and unintelligible.

I focused on a two-handed sword but received no immediate response. My interface was still zoned out, with question marks instead of levels.

As I kept staring, a pale inscription formed above the sword,

A Two-Handed Sword of a Neuro
Class: a service artifact

"I'll take it," I said.

Servoids snaked out of its hilt, sheathing my fingers. Arbido gasped, his eyes filled with instinctive fear. That was it, then. He wasn't going to touch any of these weapons, this little was clear.

Unhesitantly Charon picked up a poleax. Jurgen chose a *partizan*: a spear with a wide tip and two bladed guards at its base. Foggs studied the collection for a while, then took two short swords.

"Put the rest in your inventories," I ordered.

Arbido shook his head. "Sorry, Zander. I'll give it a miss."

"Whatever. It's up to you. Jurgen? Where do you want us to go now?"

He pointed at where the road tracing the lake disappeared into the whispering mist.

"Oh well. Let's go, then."

My armor was caked with blood. Even though I didn't feel the pain, the wound kept reminding me of itself, turning my arm numb and stiff. Had I had received a blow with the microchipped sword, I might not have gotten away so easily. Jurgen was still a terrible sight. He seemed to have aged ten years at least.

We walked in silence. The road began to climb uphill, then ended abruptly.

Arbido stared at Jurgen, uncomprehending. "Where's the junction?"

Jurgen didn't answer. He stood there gritting his teeth: his face spent, his skin a ghostly gray. Instead of the mountain locations he'd promised, we were facing the flat slope of a gigantic crater, its cracked surface still breathing fire.

Foggs cussed, dumbfounded. A wide fissure snaked just below, exuding heat. A few little hillocks looked like solidified magma bubbles. The hot wind carried disturbing odors.

"It can't be! You can't destroy all the testing grounds' equipment and its database!" Jurgen wheezed once he'd overcome his initial stupor.

There were no signs of sentient activity here. Everywhere you looked, the dull green mist mingled with the crimson glow.

Arbido's face fell. "We need to go back," he sighed. "It was a good idea. Still it doesn't look as if we can do it."

"No," Jurgen snapped. "We need to keep going!"

"Where can you go in this disaster zone?" Arbido demanded. "Can't you see? Your locations are gone! What do you want us to find? A cable hanging from the sky?"

I didn't let their argument blow up out of proportion. "We need to keep going."

I'd already spotted a strange jagged outline far ahead to our right. It looked like the ruins of a building. If Jurgen was to be believed, the access point to the Earth's cyberspace could turn out to be anything. It was too early to admit defeat. We hadn't risked all simply to turn round and go back!

"Zander, are you sure-" Foggs tried to object.

Charon interrupted him. "There's something moving!" he growled.

Arbido craned his neck. "Where?"

Charon pointed at the ruins.

Foggs tensed up. "Is it a Reaper?"

"*Nowr*! It's a human! Not tall, blond hair!" the Haash replied in his curt manner. "I can see some equipment..." he crouched and clawed a recognizable teardrop shape in the sand.

Jurgen glanced at the drawing and frowned, confused. "That's an in-mode!"

"Charon, haven't you already seen this human before?" I asked. "In the tunnel, remember?"

The Haash gave an energetic nod. A chill ran down my spine. This was too much of a coincidence. Then again, the probability of this sort of encounter was dangerously close to zero. "I'll go there on my own," I said.

"Why? What do you need to do that for?" Foggs demanded.

"I think I know who Charon's talking about."

CHAPTER SIX

THE INFOSYSTEMS CORPORATION TESTING GROUNDS

SHE PERCHED ON THE EDGE of an open in-mode capsule. Hot wind tousled her long hair. Her gray eyes betrayed fatigue.

The battered 3D Optos hung around her neck. Her bloodied fingers clutched a rusty piece of construction steel. The rocky ground around the capsule was covered in fresh scratches leading right up to the cliff's edge. The dull green mist rose from the abyss, the wind tearing at it, swirling it into unclear silhouettes and taking it away.

"Kimberly?" I stepped closer.

She didn't even startle. She just looked up at me. "How do you know me?"

Gusts of wind plucked at the tattered remains of her clothes. We were enveloped in waves of heat and still she was trying to wrap herself into her rags.

"Liori told me about you."

Kimberly sat up. "Is she alive?"

"You could say so... I suppose."

Her stare hardened in reply to my hesitation. Her fingers closed over her makeshift weapon. I had a sneaky suspicion this wasn't just any old piece of steel.

Who are you, girl? A Neuro? A Reaper? Or something else?

Madness glowed in Kimberly's gaze. This in-mode capsule which had fused with the cracked ground; the rusty piece of steel; the ancient optical device: were they her strongest memories that cemented her identity matrix? Or were they a primitive trap for my own mind?

The servoids clung tighter to my fingers, winding themselves around my wrist like living beings, helping me to grip the sword tighter.

She couldn't have survived, the dull green mist whispered at me. *All this is but your imagination. You shouldn't believe it. You shouldn't give in.*

I knew it. Our gut reactions are not always right. Still, without following them we stop being human.

"Kim? What happened here?" I perched next to her on the edge of the open in-mode like an old friend that she could trust.

With a hiss, the servoids retracted back into the hilt. The plasma edges of my sword stopped glowing.

"You were with the first twenty neuroimplant testers, weren't you?" I said. "That's what Liori told me. She was looking for you. Then she thought you must have died."

"I did," she whispered. "I did, Zander," she had no problem reading my name tag. "My identity matrix survived though," she added, staring into the green mist. "The first twenty were special cases. The neurograms of each of us were stored on a separate server. Would you like to know what happened back on Earth?" she asked with an uncomely grin, avoiding eye contact. "It was a digital apocalypse. Some corporate cretin had decided he was God Almighty. He probably thought he could add a bit of diversity to gaming worlds. Or he didn't think at all."

Kim was shaking with cold, trying to wrap the tatters of her clothes tighter around herself. Her answer hadn't explained much. We already knew about the latest update which had apparently breathed "life" into NPCs.

Pointless keeping things secret from her. I just hoped she wasn't our enemy.

I motioned the others to come out. Foggs was tense and prepared to fight. Jurgen was in shock: he must have recognized her. Charon couldn't quite grasp this latest development so he tried to stay calm, wary of not scaring the weird "human".

"Arbido, there aren't any extra clothes in that stash of yours, are there?"

"Don't bother," Kimberly's eyes twinkled with a new dose of madness. She didn't seem at all scared by my friends' arrival. "Gear won't help. I'm not cold," the words fell from her lips, barely audible. "Thanks anyway," she closed up again, deep in thought. Apparently, she didn't consider us a threat.

No idea how she'd managed to preserve a semblance of sanity and recover her neurograms in order to survive.

In the meantime, Arbido reached into his inventory like a magician and produced an old checkered plaid, threadbare in places. Cautiously he approached the girl and threw it over her shoulders.

"Kim, you know this area well, don't you?"

"You tell me why you came here first and where exactly you want to go," she wrapped herself in the plaid but continued to shake.

"We need to get back to the real world. They stopped servicing our in-modes."

She waved her hand at the edge of the precipice. "One step, and all your problems will be solved."

"Meaning?"

"You need to fall to your death. What's the point in clinging to life? Back on Earth, it's even worse. You're strong. One thing you need to remember is that for the first few minutes, your neurograms will be floating around your avatar. You shouldn't be afraid. Just do it," the way she was instructing me, you'd think I was about to jump off the cliff already. "Something might go missing but trust me, a dozen lost memories is a small price to pay."

So that's how it was, then? She'd found another way to go digital? To become part of Earth's mutilated cyberspace, adding to its agonizing technosphere?

She misunderstood my hesitation. "There's nothing to be afraid of. There're lots of neurocomputers servicing the testing grounds. I know what I'm talking about. Your identity matrix will survive. But you'll need to act fast. You must remember your name before your neurograms dissolve into cyberspace."

"Thanks for the tip. I appreciate it. Still, I don't think I'm ready yet. We need to recharge our in-modes and go back. Would you like to come with us?"

"No!" she seemed to know exactly where we meant. Her gaze alighted on the Founders' navigator. "I'm not going back there! No way!"

"But don't you understand? Here the Reapers will get you sooner or later!"

Her fingers closed around her piece of steel.

"Okay, I'll help you," she suddenly acquiesced. "But first you need to tell me why you want to go back. Is it because of Liori?"

The abyss spewed out a discharge of dull green mist. A groan resonated from the rocks. The several in-mode capsules which were fused into the cliffs flashed their indicator lights.

"Do you love her?" she asked.

"I do."

Kimberly shrank as if I'd just hit her. She shrugged the plaid off and walked over to the edge. The hot wind attacked her rags, tearing at them with a renewed force.

"I'll help you," she whispered without turning. "For this I want the neurogram of your love. This is my price."

Arbido shook a sympathetic head. "Zander, I want you to think well first."

"I only want a copy!" Kimberly stared into the abyss. "I want to be loved too. Even if it's like this... Even so..."

I didn't know what to say. The reason for my hesitation was the simple question I'd suddenly asked myself: what was love, really?

Was it a passion? Or physical attraction? Or sex?

None of those. What I felt for Liori had nothing to do with it. The words I tried so hard to summon up were all weak, unable to describe my true feelings for her.

Did that mean I had no idea what love was? That in all thirty-eight years of my existence I'd not once experienced it?

It feels so empty and cold without you...

You couldn't have said it better. *Empty and cold.* As if your heart had stopped beating.

Anxiety. Hope. My desperate desire to see Liori, to look into her eyes and realize that we were back together.

"There's no such thing as a neurogram of love," I said softly. "It can't be reconstructed. Sorry, Kim."

She turned around. "I know. I just wanted to hear your answer. I'll help you."

"What, just like that, no questions asked?" Arbido demanded. "Sorry girl, but you've no idea who we are or where we've come from! How can you trust strangers?"

"Shut up," Foggs hissed.

"He's right. You can't trust strangers," Kim now stood on the very edge, the green haze clinging to her bare feet. "This mist is everywhere now. I've learned to tap into it. I can listen in to mnemonic frequencies. This is how the Reapers seek out Neuros."

Arbido recoiled. "Does that mean you can read our thoughts?"

"Not all of them. Only the strongest," her gaze burned a hole right through me. "I know what happened to Liori. You keep thinking about her. Wait here."

She turned round and walked slowly along the jagged edge of the cliff until her outline dissolved into the acid-green mist.

* * *

"ARBIDO, are you raving mad?" Foggs attacked the old man. "Put your mind in gear before you speak! Better still, shut the fuck up! What if she doesn't come back?"

"Quit aggroing," Arbido snapped. "I couldn't help it. She looked too much like my daughter."

Jurgen walked over to the edge, scooped up the green mist and froze, as if listening in.

Charon used the opportunity to get closer to one of the in-modes. He emitted a nervous growl, then began keenly studying this sample of human technology.

I perched myself on the edge of a fire-licked hillock. Two-tone clouds swirled overhead: a depressing combination of acid-green laced with crimson. But what was that now?

A black twister spiraled through the clouds. Several black specks broke away from it. In falling, they acquired human shape, then exploded in flashes of cold light, breaking apart until there was nothing left but fading clumps of green mist.

I immediately thought of the looters we'd met by the river bank. They'd been about to throw Arbido into a well, confident that they would get some neurograms for their trouble. So that's how it worked, then?

The Neuros (which apparently meant *humans*) were now hunted and thrown into wells, caves and crevices, sacrificed to the Reapers. The fading clouds of green mist that the twister had brought were meant to be a meager reward for the murderers. Snippets of human memories and simple emotions would be shared between low-level NPCs while the players' identity matrices would end up in the location's gloomier depths where the Reapers would be awaiting them.

A digital apocalypse. Kimberly's words had pinpointed the essence of the global disaster.

Jurgen walked over to me. "I've seen it."

"Then you'd better tell me how it could happen."

"I don't think that the Corporation has anything to do with this update."

"Tell me how you see it, then," Arbido was listening in. "There're always some crazy idiots lurking in the wings, some unappreciated prodigies seeking notoriety!"

"Still, the entire scope of this is mind-boggling," Jurgen replied. "You can't write an update like this on a kitchen table. Whoever did this was familiar with the Founders' technologies," he cast a meaningful stare at my sword. "And these Reapers too — they don't at all look like unhinged mobs. I sensed their hatred — it was something irrational, almost absurd. It was as if they detested our guts. Zander, if you get the chance, can you please ask Kim how it all started? It's pretty clear that the root of the problem lies in the testing grounds. I just find it strange that Corporation workers were the first to die."

"All right. I'll try and speak to her. But this

mist, does it really work as some kind of neurogram conductor?"

Jurgen rose and returned to the edge. He reached out his hand. Immediately the green substance wavered and grew several tentacles which threatened to entwine his wrist and touch the flat of his hand.

"Does that mean that there'll be more attacks?" Foggs watched everything that was happening, drawing his own conclusions. "These Reapers, they're going to find us in the end, aren't they?"

This was a rhetoric question. But at least now we had an adequate weapon against them.

KIMBERLY DIDN'T COME BACK until much later. We'd already begun to worry when she appeared out of the mist and silently motioned us to follow her.

Soon the in-modes disappeared from sight. The shallow slope was now intersected by a web of crevices, their bottomless sides cutting through the islets of hard ground. A strong hot wind blew in our faces.

"Some terrain," Arbido looked around him. "I wouldn't say no to a levitation scroll. Shame we don't have a wizard who could cast us a bridge. No wonder the Reapers use portals!"

"It's over here," Kim pointed at a narrow crevice.

"What's this, a staircase?" Foggs studied the steps cut into the rock. "I'd never have noticed. Who made it?"

The girl ignored his question. Silently she began to descend.

The mist closed in, gradually transforming into darkness. Our torches could only illuminate a small area around us.

A *twixstworld*.

The word gave you the shivers. Here, virtual realities merged into each other, creating a new digital universe ruled by synthetic identities which placed their sole value in neurograms.

The number and variety of the NPC inhabitants of these phantom worlds were legion. Someone had poisoned them with human emotions, creating ersatz identities to whom this poison had become a drug. The lived to *feel* — their only purpose being to syphon off a great variety of experiences, each stronger and edgier than the next.

The stairs cut in the rock soon ended in a small landing. Now we had to jump from one rock ledge to the next to get down. Here, however, Kimberly's behavior became strange. She leaped onto a narrow ledge and pressed her back to the rock, edging her way step by tentative step over the precipice until she disappeared from view behind a large cliff.

"Zander, are you sure about her?" Foggs didn't look happy. "Where's she taking us?"

A blood-curdling shriek ripped through the silence, its infinite echoes trapped within the crevice. The dull green mist below rippled and bubbled up.

"Let me go first," I said.

I wasn't as agile as Kim. I took a leap but miscalculated and hung over the drop, trying to pull myself up.

My armor scraped against the rock, hindering my effort. Once again the authenticity levels had tricked my muscles into shaking from the desperate effort.

The treacherous ledge, chipped and crumbling, skirted the cliff until I reached another landing which listed dangerously to one side. A bit further on, a cave entrance gaped darkly in the rock.

Gasping, Kimberly crouched over the bodies of two Reapers. I couldn't hear what she was whispering. The red-hot piece of steel in her hands gleamed weakly.

The cave entrance exuded cold but the thin layer of ice that covered the surrounding cliffs was melting quickly.

"Kim, you okay?"

She panted, unable to speak. The brief but desperate combat had stripped her of her last strength.

Foggs appeared from around the bend first, torch in hand. Charon came next, followed by Arbido who clung to the Haash like a child.

I dropped to my stomach and offered Foggs a hand, helping him clamber up.

"Phew," he crawled away from the edge and wiped the perspiration off his forehead with the back of his hand. Then he noticed the bodies. His gaze met Kimberly's who could barely stand. The Reapers' corpses leaked green mist which began to envelop her.

Foggs leapt to his feet realizing she was somehow trying to stop the neurograms from dissolving. "What can we do?"

"Finish… them…" she croaked.

Two swords whooshed through the air, the Founders' symbols glowing bright on their blades. Immediately the mist began streaming back toward the girl's bare feet, then disappeared inside the weapons' microchips.

Kim staggered. She threw her head back and closed her eyes. "Thanks."

Her fingers slackened. The piece of construction steel she'd been grasping clattered onto the rocks.

* * *

"WHY DID YOU NEED to risk it?" I crouched next to Kimberly. "You knew that Reapers had ambushed us here, didn't you?"

"They didn't trust me," she cast a meaningful glance at Foggs and Arbido.

"You don't have to prove anything to us!"

"I wanted you to see me as an equal. Right from the start. I needed to show you what I was made of. That's how I do these things, Zander. I learned it the hard way. On Argus especially. I didn't last two months there."

"I don't understand," groaning, Arbido walked over to the edge. "What's with all the cliffs? What happened to the wastelands?"

"The location's programs are still working," Jurgen replied. "Now that their data are destroyed, they're trying to fill in the gaps by using the terrain randomizer."

"Couldn't they have made some nice flat plateau instead?" Arbido grumbled. "Much better for hiking."

"Stop moaning, will ya?" Foggs studied the indicator on one of his swords. "At least here they can't attack us all at once."

I had so many things to ask her about. Our chance meeting was too unbelievable. It felt as if someone had extracted her from my dreams and placed her into this distorted space.

"How did you survive?" I asked.

She must have expected the question. "I gradually pieced my neuromatrix together," she answered eagerly. "I was lucky that my neurograms were stored on a dedicated server. And once I realized where I was, I escaped. The testing grounds are enormous. They're self-adaptable too. So this is my home now. I really wanted to hack them somehow and get out into the Crystal Sphere. That would be so, so good," she paused, deep in thought. "So Liori is the same as me now, isn't she? An identity matrix?"

"She is indeed."

"Are you worried about her?"

I nodded. "Think you could come with us? Liori will be over the moon."

"No. Sorry, Zander. I'm not going back. I'd rather stay here with the Reapers. At least I know I can kill them."

"What's wrong with deep space?"

"Decompression," she answered reluctantly. "You've no idea what life on Argus was like at first. Nothing but vacuum, subzero temperatures and mobs that you couldn't even kill. We didn't remove pressure suits for weeks. We slept in them. The slightest cut or puncture resulted in death by decompression followed by respawn purgatory until you lost all hope and sanity. At least here you can breathe knowing that oxygen won't run out. Here I can dream of one day going back to the Crystal Sphere. Space scares me, Zander. I just freeze; I lose control. Just not my thing," she turned away.

"I'm sorry."

"It's okay. Forget it," once again she was shivering, trying to wrap herself into her rags. I gave her a friendly hug. Kimberly startled and shrank back.

"Don't," she whispered. "I'll be okay in a moment."

I didn't remove my hand. It felt so awkward and so difficult, trying to feel another person's pain, trying to take a small part of it away and replace it with some of my own warmth. All my so-called experience wasn't worth a damn... and it wasn't the first time in the last few days that I caught myself thinking this.

"How did it all start?"

"I've been waiting for you to ask," she answered softly. "Is it so important?"

"Sure."

She paused, then went on,

"One day they uploaded a model of a space station to the testing grounds. The Corporation was going to test an upgrade. I heard the techs talking about a 'hybrid' of some sort. But I wasn't really interested."

"A hybrid?" Jurgen and I exchanged glances.

"So I decided to escape to the recreation zone before they started the space simulation," Kim went on. "It's always good weather there. I started looking for a suitable data exchange channel. I envision them as roads — or tunnels sometimes. I thought, as there were some big-time tests, there'd be no one in the location so I might be able to go for a swim in the lake. So I got to the network node. I needed to get the worker's login and password but he was offline. All this slowed me up a little."

"So what happened?" Arbido asked nervously.

I hadn't even noticed how the others had crowded around us, listening to Kim.

"All of a sudden there was this cold wave. I got so scared. I thought they'd found me. I disconnected from the database, and then I saw the workers running away from the space station model. And I saw that green mist creeping along the ground. It was like a very thick aggressive fog."

"Aggressive — do you mean toxic?" I tried to clarify.

"No. It was aggressive," she repeated. "It was as if it was a living thing... a sentient thing. Then it started spewing out jets of discharge, long and strong, a bit like tentacles. Corporate workers were screaming everywhere. They just fell and disappeared in the mist. At first I thought they were logging out. But once the mist thinned out a bit, I saw their avatars lying on the ground! That's when I knew they were dead. I'd seen enough of it back on Argus. Then the defense programs kicked in and began deleting data. I had to run for my life. Whole buildings were disappearing, the ground was collapsing under me as I ran. Everything around me was leaking, only the Founders' station kept floating in the mist like a gigantic buoy."

"Didn't they try to reload the location from backups?" Jurgen asked.

"No. For a while, nothing was happening. I somehow made it to a safe location where I met up with some guys from security. They thought I was a Corporation worker who'd gone nuts with the shock. They kept mentioning some guy called Gorman — they thought he must have blocked the logout. But I knew already that they wouldn't get out of this alive. This green mist, it could come from anywhere. It seeped out of cracks in the ground or crept out into the streets from buildings' cellars. Then it would come straight for us. Its touch scalds you. It fills your head with other people's thoughts. Nothing helps against it, not even the security's unique gear."

"Did they all die?"

Kimberly's eyes darkened. "They had to fight. The Reapers descended on us from their portals. At first, the security's weapons worked fine but then they began to glitch and break down. It took the security guys ages to die. You wouldn't want to see it."

"Wait a sec," Jurgen interrupted her. "Does that mean the Reapers didn't touch you?"

Kimberly paused, then nodded. "They didn't seem to notice me at all. It was as if they thought I was one of them. Naturally, I took full advantage of the fact. I smoked three of them who were in my way and disappeared into the wastelands."

"Not good," Jurgen concluded once she'd finished speaking. "If I remember rightly, Ernst Gorman was the leader of a special squad trained to combat any glitchy mobs. His men had sufficient gear and training to smoke any NPC on the spot, regardless of its level. Their weapons just couldn't break down!"

"I'm telling you the truth! I saw it with my own

eyes!"

"I do believe you! So you think that the problem was caused by the model of the space station?"

"Yes."

"Do you know who this hybrid is?"

"No idea. I wasn't interested. Once I escaped from Argus, I kept a low profile. I wasn't trying to pry into anything. I just tried to enjoy whatever life I could make for myself."

"The hybrid is a synthetic identity," I explained. "He was created with the neurograms taken from dead players."

She gasped. "Why?"

"The military together with the Corporation wanted to establish their presence on one of the space stations in the Darg system and recreate it in all its ancient glory. The gamers apparently weren't up to the task."

"Why do you say that? We did our best to restore Argus. Okay, so it took us some time, but-"

"But you were restoring it by introducing human technologies," Jurgen gently corrected her. "And here the idea was to reconstruct the original technosphere of the Founders. You need a number of specific skills to do that: Mnemotechnics, Alien Technologies and in this particular case also Exobiology. All of which have to be leveled up to at least 100. Know many people who can do that?"

"No one," she agreed. "I only knew a few players who'd leveled up Mnemotechnics and Alien Technologies to 7 or 8."

Charon listened attentively. "Levels and abilities!" he growled. "They don't exist, do they? You made them all up. Just like you made up all these non-existent worlds."

Jurgen shook his head. "That's where you're wrong. Zander and Liori have analyzed the known interface types and arrived at the conclusion that they were all based on a single development model built originally by the Founders. It's the same for all civilizations. I'm surprised you're asking these things. Didn't you receive new levels or level up your abilities?"

"I received experience, yes. Because I was learning! I risked my life training!"

"No one's doubting that. For us it looked like a highly realistic game. For you, Charon, it must have been a battle for survival. And for the Dargians it must have been a religious experience. All of it still boiled down to one thing: we were there to study the Founders' technologies and to follow their development branches created by some ancient civilization eons ago. Every new discovery brought us new levels, skills and abilities allowing us to move on."

"Let's go back to this hybrid," Kimberly interrupted him. "Apparently, the testing of the space station went terribly wrong. I just can't see what he's got to do with it."

"Good question. I'm pretty sure that the Earth's military space forces have all the answers," Jurgen replied. "First they swallowed up the Corporation and then they began using these testing locations for their own experiments. It was they who built the hybrid."

"What is the point in combining neurograms that belong to different humans?" Charon asked. "Even I can see that it can only result in more problems."

"The risk is huge," Jurgen agreed, " but it must have been worth it. Personally, I can't see how it can be possible to extract skills from neurograms, sum up their levels and place them under the control of a cybernetic system. In this case, the only possible solution would be to create a hybrid identity matrix. Some sort of collective mind, if you wish."

Charon sniffed. "A collective mind which would immediately lose the plot!"

"Not necessarily," I said. "I think I know how the military got around it."

Jurgen gave me a long look. "How? Tell us."

"They created a dominant identity. It was a guy called Ingmud — a shop vendor who'd died during the battle for Argus. When I later met him again on Oasis, he was bent on restoring the station back to all its ancient glory. Incidentally, he had all the skills necessary for the job."

"That's interesting," Jurgen paused, thinking, then nodded to his own thoughts. "This definitely should never have worked, even if only as a temporary measure. They must have multiplied the vendor's own neurograms and integrated them into all the other identity matrices."

"Which worked until Zander returned to Oasis after his Darg mission and began applying pressure to the hybrid, provoking him with his questions," Arbido added sarcastically.

"Don't blame me! Kim, when did the disaster happen?"

"I can't tell you. Time is relative here. But still," Kimberly tried to bring the conversation back on track, "how can events in the Darg system explain the arrival of the Reapers?"

"The hybrid must have created them," Arbido offered.

Foggs kept casting wary glances around. "The Corporation couldn't have been that stupid. Didn't they realize it could all backfire? A mind comprised of a hundred personalities? It would have gone nuts the moment it was activated!"

"This is an entirely new domain," Jurgen's voice was dull. "Something as simple as a craving for revenge could have fused the hybrid's neurograms. The green mist Kim was talking about could have come into being as the result of some desperate — and possibly unconscious — mnemonic attack. With fatal consequences. The hybrid absorbed the minds of the Corporate workers who, let me tell you, were some of the most prominent experts in just about every relevant field of human knowledge."

"Yeah right," Arbido cringed, skeptical. "And by absorbing them, he immediately grew smarter, is that it?"

"Exactly. By absorbing the workers' neurograms, he received all the knowledge necessary plus the access to servers and the ability to consolidate them in order to develop and install the fatal upgrade."

"But why would he want to wreak revenge on other players? You have any idea what happened in other worlds?" Foggs seemed to be unable to face reality. He couldn't accept the fact that our civilization had fallen.

"The hybrid wasn't trying to wreak revenge on anyone. He was trying to protect himself. He was simply playing for time. He knew that the experimenters were about to destroy him seeing as the entire experiment had proven to be too dangerous and unfruitful. By merging gaming worlds and introducing this unexpected NPC upgrade which caused the deaths of in-mode-bound players, the hybrid presented the Corporation and the military space forces with a much more serious problem which took all of their available resources and gave the hybrid some time to consider his next step."

"Jurgen, you can't know any of this!" Kimberly shook her head. "What makes you so sure?"

"I simply follow the facts. The only way the security weapons could have failed was if they'd been blocked with special classified codes!" Jurgen snapped. "Their gear was supposed to grant protection from all known mobs — but it turned out to be useless! The defense programs failed to destroy the station model! Should I go on? How did the Reapers know all this? The answer's pretty obvious, isn't it? They used the Corporate workers' neurograms!"

"Talking about the station model," Charon said. "I don't think we've even seen it."

"It disappeared shortly before the Reapers' first attack," Kim said.

"Wait a sec," Jurgen sounded surprised. "Didn't they arrive here straight away?"

"Not really. It all started soon after the testing grounds had stabilized again. It might have taken a couple of days... I'm not sure."

"That's interesting. It took them a couple of days..." Jurgen repeated, pensive. "But that changes everything! By then, the hybrid was out of danger! He'd already transferred his identity to the Darg system and was about to begin restoring Oasis. What was the point in him creating the Reapers, let alone providing them with neurochipped weapons?"

"Please," Arbido raised his hands. "I'm completely lost. What do you think happened here?"

Jurgen frowned. "It's true what they say that the sleep of reason produces monsters."

"Which is-?"

"I'm afraid the situation is even worse than we thought. Kim, you say you ran away trying to escape the data destruction. Did you see anybody?"

"Of course I did. Lots of workers used personal defense programs. They look like transparent domes. I also saw some top-level NPCs which must have escaped from some database or other. The green mist I told you about eroded the domes and dissolved the NPCs. As I ran, I saw three respawn points. You can't imagine the mess. They all seemed to resurrect there, both workers and mobs. I just can't describe it."

"The green mist," Jurgen walked to the edge and peered into the abyss, "if I understand correctly, it's produced by the location's neurocomputers, right?"

No one answered.

"In emergency mode, the testing grounds should be able to support all types of identity matrices," Jurgen seemed to be speaking to himself as we listened, unwilling to interrupt him. "The upgrade created by the hybrid affected the experimental NPCs whose data was stored on the servers. As the disaster struck, they found both freedom and plenty of fragmented identities to feed upon. It must have been them who became the Reapers."

"You mean it was the excess of available neurograms that triggered their advent?"

Jurgen nodded. "Exactly."

"You want to say that they built the neurochipped weapons themselves?" Arbido cowered.

Jurgen didn't answer. He crouched by the edge. "All the knowledge we used to harvest at the Founders stations accumulated here. And then all this data got mixed up and became available to the mobs who were now capable of independent thought! They craved everything new and yet unknown. And now that the hybrid had removed all restrictions, they have none! Can't you see what's just happened?" he said, about to freak out. "Earth is gone! Our civilization is no more! The gaming worlds have all merged together — but the servers will keep working, generating this kind of warped virtual reality for hundreds of years as long as their reactors keep producing power."

* * *

BY THEN, the fine dusting of frost framing the entrance into the cave had melted completely.

Foggs ran his hand across the rough damp wall. "There're no Reapers around," he stepped into the dark. "It's warm enough. Charon, mind giving it a quick check? I can't see fuck all in front of me. Kim, you know where this tunnel is going?"

"It ends in a location I used for hiding. There's also another exit from this cave which opens up onto a road in the mountains."

"Any service lines there?" Jurgen asked.

"Loads."

"In that case, let's move it."

Kimberly activated her ancient 3D Optos and put on the tinted goggles. She glanced around herself, checking the device's work, then motioned for Charon to stop. "I'm going in first. You'd better put out your torches."

"Zander?" Charon cast a quizzical glance at me.

"Yeah, you'd better go with her. You might need to cover her if necessary. We'll follow. Arbido," I turned to him, "try to keep up."

By then, Kimberly had disappeared into the darkness.

I had a hunch that her neuromatrix too might be the result of some experiment. The military had kept tabs on everything that had happened here, that's for sure. I knew nothing about them but I knew what outer space was like. This was a hostile environment. The military space forces were staffed with experts, knowledgeable and well-trained. Somehow I didn't think they'd have overlooked something as "innocent" as one of the test subjects' sporadic identity recovery. Most likely, they had made it happen.

I wasn't going to tell her about it. She'd only get upset. She'd been eking out a new life for herself. She defied fate. Kimberly was a very strong person.

The cave wasn't that big. Soon we scrambled out of it.

The wide gray strip of cellular concrete looped downward, forming the smooth spiral of a mountain road.

Foggs stopped and raised a warning hand. "I just don't get it," he muttered, dumbfounded.

The opening vista took my breath away. It looked as if by descending we'd just crossed the mountain ridge and walked out into a gloomy sunrise.

"Zander, look," Arbido pointed at the horizon replete with a tiered urbanscape. "This looks like the megalopolis of Europe," his voice was muffled.

"Oh please!" Foggs said in disbelief. "What would a city do here?"

"He's right," Jurgen peered into the misty twilight. "This looks like a model of the real world. We seem to be in the Alps. It's one of the mountain ranges back on Earth, in case you didn't know. I remember because these mountains hindered urban development. There was a lot of fuss about them until one day the Corporation bought them out. They cropped a few of the more famous summits and built their technoparks on top. Kim? The location where you used to hide, where is it?"

"It's a bit further on," she replied. "Once we turn the corner, you'll see it."

Charon alone didn't speak. He didn't even look around himself, just kept blinking and shaking his head.

"Are you okay?"

"The mind expander," Charon wheezed. "It came on, but only for a few seconds. Then it disconnected again."

Jurgen heard us. "Impossible," he snapped.

Charon shook his head again.

"Could it be your eyesight playing up?" Arbido asked, sympathetic.

"*Nowr.*"

"Can you walk?"

"Don't worry, I won't slow you down," Charon strode ahead, unwilling to discuss it further.

I too tried to concentrate on my own

sensations. Still, I couldn't detect any obvious signs of my implants working.

"Keep to the road," Kimberly warned. "The roadsides are full of deformations and unstable areas. You won't like it if you get caught in one of them."

We turned a bend and faced a totally new panorama. Just as Jurgen had said, the artificial plateaus were densely built-up and interconnected via a complex road network.

I stopped and took a peek down. My heart dropped.

The dull light of daybreak was seeping onto a small mountain location.

The familiar lake was framed by a thin strip of golden sandy beach. No signs of ice or snow anywhere. I could just make out some overturned deck chairs lying around. Further to my right lay a park, its branches enveloped in the crimson of autumn leaves.

The buildings looked long abandoned.

Kimberly stopped next to me, gasping in excitement. Jurgen, Arbido and Foggs stared at the familiar scene, dumbfounded.

"We've been here already, haven't we?" Charon looked confused.

"I don't think so."

"But this place looks identical!" Charon insisted.

"The lake isn't frozen," Jurgen's voice was hoarse. "But we kept descending! How come the recreation zone is now below us?"

He paused. "What if this city isn't a location setting?" he suddenly suggested. "What if this is the frontier between virtual reality and the real world?"

"Are you freakin' nuts?" Foggs said.

"No, I'm not. If you use the Founders' technology, that could make it possible. Remember Darg! Didn't your identity matrix interact with the planet's real world?"

"I just try not to dwell on it," Foggs snapped. "Questions like that aren't healthy."

"But you do realize, don't you, that the Founders' stations are material objects?" Jurgen asked.

"Honestly, I don't know. I'm not sure. Is it so necessary to discuss it right now?"

Arbido smirked. "See no evil hear no evil?"

"Piss off," Foggs said.

I understood him really well. All we'd wanted to do was play a game in a new exciting virtual world. Instead, we'd got ourselves caught between the millstones of an alien civilization. None of us had been prepared for this turn of events. So what were we supposed to do now? Ignore the inexplicable? Or just try and find a few answers?

CHAPTER SEVEN

THE CYBER SPACE OF PLANET EARTH

" ALL RIGHT, ALL RIGHT, let's go and take a look!" Foggs took a few steps and stopped, staring at his hands in terror. Without making a sound, he collapsed to the ground.

Charon darted toward him.

"Charon, no!" I shouted.

"He needs our help!"

"Let me do it!"

The location was quiet and deserted. None of us understood anything.

My clothes and my hands began to surge with bluish light. My mind expander sprang to life, then disconnected again. The surrounding air exploded in a multitude of object signatures which faded almost straight away.

Foggs wheezed, stirring. "It hurts," a groan escaped his chapped lips.

I was shuddering. My left arm became transparent, flickered, then disappeared. My left sleeve hung empty. The elements of gear connected to it clattered onto the road.

"Zander... your face!" Foggs' eyes filled with fear.

Three translucent figures materialized nearby, floating in the air. They resembled ghosts after being attacked by an apprentice wizard who'd failed to summon them properly.

"Reapers!" Kimberly made a dash to help us but couldn't move.

I pulled Foggs to his feet. "Can you walk? Turn back, now!"

"And you?" his insane stare searched for his weapons but found none. His unique swords were gone. His clothes and gear kept fading.

The invisible line dividing the two realities seemed to be here somewhere. Yes, I know it sounds crazy but the Founders' technologies could make cyberspace interact with the real world!

This was my chance. The warped cyberspace of the testing grounds had offered us no exit into reality. We could travel them forever with zero results. But my Darg mission was living proof of our identity matrices being able to engage with the real world.

All I had to do was overcome my fear. I had to try.

"Zander, where're you going?"

"I just want to take a look what's there. I'll be right back."

"That's crazy! You're gonna die!"

"Get back *now*!" I shouted.

Mechanically, Foggs obeyed the order and

staggered back. His outline rippled as if he'd crossed an invisible barrier.

I did exactly the opposite and ran down the slope. The "ghosts" hovering nearby seemed to be very happy with my unwise behavior. They came for me.

The descent became a struggle.

If I'd been wrong, it would have been the end of me.

My legs gave under me. I dropped, rolling to a halt down the slope. My body slackened. I couldn't use a single muscle.

Familiar icons glowed in my mental view. This was my interface coming back on! Jurgen had been right! The city wasn't a setting. I had just crossed into the real world!

The Founders' navigator flared up and disintegrated, its particles forming the vague outline of my own body.

You have left a cyberspace incompatible with your interface.

Your identity matrix is stabilized.

Your combat ability The Call has been activated.

The Call worked like a dream, pulverizing the three ghostly figures into a shapeless cloud.

You have received 70986 nanites.

Your neuroimplant version is out of date. Conditions for new ability activation met.

A mind expander malfunction has been detected. Now attempting to rectify the problem.

Warning! You don't have enough nanites to replicate your human form.

New function activated: Interaction with Environment.

You have arrived at the planet: [...]

Navigation error. No data received.

Now scanning the area for available source material to commence replication. No source material found.

New ability received: Pioneer.

Level: 1

In order to advance to Level 2, you need to visit a new yet unexplored planet.

New ability received: Interaction.

Your integration into the planet's environment is currently minimal. In order to improve it, you need to increase the number of nanites.

Reality — naked and at its ugliest — fell upon me like a ton of bricks.

My hand felt the rough surface of cellular concrete. The jagged stump of a multi-level highway junction was listing, barely supported by two leaning trestles.

The ruins of a building rose over the cliffs' precipitous outline. Its façade had crumbled but the framework had survived. Indicator lights glowed within the darkness of some of the rooms: apparently, some of the equipment was still working.

Charon, Kimberly, Arbido, Foggs and Jurgen — they were all gone. All I could see overhead were fat bundles of optic cables swaying in the wind.

Here it was, the border between two realities! My friends had stayed in the virtual world — they were all still there, inside the fraying lengths of optic fiber. They had no nanites available which meant they couldn't cross.

Once again sickness overcame me. Reality blurred. Still, I knew this was only temporary. I'd have to reconsider lots of things. This glitch in my perception had nothing to do with any old ideas about health.

What I felt was stunning. The nanites weren't dense enough and I could literally sense the morning breeze blow right through me. Now I knew how Liori must have felt when she hadn't had enough nanites for a complete materialization.

My heart was pounding. These authenticity levels were way too high for me.

Unable to help myself, I reached out to touch the cellular concrete of the parapet. It was rough — cold and damp. Touching it almost gave me an electric shock.

I was back on Earth. The realism of my experience was mind-blowing.

By then, the diagnostics of my mind expander was complete. The cyber modules of my mind worked at barely one-third of their potential. Until I laid my hands on more nanites, I'd have to make do with using the good old five senses.

Gradually I stopped shivering.

I took my bearings.

What I'd taken for a "mountain range" was in fact a man-made skyline. The silhouette that I'd mistaken for jagged cliff ledges in the mist were pyramids of tiered skyscrapers.

A holographic road sign blinked nearby, its 3D surface rippling and expiring, then turning back on. I struggled to make out the letters,

Infosystems Corporation. Mont Blanc Service

Facility

The arrow was pointing down to the right.

Dawn was breaking, a new day justifying its presence. The skyscrapers were enveloped in sheets of fog which drifted past, avoiding the recreation zone to my left below: it must have had some artificial climate device installed. I could use this location as a reference point. Jurgen had recognized it, hadn't he? Hadn't he said that his and Frieda's in-modes were somewhere nearby?

The road spiraled smoothly downward. My bare face was exposed to a light drizzle. I had no weapons. Every little sound made me jump.

My nerves were not good. I bent down and picked up a piece of construction steel. The nanites reacted by regrouping to reinforce my hand. Strangely enough, the sheer weight of this useless piece of steel added a touch of confidence. I know it sounds stupid but that's the way it was.

The spiraling road joined an elevated highway. The roofs of the skyscrapers served as parking lots, connected to the road by short exits guarded by security checkpoints.

I gulped chestfuls of mountain air, cold and slightly rarefied, emission-free. All my danger indicators sat snugly in the green.

The sun was rising over the Corporation's domain. Diffused by the buildings, its light illuminated the fine web of multi-level highways below. Not a stir anywhere. The world froze in a crystal-clear silence.

The crimson disk of the sun sported dark diamond-shaped spots.

I didn't think much of it. I gathered it must

have been some of the technopark installations obstructing the view.

The mist began to fade. The nearest parking lot was crowded with the latest models of luxury flybots. The digital disaster must have struck at the height of the working day.

Further on, I could see a cluster of gravity elevators. They were exactly what I needed.

My plan was simple: I wanted to penetrate the building and find the lab where they'd experimented with nanites. In order to replicate them, I needed suitable source material.

I scrambled past row after row of parked cars. The wind screeched over a loose sheet of steel. The taut cables supporting some sort of latticework tower were vibrating, emitting a low-frequency hum. Not a soul in sight.

Just when I thought about it, I noticed a group of dark specks in the sky, quickly approaching from the west: winged creatures looking suspiciously like harpies.

Where the hell had they come from?

You can't surprise a player of my experience with a mythical beast, and still my blood ran cold. Realities had merged completely! Our skies were circled by monsters we'd built using alien technologies!

One of the harpies noticed me and banked, coming for me. I'd barely had time to dive under a car when the monster's claws screeched against its bodywork, tearing it apart.

Squawking indignantly, the harpy soared upward, preparing to strike at me again. I'd dropped my piece of steel. A film of cold sweat clung to my body. Who was I afraid of? These were ordinary mobs! And — they were an excellent source of nanites. I was pretty sure the Call should work against them.

A burst of a submachine gun rattled nearby. I heard the sound of something heavy plopping to the ground.

I crawled from under the car and darted for the nearest cover. The flock of harpies was panicking, trying to escape. One of them lay dead about fifty feet from me. Its body rippled with interference, its claws still scraping on the concrete. Its sprawled wings were rapidly dematerializing.

The mist was fading away, dissipating into the finest haze. The visibility had improved dramatically. I could now see seven people stealing past the rows of cars. They were armed with stub-barreled pulse guns. I didn't recognize the make. The combat visors of their battle helmets concealed their faces. Their clothes were threadbare, their gear tired and covered in dark brown spots which looked suspiciously like caked blood.

Survivors?

37,549 nanites detected. Status: deactivated, inoperative. For immediate re-use, enter reload code.

By then, the silhouette of the downed harpy had faded into nothing, leaving behind a small puddle of gray liquid on the damp roof. I lingered, wary of activating the Call for fear of attracting attention. I had no reason to trust Corporate staff.

I watched them.

The strangers acted in calm confidence. They didn't look like researchers. Security, probably. How on earth had they managed to shoot down a nanite-generated harpy with a regular pulse gun?

"Keep looking!" a voice said nearby. "Keep looking."

One of the men stopped by the puddle of gray liquid and doused it with a spray can. The liquid foamed. The man unclasped a small cylindrical container from his belt and began collecting the foam into it, then screwed the lid tightly back on.

He'd taken the remaining nanites. What a shame.

"Sector scanning completed. No targets detected," the fear and confusion in his voice were palpable.

"Same here," another voice reported calmly, as if the speaker was past caring.

Another burst of gunfire rattled through the air.

"Don't waste your ammo!" the group leader snapped at the man for firing blindly.

I didn't like their aggressive attitude. The men were apparently busy mopping up the area. They would shoot anyone on sight. I might not even get the chance to explain myself to them.

Nanites were my flesh and blood, and right at the moment, I simply didn't have enough. My combat and defense ability icons were colored gray. In order to negotiate with them on equal terms, I needed more nanites.

A single shot rang out in the silence.

The bullet hit one of the men in the head, striking sparks from his combat helmet. If that wasn't enough, his gear began to blur and fade, rapidly covering with interference. The man's body began to melt into thin air.

"Neeeeuuuuro!" the already familiar blood-curdling shriek echoed from the surrounding walls. A shadow strobed behind the windows of a nearby building, followed by more bursts of automatic fire.

So much for survivors! These were Reapers!

"I found another one!"

I barely had time to duck, shattered glass showering me from windowpanes above. They were firing at me now!

You've lost 13,000 nanites.

You've received a fragment of an unidentified control code.

The lone sniper's bullet rang out again, cutting the burst of automatic fire short. The fake "Corporation worker" waved his hands in the air before collapsing to his knees. A large round hole gaped in his chest, its fire-polished edges glowing red with heat. An incandescent haze slithered around it.

The Call: activated

It didn't work! I darted off, weaving between the cars. Bullets chased me, thudding through the metal. The mysterious control code kept popping up with every near miss. I kept losing nanites and I couldn't do anything about it!

Now I knew exactly how the Reapers had shot the harpy down. Well, they weren't stupid, that's for sure. Their bullets must have had built-in transmitters.

As a last resource, I activated Steel Mist. The

number of the nanites stabilizing my neuromatrix dropped to critical. But at least the Reapers' scanners couldn't penetrate its fine veil.

It looked like I'd lost them.

I stopped to catch my breath. Mechanically I leaned my hand against a taut cable. My fingers went right through it. My hand smarted with a burning pain.

Your perception levels cannot be decreased

This system message definitely had something to do with that Pioneer ability. I had to look into it. Still, it would have to wait a little.

The Reapers seemed to have given up on me. The firing stopped. There were five of them left. No idea what had happened to the mysterious lone sniper.

* * *

A WARY, DECEITFUL SILENCE hung over the parking lot.

I watched the enemy, trying to second-guess any future scenarios.

The harpies circled the sky at a safe distance. None of them had ventured to approach the arena of the recent combat. How on earth had they escaped into the real world at all?

In the meantime, the Reapers had split. Three of them stayed with the dead bodies. They were busy talking — apparently, not afraid of the mysterious sniper anymore. They must have believed him dead too. Two more headed towards the service vaults at the east side of the parking lot.

They were back almost straight away, carrying a plasma torch.

Now what would they need that for? I crept closer. I could just about make out the two misshapen human outlines of the defunct "Corporate workers" lying amid the deformed cars. Their gear had already melted and solidified in fancy patterns of purple-tinged metal.

This was cargonite!

No idea what kind of weapon the sniper had been using but it must have had something to do with alien technologies. No bullet in the world could provide the energy required to completely disintegrate nanites.

None of the Reapers seemed to possess the Mnemotechnics skill. Good. I wasn't going to risk losing my chance.

"Can't you cut any faster?" the leader's voice rang with irritation. "I want all of it, every single crumb. Move it!"

No one answered. His men were working hard, struggling to cut through the high-resistance metal, but they were too inexperienced and clumsy.

Who were they? I kept thinking of them as Reapers but these couldn't have been NPCs.

What if these were some of the dead Corporation workers, their minds and their appearance preserved in nanites? Come to think of it, I had no idea of how the disaster had unfolded in the real world.

They seemed to behave like human beings but this didn't count anymore. They must have inherited their hosts' identities together with their neurograms.

The leader was confident — arrogant even. He was also quite careless, standing there in full view with his rifle slung behind his back. One of his men, however, kept casting wary glances around, constantly on his guard. The remaining three weren't exactly all there. They didn't seem to know what they were doing, freezing deep in thought, then continuing to hack through the cargonite carelessly, at the risk of taking off their own fingers.

My heart clenched with a momentary sympathy. Then I asked myself a legitimate question: where were the devices supporting their identity matrices?

At the risk of exposing myself, I restructured the Steel Mist, thinning it out, and sent a small group of nanites to investigate.

Five neuronet connections detected.
The source of data is located outside the effective scanning range.

Immediately the group leader sensed something. "Neeuuro?"

There was nothing human left in his dull voice: it breathed cold and dread. These creatures were neither NPCs nor humans: they were of a third gender, a new life form that had sprouted out of the marriage of human and alien technologies. We really shouldn't make a mistake in their respect.

I attacked them with Replication. This nanite-making ability had saved my backside quite a few times in the past. Now too it lived up to its name.

The air exploded in flashes of blinding light which rose in roaring pillars of fire. The plasma torches' power units blew up. The blast overturned the nearest cars, some of them crashing down into the abyss separating the buildings. Others went up in flames. The newborn nanites streamed toward me, pouring into my fading body, activating the skills and breathing life into me.

The Reapers may have survived the crushing blow but their weapons hadn't. Not a single shot sounded in response to my attack.

Dropping flakes of oxidized steel, four of them came for me, furious. Their appearance was awe-inspiring; their expressions made your blood run cold in your veins.

I met one with a Plasma Blast. Then things didn't go according to plan. My attackers recoiled, their bodies dissipating in a fine veil of nanites that enveloped their leader.

His gaze was cold and emotionless, as if he was studying an insect. This wasn't a common nanite hunter anymore. It seemed as if I'd just invited the attention of someone much bigger than this group leader.

Exactly. There was only one data communication channel left, but its traffic had grown tenfold. The source of the signal was still outside the effective scanning range. Did that mean that my opponent was nothing but an avatar, controlled by an identity safely out of my reach?

Didn't that sound familiar. The only difference was that the world had shifted on its axis. Its poles had inverted. Just like him, I used to be a bored top-level player, fed up and asking myself whether the meager XP and penny loot were worth taking on another mob. I used to give them the same kind of look he was giving me now.

All right, but who was he? Definitely not a Reaper. They never declined battle, always on the prowl for yet more neurograms. They attacked you when they saw you and didn't bother to stare their victims down.

The fact that all this was happening in real life made me uneasy. I was surrounded by the deserted towers of buildings and technoparks. The sun continued to creep toward its zenith. The dark diamond-shape spots on its surface were still there.

You might think I was taking my time because I was too scared. That's where you're wrong. All of the above had only taken a few split seconds. Time seemed to have compressed. Droplets of molten cargonite hit the damp tarmac, rolling, steaming and hissing.

The blast detonated a couple of blocks away, spewing an ash-white cloud of debris into a sky permeated with flames.

The degree of surprise in the fake "Corporate worker's" stare was enormous. He definitely didn't view me as an insect anymore. Apparently, he hadn't expected to come across an opponent in possession of the Mnemotechnics skill. He'd failed to realize that I'd been using their communications channel as a homing beacon for my nanites who had been programmed with System Failure and Critical Damage.

You've received 2,385,000 nanites!
Now configuring the Replication matrix. Your integration into the environment has increased to 100%.

You've received a new level!
Your Mnemotechnics skill has grown 2 pt.!
New ability available: Colonizer
New nanite control code available!
New ability available: Self-Replication

* * *

THE FIRE AT THE PARKING LOT went out quickly.

I felt remarkably well. The Founders' interface worked just fine. All my skills and abilities were active. I had plenty of nanites at my disposal; still, it was probably time I ditched some old habits. I created some comfortable lightweight clothes for myself, restored my personal navigator module and stopped at that — for the time being.

I had to think and act fast. I checked the mnemonic communication channels. The planet's mnemosphere responded with a dull silence. All channels were dead; my friends were still out of range.

I scanned the nearest buildings. Immediately the world around me lit up with a multitude of signatures. The top floors were occupied by some large spacious halls. Below them, the density of the equipment filling the floors grew; power consumption also grew respectively. No people anywhere.

Finally, on Floor 50 I discovered some rooms housing in-modes. My hopes soared, only to crash the next moment as the in-modes' equipment reported critical failures.

The fate of the mysterious sniper was still unknown. I'd have loved to have known who he was.

A lucky survivor from among the Corporation staff? A player whose identity self-replicated in nanites? Had he managed to escape the Reapers' attack?

In any case, I had to find and study his weapon. I glanced at a nearby tower. One of its floor-to-ceiling windows was broken. That's where he'd fired from.

Ten floors below, my scanner offered a clear view of server rooms. Just what I needed! Nanites would help me gain quick access to their equipment. So that's where I needed to go, then. I would first study the position of the anonymous sniper; then I'd enter the city network and connect to my own apartment. I'd have to hack the nearest vending machine. Using their principle of molecular replication, I'd create some exo and cartridges. Then I'd get a few service robots off the street to help me recharge my in-mode and run a quick maintenance.

But first I had to sort out my new skills. In this situation, the Founders' interface was my sole survival tool.

First off, I opened the Mnemotechnics tab.

After all the fiddling around with nanites while repairing the interstellar communications module on board the Relic — and especially after building all the personal navigator devices — my Mnemotechnics skill had grown 5 pt. Still, the Active Shield ability was highlighted in gray.

Requires an implanted artificial neuronet module

I had one, didn't I? I'd been saving it in case my in-mode failed completely. It looked as if now was the time to use it.

I activated the artificial neuronet and allowed it access to my mind expander. I concentrated on my sensations but it seemed okay. The loathsome identity of the ancient AI had apparently been exterminated.

Your Active Shield ability has been activated.
Now redistributing nanite groups.

Excellent.

Let's have a look at the skills I'd received by crossing into the real world.

Pioneer: you've completed your first independent journey from one star system to another.

I smirked. So Darg didn't count then, did it? I wonder why?

I kept reading,

Upon arrival on a new planet, you will receive a new ability: Interaction.

Both the degree of your integration into a new environment and your ability to interact with it directly depend on the numbers of nanites under your control. Try not to waste them: unexplored planets offer few available replication sources.

Suggestion: Use your personal navigator device in order to search for automatic stations and stocks of replication source materials prearranged by AI suppliers. If your navigator fails to locate such stocks in a star system, proceed with extreme care. You might need to use Object Replication to create a recon probe and send it in search of any potential sources of cargonite. Failure to obtain them might result in your being forever stuck in an alien world!

Suggestion: Use your personal navigator device in order to communicate your coordinates to the AI of the central network node and set up a timeout period. Upon its expiry, your identity matrix will be restored from backup at your point of departure.

Which, if I understood it rightly, was Phantom Server!

Amazing. What a shame I didn't have an identity matrix backup! Besides, the central node of the ancient interstellar network had long become a myth. It was probably long gone, destroyed like all the Dargian stations.

Colonizer. You currently have over 2,000,000 nanites under your control. If you would like to allow other space travelers access to the new world, create a navigational beacon and set up an arrival point. Please bear in mind that you need two or more nanite colonies in order to support an identity matrix. Each new arrival will necessitate three nanite colonies, not including the nanites required to recreate the travelers' physical appearance. In order to receive their spaceship, you will need plenty of cargonite stocks, a communications station and an AI responsible for the travelers' materialization.

Each navigational beacon, resurrection point or wormhole exit you create raises your status in the Colonizers Council.

Warning! If a planet you've discovered already hosts sentient or pre-sentient life forms, proceed with caution. You will need to consider any potential consequences of your every action and their possible effect on the indigenous civilization. The Colonizers Council may hold you accountable for any fragrant interference affecting the evolution of endemic species or any other acts inconsistent with the Council Code.

Please note:

If you would like to open a planet for free unlimited visitation, at least 90% of its surface has to include nanite deposits. This would guarantee complete interactivity, allowing any traveler or even his or her identity matrix to engage with the new environment.

* * *

I LIKE DISCOVERING THINGS. Even in my past gaming life, I loved solving complex non-linear quests, enjoying the challenge of unraveling their riddles one step at a time. But this ray of truth glimmering at the edge of understanding was akin to a shattering informational blow.

I could finally stop wondering how we'd managed to interact with physical objects back on Darg or how we explored space stations, confronting alien invaders.

Nanites were the answer! We'd had no idea of their main and primary function!

Nanites were the mediator between an identity matrix and the real world. This was how the Founders made the entire Universe interactive!

The Founders' AI-controlled avant-garde fleets had visited star systems which they then impregnated with nanites. Scattered in space, nanites automatically sought the elements necessary for their self-replication, after which their masses landed on planets and switched to energy saving mode, patiently awaiting their activation for millions of years.

A "traveler's" arrival would activate them. The fact that the network's creators had been long gone was irrelevant. The nanobots can't tell the difference between identity matrices: a Founder, a Haash, a Dargian or a human being are all the same to them. And that includes in-game monsters infected with original neurograms.

A shiver ran down my spine. Nanites didn't care. They would support any identity matrix at all. They had no idea of the millions of years that had elapsed; of new civilizations flourishing on once virgin planets — civilizations which had already evolved and invented their own cyberspace and neurocomputers, having learned to build and digitize their own *fantasies*.

I cast a look around. The harpies were still circling the sky.

Our dreams, our myths — the Founders' technologies had inadvertently brought them into being, allowing them to flood the real world.

Too late to try to change it back. I couldn't even imagine the number of star systems visited by the ancient AI-controlled fleets delivering cargonite to places which would have never had it otherwise.

Did that mean that the disaster that was engulfing Earth had been predetermined long before our ancestors had learned to control fire?

My fingers touched the navigator, lighting up a few icons of the outer ring.

Navigation beacon: not detected
Arrival point: not detected
Wormhole exit: not detected
Would you like to colonize the planet with nanites?

I snatched my hand away. The symbols of the ancient language faded obediently.

* * *

THE CORNER of the nearest building had collapsed. A few of the structural beams listed, reaching across the abyss toward the opposite tower. A perfect shortcut.

Trying not to look down, I ran the whole length of the shaky walkway and jumped down into the collapsed room.

Its floor was littered with broken plastoglass and concrete debris. All furniture had been swept into the opposite corner. Nothing of interest.

I walked out into the deserted corridor. A damaged light switch sparked in the silence. The walls and ceiling bore occasional traces of fire damage. Puddles of water on the floor were framed with the recognizable white crust of chemicals from the automatic fire extinguishing system.

The office next door was virtually undamaged. Its ex-owner had lived in a world far removed from our cramped capsule flats. You could probably billet a hundred people in the enormous — by city's standards — space he'd had all for himself.

Water cascaded down an installation of terracotta terraces at its center, pouring into a small artificial pond inhabited by fearful bug-eyed little fishes. The pond was surrounded by real potted plants.

The room's molecular replicator — one of today's must-haves — didn't work. Its casing was deformed and had been ripped off in places. The room's walls looked gray and bare compared to its lush décor. No wonder: normally they'd be covered with holograms but now that power was down, their meticulous design was gone too.

What was there on the floor?

I crouched. Fresh drops of blood led from the broken window to the door. So that's where the lone sniper had fired his second shot, then. That's where he'd been wounded.

I followed the trail to the spot where the mysterious sniper must have stood for a while, holding onto the wall. His wound was serious. He'd lost a lot of blood.

The door was open, its lock shot out.

The familiar rustle of a pulse gun being cocked came from inside the room.

"Hey! I'm a friend!" I stepped away from the door just in case. His weapon was extremely dangerous in my state.

"Name yourself," his gargling throat wheezed.

"My name won't tell you anything."

"Piss off, then. I know all my friends. And my enemies won't get me here."

"All right. I'm Zander."

"What's your nickname?" I heard the sound of metal against plastic. He had the doorway in his crosshairs. "Give me your squad number or leave now. You've got nothing to gain here. I have no nanites."

All right. He must have taken me for a Reaper. Why wasn't he shooting, then? Was he waiting for me to appear in the doorway for a positive kill?

The sounds behind the door ceased. I didn't trust this silence. Still, nothing seemed to happen. I waited for a while but couldn't hear a thing from inside.

I had to chance it. I had no desire to waste my time hovering in the corridor.

I sacrificed a group of nanites to create a copy of myself. It was low-resolution but it'd have to suffice.

My nanite twin stepped into the open door. No shooting followed. The nanites forwarded me information and returned, forming an extra protective layer over me.

I entered. The room was small, barricaded with piled-up computer terminals. A man was slumped behind them. He wore the uniform of a space forces Major. His helmet lay on the floor nearby. His face was gaunt and pasty, his chapped lips pursed together. He looked about forty or forty-five. Blood caked in his prematurely gray hair. His eyes were closed.

I crouched to study his wounds. They didn't look good. Two bullets had breached his armored suit. One was stuck in his right upper arm, the other in his chest where the multilayered fabric of his suit had already been damaged.

I ran a quick scan. The Major was still alive. I had to remove the bullets, stop the bleeding and dress his wounds but I had nothing to do it with. No surgical tools, no dressings. All I had was nanites.

But what if I used his own gear resources?

His life support module proved to be completely dead. All cartridges empty. Same with the automatic first-aid kit. He had no metabolites. A more thorough search revealed three more holes in his suit. The wounds below them had already healed. The guy had had it rough in the last few days. Hadn't we all.

He was dying. My medical skills were rather symbolic but I had to do something!

Supporting his head with one hand, I ran the other over his wounds. Nanites flooded in, streaming 3D pictures of the wound canals. I acted on a hunch, sending direct mnemonic commands to patch up damaged blood vessels. Luckily, all I needed to perform these minute surgeries was a clear-cut mental image and a mental command. I focused on microscopic ruptures on the 3D model, marking them, then activating the Restore From Sample command.

The bleeding seemed to have stopped. Now the bullets. On my orders, the nanites began to utilize the deformed slugs. Did it sound like I was *repairing* him? Well, what else could I do? I wasn't a surgeon!

It was a good job he was unconscious. I don't think he'd have appreciated my first aid techniques.

Whew. The bullets were gone. What next? He was still too sick. For all my help, he might die without regaining consciousness.

Should I use exo?

Well, what other options did I have? I thought I'd seen a molecular replication machine in one of the offices but I wasn't sure it still worked.

I activated Piercing Vision.

There it was! Its casing was ripped off — a mob's work, judging by claw marks. Let's have a look what's inside.

The cartridges were there. The machine was out of power, a few of the connectors broken, but its core was undamaged. I might try and repair it, seeing as I had its scheme in my Technologists Clan database.

I reached for the Major's gun and removed the power unit. The nanites picked it up and transported it to the replicator.

Excellent. Now I had to repair the broken connections. Then I'd try to upload Novitsky's formulas to the machine's memory. They just might work.

A dry click made me flinch.

The gun's muzzle touched my temple. The Major's hands shook with the effort.

"Put it down," I said. "It's not gonna work. Don't exert yourself. Better tell me your name."

Slowly he lowered the gun and crawled back to the wall. His eyes couldn't focus. "Fuck you..."

Exhausted and frustrated, he had taken me for an enemy.

"I'm not a mob," I said. "I didn't escape one of your test labs. All right?" suddenly I felt angry. Why is it that two human beings can find it so hard to come to an agreement? It had been so much easier with the Haash!

"Do you know who I am?" I asked.

"Surprise me," the Major croaked.

"I'll try. Just let me do my work," I focused back on the nanites. "What's your name, tell me."

"Dominic," he struggled to stay alert.

* * *

I KEPT NOTHING back from him. The brief story of my life seemed to have perturbed him. He definitely knew of the events I'd mentioned.

"So how do you like my side of the story?" I finally asked.

He didn't reply, just glared at me with suspicion. His standard-issue holographic sleeve patch sported an additional small icon. I knew what it stood for: Deep Space Communications.

Could he have been the one who'd been monitoring our progress in Phantom Server?

"You don't have a clue," he croaked.

I didn't take offence. "Maybe I don't. But I do have lots of questions. I just hope that you have the answers."

By then, the molecular replicator had rebooted itself. One little thing left to do. I had to make it synthesize an alien metabolite using a formula from the Exobiologists Clan's database.

"We were forced to choose the lesser of two evils," the Major wheezed.

Oh no. He wasn't going to get away with empty rhetoric. "Creating the hybrid, breeding the Reapers, killing billions of people — is that a lesser evil? What was your objective, may I ask?"

"Expansion into the Universe," he answered self-righteously. "As well as the survival of humanity."

His last words drove me mad. "Some survival!"

"You don't know," he repeated.

"Okay, tell me, then! Your turn to surprise me! Where did you get the neuroimplant prototype from? Where did you find cargonite?"

"By accident," he struggled to speak. "On one of Jupiter's moons... deep in one of its subglacial oceans. An alien spaceship... wrecked..." blood boiled on his lips.

"Okay, don't! Keep quiet. I'll fix you up in a moment. Then we can have a talk."

"I won't live."

With a startle, he stared at me as if he'd seen a ghost. Red spots covered his cheeks. He blinked. Had he recognized me?

"Don't worry, Major. I'll patch you up like you won't know yourself."

He gulped, then glanced at his gear indicators flashing red. The sight must have discouraged him a bit. He mustered up his last strength to wheeze,

"Zander, you tell me what you would do had you laid your hands on the information about a hundred and eight alien races compared to whom we're still living in caves? What would you have done knowing that space is teeming with creatures whose technologies are far superior to ours? Would you have shelved the whole thing in some classified vault?" he croaked and burst out coughing, spitting blood.

"I would have tried to find out more," I said without hesitation. "Please pace yourself, man. Just a couple more minutes."

He didn't listen. "That's exactly what we did," he hurried to pour everything out believing he was nearly dead. "We managed to study the neuroimplant prototype and restore the ship's interstellar communications module. By activating them together, we hoped to receive some data that might confirm the existence of the Founders' network."

"I know that part. You don't need to tell me."

As I listened to him, I simultaneously controlled the molecular replication process in the other room. The machine kept glitching; the office was now flooded with byproducts of the reaction. The plants framing the artificial pond began to wilt. "I know that your experts didn't survive under pressure. Was that when you decided to bring gamers in? Like, because of our high mental adaptivity levels? But why the fuck did you have to block the logout? Why did you have to stop servicing our in-modes?"

"No one blocked your logouts," he wheezed. "Activating a neuroimplant via the Founders' network is a one-way ticket. We had no idea how to bring an identity matrix back undamaged. You're the first to come back."

I very nearly lost control of the nanites. "You're a liar! I did come back, twice! First time was just when I started out, before the Dargians caught me. And second-"

"Zander, your identity remained in the Darg system. By then, we'd learned to read neurograms and kept adding the necessary data from here. We didn't want to disrupt the illusion of you all playing a game."

"Does that mean that whatever I saw — all those deserted cities, the abandoned Earth — was a lie? Was that a figment of my imagination?"

"No," he could barely speak. "It wasn't."

"Enough! Keep still. You need some rest."

The exhausted Major fell silent. As I waited for the replication process to complete, I couldn't help thinking.

Now I knew why I'd received my Pioneer ability. Our planet hadn't yet been impregnated with nanites, and the only source of cargonite we had were the remains of the mysterious alien ship.

Not that it changed anything. We could still hope that the numbers of both Reapers and mobs which had crossed over into the real world were limited. It still left us with a lunatic hybrid and the mass death of all the in-mode-bound people.

The arrival of life support cartridges distracted me from my heavy thoughts. They came floating through the air, surrounded by a veil of the nanites transporting them.

Seeing the cartridges, the Major struggled to sit up, propping himself up on one elbow. "Where did you get them from?" he asked warily, apparently suspecting foul play. "They're unmarked."

"I made them. I used a molecular replicator. Be warned: they're strong and they act fast. They're charged with alien metabolites. That's how we survived back on Darg. We know this formula."

"Okay," he clearly realized he had no other option. He'd lost too much blood for his body to survive without help. "Shoot me up."

* * *

You've received a new level!
New skill available: Exobiologist.
Accept: Yes/No

The Major's shrieking echoed endlessly through the room as the metabolites kicked in. His eyes popped out; his body shuddered and convulsed.

"Steady!" I pinned him to the floor, watching

him closely for any signs of respiratory failure. The risk of allergic shock was huge. I should have thought about that. Back in cyberspace we'd never had to deal with anything like it.

Decision timeout. You've received a new skill: Exobiologist.
Current level: 1

I was furious. I had enough exo formulas to flood this place with but no proper human medications!

"Shit... shit..." Dominic breathed in shallow fits. His reddened eyes streamed with tears. The indicator lights on his suit's panel flashed hysterically.

Soon his convulsions ceased. His breathing stabilized.

"Let me go," he wheezed. "I want to sit up."

"How are you feeling?"

"Like I've been boiled alive. But I feel better. I can think straight," he said in disbelief.

"You'd better not move."

"Yeah right! I feel like I can punch through this wall no problem! How long does this shit last?"

"Five to six hours. Depends. Your reactions are not typical."

"I'm fine!" he was shuddering again, this time with excess energy. "Mind giving my power unit back? I feel sort of naked without a gun."

"I've used the battery up. I'll make you a new one now. Have you got any micro nuclear batteries?"

"Only a few. Can't you hook up to the mains?"

That was a thought! I searched for the building

distributor's signature and sent a command to the nanites to use it as a power source. Using Object Replication, I made two batteries for his pulse gun.

"I meant to ask you, what's this type of gun you're using?" I said.

"I took it off a dead special-forces guy," the Major replied. "Shame there isn't enough ammo. I only have five slugs left. No idea what they're made of but they seem to break atomic bonds on impact. The amount of energy it releases is enough to blow up a brick shithouse."

"Can I have a look?"

"Sure," he unclasped the clip and produced a bullet.

"So you're trusting me, then?"

"I recognized you."

"Oh did you?" I scanned the plain-looking cylinder. Inside was a scheme of an unknown device and a tiny capsule filled with some strange substance.

"We first heard about you when we'd just launched the hybrid's matrix and were about to prepare an Oasis upgrade. Not many can boast the Mnemotechnics skill. Whoever receives it, immediately comes under close surveillance."

"Does that mean you followed my every step?"

"We were there only to help you," the Major replied. "But those Outlaws screwed everything up! Five years of piecing data together, restoring Argus, helping you in every each way we could! You shouldn't think we were sitting here rubbing our hands together as we watched you explore a new star system!"

Honestly, I was taken aback. I'd never looked at it that way. "Helping us, were you? What with, may I ask?"

"We provided information. Neurogram analysis, data collecting and processing... Do you really think all those clans and corporations back on Argus just sprouted naturally by themselves? Oh, no. The Founders' technologies, device schemes, repair procedures — we studied it all here! You can't imagine the sheer number of people working for you. Not only the Corporation's entire technical pools, but all of the military space forces' data processing centers all over the world. Then we sent the processed data back to you."

"Do you want to say that all the players knew where they were and what was going on there?"

"I wish," he answered in all honesty. "Most of them sincerely believed they were the ones responsible for all the discoveries. Which was sometimes true. Jurgen is a prime example. He is a top technologist, make no mistake. Zander, please! No one was going to abandon you. We had a plan."

"You did abandon us, though."

"It wasn't our fault, don't you understand? The Outlaws lay their hands on the Founders' identity-copying module which allowed them to wrest their identities from our control. That's when all the problems started!"

I immediately remembered the conversation between Jyrd and Khors. "From what I heard, they had some clout here?"

"Sure. Some of the top brass didn't like the fact that the military had full control of the project, letting all those technologies slip through the Corporation's fingers. So they decided to take their share behind our backs. They were uncovered pretty quickly though but by then it was too late. The Outlaws had already used the identity-copying module to digitize themselves. Then they created Avatroid. Shitheads! I assure you that no one here expected Argus to be attacked by Phantom Raiders. That was a complete surprise!"

He sat up and hung his head. "When we realized that Argus was bound to fall, we had to urgently prepare the hybrid's identity matrix even though his artificial intellect still had a lot of growing to do! Actually, I was against this decision. We still couldn't properly control such synthetic identities. His introduction hadn't even been planned until the arrival of the Second Colonial Fleet next year but we had to push it. You understand, don't you? After the Raiders' attack, the only way we could help the survivors was by restoring Oasis."

"So what was your original plan, then?" I handed the cylindrical bullet back to him. The scanning had been successful: my databases were now one file richer. But this particular object was way too complex for my Technologist level to replicate.

"The 'arrival' of the Second Colonial Fleet wasn't planned until next year," he repeated. "It was supposed to turn the tables. Can you believe that we were one step away from building our own interstellar server? All of you would have gradually been called off and replaced by military personnel. But the arrival of Avatroid ruined everything!" he shrugged. "The emergency measures we took only made the situation worse. The hybrid took on a life of his own. As for our updating of Oasis, all it served was to awake more AIs."

"Wait a sec," I said. "We can send information

via hyperspace but not a physical object. This I know for sure. How did you manage to react so quickly to the Raiders' attack? Didn't the Second Colonial Fleet arrive in the system immediately after the attack? Or have you solved the Founders' mystery?"

"Nope. We can't jump a ship via hyperspace. The technology is still under research. Let me explain," he reached for his nanocomp bracelet, activated it, entered a password and began searching for information.

He was considerably better now. His condition had stabilized. The feverish red of his cheeks was gone. His gaze cleared, his movements gained precision.

"Look," he activated a holographic model.

I faced a weird structure. A small oblong platform devoid of familiar hull structures and docking quays didn't at all look like a space station. It was enclosed within several spheres. The entire structure resembled a collection of geometrical figures slowly moving against a backdrop of stars.

I frowned. "What's this supposed to mean?"

The Major fiddled with the settings. The objects' thick hulls became transparent. Now I could clearly see the decks, the power units and the engines. The remaining space was chock full of all sorts of equipment without as much as a tiny passage left for a human being. The tightly packed machines were entwined by power cables, data exchange channels and service communications for maintenance robots.

"This is the Second Colonial Fleet," the Major explained in response to my growing bewilderment. "It set off fourteen years ago, as soon as we received the exact coordinates of the Darg system while deciphering the data on board the alien ship."

"Wait up. What about the cryogenic platforms? The cruisers?"

"These, you mean," he pointed at the spheres. "The Eurasia is only about its cyberspace-generating servers. The automatic interstellar stations that carry them are primitive but trustworthy. Flying at sub-light speeds, they in due time reached the Darg system and took their positions at its edge awaiting their turn."

"What was the point?"

"Don't you understand? The Founders' technologies are based on nanite control. And their use is limited to sentient living beings."

"That's not true! I've seen AIs manipulating nanites too," I interrupted him.

"They can. But their control of them is limited to say the least. I repeat: only an identity matrix of a living being is capable of leveling up sufficiently to unlock all of the nanites' potential."

"So what was this so-called Second Colonial Fleet busy doing, then? Was it just cruising the system's edge waiting for players to log in? Why didn't you use it immediately on arrival?"

"Because we didn't know anything about the Founders at the time. Our pioneers had only just started to settle on Argus. Neuroimplants were still undergoing testing in the Crystal Sphere. Automatic long-range scanning stations were busy collecting data on Darg. The artificial intellect best known to you as Admiral Higgs was the one who studied the various methods of nanite control, using the data received from Argus-based clans and corporations.

Under his leadership, the Eurasia and the "ships" that were supposed to have escorted it were gradually being completed, growing in both purpose and appearance. This was a lot of painstaking daily work. We planned to power up the servers to their full capacity as soon as conditions on Argus improved enough to allow us to introduce new 'colonists'."

"This Admiral Higgs, did he also get out of hand?"

"Oh, no. Our attack on Darg was just another hasty decision made by the top brass. They'd panicked. Between the Phantom Raiders' assault on Argus and the failure of Project Hybrid, the situation became uncontrollable. We did our best to contain the Reapers hoping to save the players. By then, cyberspace had already merged with the real world. Still, we kept sending special space forces to Crystal Sphere with one objective alone: to hold any defense-worthy locations and unite the Neuros until we found a solution."

"Was there a solution?"

"There was indeed. In the five years of exploring Argus we'd learned to use the interstellar network. We knew enough to be able to transmit identity matrices. The big question was, where to? Eurasia station was only a transit point. It couldn't accept more than a few thousand players at a time."

"That's when you decided to use Darg?"

"We had no other option! This was our last resource. We were desperate. The plan was to eliminate slavers and take over the Founders' equipment. We were going to transport the few in-mode-bound survivors to the military space backup center and send their identities to Darg in order to start a colony. But their command didn't reckon on the Disciples ever being a power. Lots of mistakes were made. You know the result," he fell into a sullen silence.

"What happened to the groups sent to the Crystal Sphere?"

"Dunno. We've lost contact. Last thing I heard, the Reapers were prowling everywhere."

"Not a single one of them managed to log out?"

"Oh yes. Some of the more experienced gamers did. But what were they supposed to do in real life? Bore themselves to death in their capsule flats? You were the same, you should understand. We did warn them about the dangers. Still, every single one of them logged back in."

"To face the Reapers in one last battle," I added, thinking of the river bank strewn with the avatars of dead players.

The Major startled but didn't say anything. He threw his head back, his glare filled with desperate hope. "I still think we have a chance. I need to get to the communications station. I tried to fight my way through but I couldn't. You have Mnemotechnics. Together we might just make it. Think you can help me?"

We still have a chance? Was he delirious? He must have been suffering the mind-crushing effects of exo multiplied by the gravity of his wounds.

"Where do you keep the first twenty players?" I demanded.

He knew very well what I meant. He fumbled with the settings, opening a holographic image of what looked like some sort of bunker.

"Whichever of them you mean, they're all

there," he ticked a few adjacent rooms. "The communications station is just next to them," he said, highlighting it too.

It looked as if he'd been right: we were heading in the same direction.

"Where's this place?" I asked.

"It's right here. In the technopark."

"You mentioned this military space backup center. Can we move the in-mode capsules there? Mine included?"

"We sure can, provided we can get to the communications station," he answered unhesitatingly.

He wasn't telling me everything. I could see it in his eyes.

Quest alert: Shadows of the Past. Quest failed.

New quest available: The Nature of Avatroid

You've found out the truth about the recent developments in the Darg system. Now you need to use this knowledge to find out the development route taken by the ancient artificial intellect known to you as Avatroid.

Deadline: none.

CHAPTER EIGHT

EARTH

INFOSYSTEMS CORPORATION TECHNOPARK

TWO WORLDS that had finally come into contact. Two views of the same problem. Two realities that had merged.

My incidental discovery of Phantom Server combined with my insatiable urge to play this "game of the future" had given me no inkling of what I'd been about to get myself into.

The sun had already risen, hanging high above the buildings. The rarefied air was fresh and cold. Infosystems Corporation used to build its complexes safely above the emissions layer.

"Where's the entrance to the bunker?" I asked.

Dominic pointed in its general direction. "You can't see it from here. About a thousand feet as a crow flies. First we need to find a suitable position, then I'll show you exactly where it is. I tried to fight my way through to it twice. It didn't work. I tried to get there via a magnetic monorail line but I walked right into the harpies. I just about made it out."

"I still don't understand how mobs managed to get out. How did they materialize? I thought that nanites weren't supposed to interact with such primitive creatures?"

"You're dead right there," the Major headed for a service stairwell which took us one floor down toward the monorail looping around the nearest towers. "They have nothing to do with gaming. Those monsters escaped from our AI labs."

"They're *sentient*? Jesus, why?"

The Major forwarded me a file containing the images of a harpy and about a dozen similar monsters. Some seemed familiar from my gaming experience; others looked like nothing I'd seen before.

"They're alien," the Major commented. "We discovered their images in the Founders' databases. We created their avatars in case of first contact. They're generated by a device which contains a nanite unit which the operator can use to control the creature via a mnemonic interface."

He spoke matter-of-factly, but for me, his every word was a revelation.

The mythical creatures that the gaming corporation had borrowed from various intercultural legends — did they really exist? Had they visited Earth at some point in the past? That could explain their presence in our mythology.

"I know it's hard to believe," the Major said. "You don't need to. Just accept the fact."

We walked a narrow bridge across the abyss separating two of the towers. Far ahead, dark dots circled the sky.

"What makes them so aggressive? These aren't the properties one would employ in a successful first contact, are they? Or am I missing something?"

"No, you are not. They weren't supposed to be aggressive. I don't know much about it," he admitted, "but I did hear about some glitches in the system. Whenever the operator ceased controlling them, the avatars' behavior became unpredictable. Apparently, nanites were the problem. The current theory is, alien nanites are capable of preserving information of both their alien hosts' appearance and their character."

He didn't have time to expand on it further. We reached a balcony and used it to enter the building. Immediately we became aware of suspicious noises. The sound of heavy footsteps and the whine of servomotors... it sounded like robots... or human beings wearing armored suits.

I gestured to the Major to take cover while I activated Piercing Vision.

The nanites infiltrated one of the rooms. The sound of heavy footsteps and the screeching of servomotors grew closer.

The glow of 3D monitors seeped through the gloom. A man sat in a chair by a desk: his arms hanging listlessly, his head tilted, his eyes wide open.

Dead.

The floor and the walls seemed to be vibrating. The sounds came from powerful speakers built into the walls. One of the screens showed what seemed to be a cyber lab. A futuristic robot was pacing the middle of the room.

"Whew," the Major's face was pale. "It's only a model. Come on, then. This way," he checked the plan and pushed an unlocked door. I glimpsed an emergency staircase.

* * *

WE CLIMBED OUT onto the roof. This building towered over the technopark structures.

"This is the Corporation's HQ," the Major didn't mince words. He pointed at a de-energized flybot motionless in the center of the landing pad. "If only we could find some way to charge it up, we could go there directly."

Sounded tempting, no doubt about it, had it not been for the gang of harpies circling the sky nearby.

I noticed some cables snaking around a service vault. "Let's switch on the mains first," I said, "and worry about it after."

"They'll see the signature. Think you can camouflage it?"

"Easy," I selected a nanite group and activated Steel Mist.

"You know how to use them, don't you?" the Major asked. "What's your skill level?"

"Fifty-seven. So where's this entrance to the bunker?"

We hid behind a low concrete glass parapet.

"See the road junction?" he asked.

"Yeah."

"Below it there's an airlock. That's the entrance."

The view was distorted by the haze of a force field. I had to send some nanites there. Soon they began streaming data to my mind expander.

The Major struggled peering into the distance. I forwarded him the data.

The airtight gate was shut. I could see some armed people standing next to it. I read their signatures. Reapers. There were about twenty of them outside. I could only imagine how many there were inside.

The view slowly shifted in my mind's eye. Magnetic monorail lines intertwined in the gossamer lacework of a transport junction. The scarlet outline of laser turrets surrounded the installation's perimeter. I made out numerous fortifications behind the veil of the force shield. Made of armored plastic and camouflaged with holograms, they resembled cliff ledges, perfectly unnoticeable to the naked eye.

"Dominic?" I asked the Major. "D'you have authorized access? Think you can open the gate remotely?"

"I tried to already. It doesn't work. The hybrid must have changed the codes."

I studied the gate. I could probably use Disintegration to knock it out. And then what? Would I have enough nanites left? "Any other access?"

"Here," he marked them on the plan. "The gravity elevator and the cargo terminal. The elevator is being closely guarded. The terminal is shut down."

To the right of the airlock I indeed saw a monorail station. I redirected the nanites to scan the station's equipment. It still had power but the Major was right: the only thing still functioning was the security system which was controlled autonomously by computers independent of the network.

"Why don't the turrets react to the mobs?"

"The security system is adaptive. What's the point in shooting at holograms?"

"Well, some of those harpies look material enough," I said.

"They're not stupid, either. They keep a safe distance, as you can see. It's not the turrets they're afraid of though. It's the special-purpose ammo that the Reapers have found there."

I began a repeat scan, this time creating a detailed model of access routes to the installation. "How much cargonite did you recover from that alien ship?"

"About twenty tons, or so I was told," the Major replied.

"Why so little?"

"Most of the cargonite was part of their equipment. For that reason, it couldn't have been utilized. All the equipment is stored in the lower levels of the bunker. They only used the ship's hull to harvest cargonite."

I glanced at the harpies. Their steely wings glistened purple. The bodies of a few seemed to have higher nanite density than the rest; their behavior was marked by a calm confidence as they circled the high-altitude sky.

"Do you happen to have the remote avatar control codes?"

"No."

"Never mind. We'll think of something."

I sent a mental command to build a microscopic probe. I entered an emergency command sequence for nanite control and selected the weakest harpy as target. It was little more than a translucent outline. Dominic was following my actions through the combat scanner but refrained from asking any questions.

Having received my freebie upgrade, the creature soared into the sky, then banked rapidly, attacking the nearest mob. The harpy's claws broke out in bluish flames as it sank them into its victim.

The Major cussed, watching in amazement as the monster devoured its opponent. Immediately it attacked again, this time in vain. Sparks flew everywhere, but still the harpy failed to get hold of more nanites.

"Easy, man," the Major said warily. "Make sure you know what you're doing. Or we might end up with the kind of mobs that make the Reapers look like Mickey Mouse."

"It's only a one-time code," I reassured him. "We don't have enough ammo to fight everyone. This might level our chances up a bit."

"You want to use the harpies against them? They're not that stupid, you know. They've already burned their fingers. They don't get anywhere near the junction."

"You mean they won't even chase a flybot?"

He apparently didn't like my idea. Still, he didn't let his skepticism show. Instead, he asked, "All right, then. Spit it out."

* * *

YOU NEED TO USE your old skills. Charon's words had served me well in these last few days.

Dominic didn't like my plan at all, I could see it. Still, he didn't say anything. He paused, thinking, then nodded his agreement and headed for the flybot.

Me, I had nothing left to lose. But his motives were a mystery. Was it his sense of duty? Guilt? Or just being stubborn?

Why was he so desperate to get to the communications station? Did he hope to use it to contact his family?

I had no idea. Nor did I have the time to second-guess his actions. My brain was struggling to embrace both realities as it was.

Hissing, the door of the flybot's passenger compartment slid open.

"Buckle up," Dominic's voice echoed in the earphones from the already sealed pilot's compartment.

I climbed inside and clicked the seatbelts shut. "Mind sharing the data?" I asked. It had already become part of me.

A new operative window opened in my interface. I looked over the on-board systems. A powerful hydrogen engine, two antigravs, new improved G-force absorbers and an armored hull. No integrated weapons though. This was a purely civilian vehicle with a penchant for the utmost in comfort.

"I'm done."

Dominic activated the manual controls. Camouflaged by Steel Mist, he lifted off and made a few U-turns to test the antigravs, hovering just a few feet above the roof.

"It's working fine," he said. "Shall we go?"

"Yeah. Pick up the nearest harpies."

An unpleasant chill ran over me, indicating a rapid change in altitude. The flybot dove under a bending monorail and headed for its target.

I removed the camouflage. Immediately the harpies noticed us.

Dominic banked into a steep turn. He was an excellent pilot. You'd never think he'd worked in communications.

He spiraled us around the tower, all the way down to the ground, then back up, weaving a path amid the towers. Despite the functioning G-force absorbers, the flight took your breath away.

"Zander, I'm on course! The beasties are following. There's at least fifty of them!"

"I can see."

The harpies chased after us, following in our wake like a heap of dry leaves raised by a gust of wind.

* * *

ANOTHER GROUP OF HARPIES came for us head-on.

"Dominic, keep to the right! Try to avoid them!"

The flybot ducked dangerously to one side and brushed the corner of a tower, striking up a cascade of sparks.

"Zander, send them the code!"

"Too early! All they'll do is fight between themselves! We don't need it!"

Dominic cussed under his breath as he maneuvered every which way, aggroing the mobs. He did well. Their numbers kept growing.

"That's it, the engines won't take any more," he wheezed, changing course, as he rapidly approached the installation.

We were met by bursts of submachine gun fire.

Bullets plastered the flybot's frontal armor plate. The fake Corporation workers took up their positions by the massive airlock. Come on now...

A shuddering blow threw our vehicle off course. The starboard hull was sliced into uneven strips as the creature's cargonite claws ripped through the metal with ease.

"Try to get to the cargo terminal!"

Dominic was doing his best. We were thrown from side to side. The starboard antigrav began billowing thick smoke.

"We're losing altitude!"

The harpies dashed overhead, then scattered in all directions, maneuvering amid the interweaving monorails.

Now.

I had groups of nanites ready. They headed toward their selected targets.

"I can't lift her up!" Dominic croaked.

Dammit! I'd counted on the cargo terminal's emergency protocol. Its automatics were obliged to rescue a civilian craft in distress and land it safely using specially configured power fields. But we were flying too low for them!

I noticed a small gap between two loading lines. "To the left!"

Overloaded, the second antigrav too began billowing smoke. We weren't descending anymore: we were falling.

My heart throbbed, clocking down the moments until impact. The Reapers must have decided we were toast and switched their attention to the harpies. Just what I'd been waiting for. Their weapons were very effective against nanites.

Immediately a few of the harpies' outlines rippled and began to fade.

We'd lost our pursuing tail but we continued to drop toward the terminal buildings, unable to maintain altitude without the antigravs.

The flybot crashed into the fine latticework of loading machinery, breaking manipulators and ripping out supports. A few beams impaled the vehicle, penetrating both compartments.

The deafening rattle was followed by relative silence.

"You okay?" Dominic unbuckled and scrambled toward me, rubbing his injured shoulder.

"I'm fine."

"Did it work?"

"It did! They began fighting each other."

Indeed, the submachine gun fire rose to a crescendo and didn't die down. The Reapers put up a good fight but the mobs in possession of the emergency command for nanite control kept pressuring them.

Dominic opened the emergency hatch and climbed out. He proffered me his hand.

I scrambled out too and took a look around. The flybot was firmly stuck in a tangle of construction beams. Its engines billowed smoke. The vehicle's hull was breached in many places where some of the loading supports had pierced it.

The harpies circled overhead, their ranks considerably thinner. They would soar upwards, then dive, their bodies filling out with nanites with each attack, becoming more and more dangerous.

"What's gonna happen once the codes expire?" Dominic asked warily.

"They should have done so already," I honestly replied.

"Are you going to interfere?"

"Not yet. Let's get closer."

He cast another wary glance at the harpies. What was he so unhappy about? Let them clear our path.

We climbed down using the broken ends of cables. Now we were about a hundred and fifty feet away from the airlock which was slightly to our right.

"It's there," the Major pointed at a squat fortification next to the cliff's edge.

* * *

UNEXPECTEDLY, the melee by the bunker took a new turn.

By now there were only five harpies left but now they easily sustained damage without losing any nanites. Had they evolved? Were they blocking some controlling code unknown to me?

I'd have loved to intercept it but I had no idea how to do so. Frequencies were packed with interference. Scanning produced no results. The micro transmitters that the Reapers were firing had a very small range. That was the whole idea, otherwise creatures other than the target might suffer from the transmission too.

Never mind. I was pretty sure that this bunker of theirs held prototypes of all sorts of weapons.

The mobs were getting desperate. Their cargonite claws ripped through the armored plastic of bunker fortifications with ease, making a quick job of the fake Corporate workers in passing. Their every blow tore out a large chunk of the Reapers' technogenic flesh that would dissolve in cascades of fine purple spray.

The Major didn't seem to like the harpies' rushed evolution at all. "Zander, isn't it time you interfere? Are you in control of the situation or what?"

"What's your problem?" I pointed at the gravity elevator next to the airlock. With a popping sound, about a dozen Reapers were forced out of its depths onto a small platform at the center of the bunker's upper structures. "Everything's going according to plan. These bastards are smoking each other!"

"I think you're making a mistake," he prophesied. "It'll stop any minute now. The Reapers aren't that stupid. They'll soon realize that their weapons aren't effective anymore. Then they'll retreat into the bunker. And we'll be left here to face the monsters you've just built!"

I didn't reply. Instead, I tried to activate Friendly Contact in an attempt to control one of the harpies. It failed. Friendly Contact was supposed to have worked! But somehow it hadn't.

"Zander, what the hell is going on?"

"The mobs have evolved! They're blocking the control code I sent them!"

"I told you!" he snapped. "Harpies are based on an AI prototype!"

Sending them the control codes had been too careless of me. That's exactly how the Outlaws had lost control of Avatroid. I should have thought about that!

Shooting back, the Reapers retreated toward the elevator. They were too calculating to fight to the last man!

The five harpies drew near them, forcing their way into a narrow gap between two massive concrete glass structures. Their heavy wings flapped, raising clouds of white dust. Threads of electric charges crackled between their claws. The rapid increase in nanites had led to their developing new abilities!

"Dominic, I want you to stand close to me."

The world faded into a distance. My mind expander reached its peak processing speed.

I focused on nanite control, taking the creatures' steely wings into my grid sights.

I attacked with several Disintegrations in a rapid sequence. A series of blinding flashes obscured the sun. The nearest structures cast sharp deep shadows. The figures of the Reapers burst into fountains of molten steel. With a thunderous roar, the top part of the elevator shaft collapsed on itself. A web of deep cracks ran across the concrete glass.

The towers shuddered with the shock wave, dropping fragments of their façades.

My Active Shield ability kicked in. Flames flowed around us without touching.

You have used 784,578 nanites.

Your actions have had a destructive effect on a habitable planet's environment.

Your Colonizer status has been temporarily blocked.

Warning! The Colonizers Council may decide to lower your Mnemotechnics Skill 10 pt.

For your information. The Colonizers Council isn't available. The investigation and judgment of your case is not possible.

Your status has been restored.

The smoke of hundreds of fires obscured the panorama of the technopark.

Dominic and I stood amid the ruins of the installation at the very center of a fire-ringed circle that marked the boundaries of the Active Shield that had saved our lives.

The part of the road leading to the gravity elevator was no more. The enormous airlock gate had been deformed. Its supports had crumbled into shapeless chunks of concrete glass.

For no apparent reason, Dominic felt his helmet with his hands. He cast me a glance and turned away. A gust of wind blew the plumes of smoke aside, revealing the jagged outline of dozens of towers sporting collapsed upper stories.

I knew he was thinking I'd failed to keep my skills under control. He wasn't right though.

In outer space it had been different. Ditto for space stations. Even when I'd had to attack Phantom Raiders, I still hadn't had to utilize the same quantities of nanites, throwing them into the furnace of Disintegration. There it had been enough to burn through a small area of the ship's hull, end of story. The ship's equipment would immediately begin to fail, completing the damage.

Another deafening roar sent clouds of white dust into the air.

The massive airlock gate finally parted from its deformed frame, thudding to the ground.

* * *

GRADUALLY THE DUST had settled. A dull red light seeped from inside the bunker. I could hear the far-off rumble of a rockfall.

I could scan traces of cargonite everywhere. The bulk of the precious substance had been lost to us but we had to try and collect what we could still salvage.

I activated Self-Replication (the ability I'd received at the same time as Colonizer). Soon a vague haze of newborn nanites enveloped me. A new indicator appeared in my interface: a shimmering bar which kept growing, the digits next to it showing the increasing number of nanites under my control.

"Shall we go now?" Dominic shuffled his feet, casting occasional glances into the darkly crimson depths of the elevator.

"Wait a sec. If you have something to say to me, you'd better do it now."

He cracked a nervous smile. "Zander, I understand we couldn't have destroyed the harpies any other way. They were made of nanites, weren't they? You couldn't have done it any other way. But I'm afraid it might not work down in the bunker. Do you have anything less spectacular?"

"Against the Reapers? I don't think so. They're immune to both System Failure and Critical Damage. The best thing I can do is Plasma Blast."

"Then we have problems. We can't just scorch everything in sight down there. The place is packed with unique equipment. We need to save it."

"Save it for whom?"

"How about those who're stuck in the virtual

world?"

"Okay. Let's have a think. Are there any labs anywhere near that used to study nanite control codes?"

He gave a confident nod. "Yes."

"Change of plans, then. We need to check them first."

"What exactly do you expect to find? From what I heard, there're lots of codes. The problem is, most of them are fragmented."

"Then we need to see, don't we?" I said. "Show me the way!"

EVERYTHING WAS BATHED in a dull crimson light. We walked up and down some tunnels, wide and deserted. The walls on both sides of us were lined with dozens of closed armored doors that led to all sorts of science and research centers. Our advance was occasionally hindered by emergency bulkheads. Those we had to bypass using a cramped system of service tunnels.

"It's here," Dominic checked against a scheme and opened one of the hatches.

We climbed down a vertical well to the level below and secreted ourselves amid the bundles of cables, listening.

An intense hum kept growing stronger, then weakening again as if someone in the room below was playing with a switch of a giant electric transformer.

I cast Dominic a quizzical glance. He shrugged. "No idea," he mouthed.

Warily he opened the hatch a crack. A narrow

strip of light cut through the gloom of the utility lines.

I touched his shoulder. "Wait."

Earlier, we'd agreed only to use nanites as a last option. Dominic had warned me that most research equipment was fitted with sensors which raised the alarm whenever they detected any stray nanites. Such precautions were perfectly understandable, considering the kinds of technologies they had studied here.

I read the equipment's signatures, trying to locate the alarm.

I found it. It was disabled: by the Reapers apparently, which was only logical.

So what was that hum down there?

The room was large, separated into several work zones by translucent floor-to-ceiling screens. Processor columns crowded its center. The room's perimeter was lined with the square chassis of neurocomputers.

Directly below us in the room the floor was raised, forming a pulpit-like platform. It was connected to a multitude of cables and pipelines that ran under the flooring.

I continued scanning, engaging some nanites to help me with the data harvesting.

"The Reapers," Dominic mouthed.

"Quiet. I can see them."

Ten security guards in full military space uniforms paced the equipment-free area holding the already-familiar pulse submachine guns. I focused on their matrices. Those were Reapers, no doubt about it.

My mind expander outlined their weapons in red as factory-made. The rest of them were nanites, armor suits included.

Here too the odds weren't in our favor.

I selected them as targets, allowing my mind expander to monitor them.

The enormous screens were filled with first-person views of various virtual worlds. Each picture contained additional information: the place's coordinates, its correlation with location maps, and the distance to certain objects marked with unknown symbols.

"Dominic? What are those signs?"

"These are our bases in the Crystal Sphere," he replied. "They'd been created before we started testing neuroimplants."

And I'd thought I knew the Crystal Sphere inside out! "Are they still holding?"

"Destroyed. But not all of them are marked down here. There's still hope they failed to locate a few."

The hum returned. More monitors lit up. The configuration of indicator lights on both the processor columns and the neurocomp boxes changed.

"*Attention all personnel for an incoming arrival,*" said a cybernetic voice.

The power consumption soared. Data flooded the channels.

"*Coordinates confirmed. Now commencing hyperspace jump.*"

The dome of a power shield unfolded over the platform at the center. The familiar dull green mist filled its interior, forming a human outline.

Invisible vents ejected a cloud of nanites which mixed with the mist.

The hum died away, replaced by the hiss of

compressed air.

"*Materialization successful,*" the cybernetic voice reported. "*Reverse in ten seconds. Dematerialization. Aborted. Security protocol failure. Multiple identity matrices transportation impossible. The experiment cannot be continued.*"

None of the guards seemed to be interested in what was happening. They paid no heed to the system messages. The power shield collapsed, leaving behind a perfectly normal-looking man made entirely of nanites.

His clothes surged with interference, then stabilized. The stranger turned and headed for the exit.

The servodrives of an airlock thudded, unsealing the hatch. Its armored shutters parted, letting the newly-arrived Reaper out into the corridor.

* * *

"I HAD NO KNOWLEDGE of these experiments, I swear," Dominic managed.

The machinery kicked back in, reopening the hatch. Two Reapers rolled in a trolley equipped with a built-in antigrav. The trolley was loaded with a neat pile of broken armor and pieces of equipment.

Cargonite.

A deep bay opened in the floor. Two Reapers began to unload the platform, placing the pieces of the alien ship into the converter.

The doors of an elevator slid open with a melodious jingle. A warrior walked out, clad in top-level armor. I used to know the artisan who made it;

actually, I used to wear a very similar set of gear once, famous for its excellent characteristic-boosting stats.

"Wait up," his dull voice ordered.

I couldn't see his face behind the richly decorated helmet. The scanning results brought more bad news. This one too was made of nanites.

He touched a few sensors, entering a command sequence, then stepped onto the platform. The power shield activated again.

"*Attention all personnel. The object is about to be dematerialized,*" the level cybernetic voice said. "*Reception of neuromatrix transfer coordinates acknowledged.*"

"Watch the screen," Dominic whispered.

One of the 3D monitors blinked but showed nothing.

A flash consumed the insides of the shield dome. Wisps of the dull green mist shot up, then dissolved into the air.

150,000 active nanites detected.

The Reaper disappeared. The remaining nanites were sucked into the same microscopic vents. The green monitor screen rippled with interference. The picture of a carved stone arch filled the screen. I recognized its chiseled patterns. Behind it, a crooked pole fence listed to one side. I could make out the corner of a log cabin complete with a cat sleeping on the porch.

This was one of the Crystal Sphere's standard-issue respawn points. There were hundreds of them over there.

"Have you been to these labs before?" I asked.

"Absolutely not," Dominic seemed to be equally shaken by what we'd just seen. "I've got nothing to do with this place whatsoever. But I did hear something about Sector 14 experimenting with nanite codes," he tried to explain his choice of itinerary.

"Okay. Give me another couple of minutes," I continued studying the mysterious lab.

Now I could understand how Reapers had crossed over into the real world. But what was their business in the military space bunker? Why did they keep sneaking in and out of cyberspace?

As I pondered over this, my mind expander had created a detailed scanning file.

I honestly expected both my Technologist and Alien Technologies levels to soar. No such luck. I'd received a bare minimum of XP.

Did that mean I'd already come across this device in the past?

I ran a search of all my databases and promptly received my answer. The respawn points at the Founders' stations had almost identical signatures.

In the meantime, the Reapers had unloaded the cargonite they'd brought in and set off to get the next load.

Dominic touched my shoulder, attracting my attention.

"Yes?"

"We need to go," he said. "There's nothing for us here."

"Then what do you want us to do? Keep wandering about all these service corridors?"

"We can't take on ten of the enemy," he wisely assessed our situation.

"You really think that the communications station or the in-mode room are less protected?"

"I suggest we try the Alien Technologies sector," he said. "I have a funny feeling that's where they used to make the special-purpose ammo," he cut himself short as the power shield sprang back to life.

"*Attention all personnel for an incoming arrival,*" the calm cybernetic voice sent inexplicable shivers down my spine.

This time not one but two Reapers appeared under the dome shield. How could I forget their armor — or the battle by the frozen lake.

In an eruption of green mist, lights began to flicker because of the peak power consumption.

Nanite control code intercepted: Object Replication, level 20.

In a hiss of compressed air, the two Reapers began to materialize slowly and laboriously. Apparently this time the process didn't go as smoothly. I focused on them, reading their fading name tags, then activated penetrative scanning at the risk of exposing myself. Luckily, they didn't seem to be in possession of Mnemotechnics. Good.

In which case, who or what had activated Object Replication and for what purpose?

The green mist filling the power shield began to disperse. The two Reapers were carrying some semblance of a two-handed trunk similar to neurocomp modules. Building it had taken over 300,000 nanites which had formed permanent links and couldn't be reused.

What was inside it, then?

My implants-enhanced vision struggled to pierce the protective covering.

Neurograms!

A few scraps of other people's mental images singed my mind, even though the memories themselves weren't traumatic. Judging by the plethora of complex machinery inhibiting them, I was looking at the inside of research labs.

That was the extent of it.

I just couldn't get it. What was the point? Who were those people and why were the fragments of their identities so important? Why were they brought back to the real world, wasting precious and hopefully non-renewable resources?

"Connect it over there," a stifled voice said.

Two guards picked up the box and placed it on top of a stack of identical ones.

"Testing."

The Reapers didn't waste time. Indicator lights glowed behind the box's dark housing. New monitors lit up, showing some schemes and diagrams.

"Not enough," the other arrival said. "He won't make the next skill level."

"Shame. We'll have to go back and search for more."

* * *

HELP... ME...

Filled with inhuman suffering, the barely audible whisper cut me to the quick.

Help...

"What's going on?" Dominic cast anxious

glances around.

He kept refusing to use mnemonic communications on the pretext that the Reapers could tap into the unique frequencies. Well, well. He definitely had something to hide. His neuroimplant only worked in reception mode: all transmission was blocked.

"Did you hear it too?"

He nodded. "This is the emergency mnemonic frequency."

"Were any of the military space personnel in possession of Mnemotechnics?"

"A few, yeah. But their advance was negligible. Level 2 or 3 at the most."

"Did they work in the virtual testing grounds? Were they involved in the Hybrid project? Did they have anything to do with the Oasis update?"

He gave a reluctant nod. "We're not going anywhere, are we?" he peered into my eyes.

"Not yet. I need to understand what's going on. If you have something to tell me, now is the best time to do it."

"Zander, I didn't work here! I've no idea where this voice in my head has come from! It might be a mind expander glitch! You'd better tell me what these creatures want. I thought they were just some dumb NPCs with a craving for neurograms. But it's much worse than that, isn't it? Are they trying to build another hybrid?"

"They're trying to finish what you started!" I snapped. "They're building a special-purpose computer. They want to make a machine with mnemotechnical abilities."

"A machine cannot control nanites!"

"Oh yes it can!" I remembered the alien shipyard and the drones busy restoring the ship's hull using Object Replication.

"There must be somebody controlling them! They're only NPCs! They can't have evolved so rapidly!"

"Some of them could have done. The neurograms they've consumed are not only emotions. They're also knowledge," I repeated what Jurgen had told me. "The problem is, the Reapers weren't the first. Do you know what this is?" I highlighted a section of equipment.

"No idea! This has nothing to do with my job description!"

"This is a respawn point! And it's identical to those on the Founders' stations. The funny thing is, it has some neurocomps connected to it. Now I wonder what could be inside them?"

Dominic turned pale. "No need to aggro me, man."

"Well, I think that these comps contain a human identity. It may be mangled and fragmented but it still might preserve certain skills. It has to be someone from Argus. You *built him into* the computer!"

Dominic kept a broody silence. What could he say? Most likely, he'd indeed known nothing about the experiment. Still, making a neurochip called for at least 100 in Mnemotechnics. Question: how had the military space forces managed to organize their *mass production*?

"How many serviceable implants were found on the alien ship?" I asked him.

"Twenty..."

* * *

THE FIRST TWENTY.

Of them, Jurgen and Frieda were the only survivors. The others had died; still, their identity matrices had been pieced back together from their neurograms, crumb after laborious crumb.

They'd left Kimberly alone — she hadn't lasted on Argus long enough to have completed the necessary development branches. Jyrd had founded the Outlaws. That left sixteen people whose names I didn't know.

"Dominic, I want you to keep an eye on the Reapers. I'll try to find out who it was speaking to us."

My mind faded as I opened mnemonic communication channels, searching for available connections.

A gust of gray wind swirled around me, twisting and pulling me into a rapidly forming vortex.

This reality resembled shards of a broken looking-glass, with many of its fragments missing. I could see a cramped personal module, its bulkheads haphazardly patched up. The air was cold and acidic.

The creature hunched up in a corner couldn't be called human anymore. Its flesh and its cyber modules had long fused into each other.

I knew how it must have happened. They couldn't have had enough neurogram fragments to build a fully-fledged identity. A few years ago, they hadn't had enough experience with these things, filling in the blanks with all sorts of technological data. The result was repulsive. This was a case of appearance reflecting reality.of the First

"What's your name?" I crouched next to him,

unwilling to tower over him.

"Kyle."

"Kyle, did you call me up? Did you ask me to help you?"

"I'm cold. They keep coming and telling me what to do. I can't say no. This is what they leave in return," his prickly glare shifted to a small messy pile of slimy flesh in the room's opposite corner. "I won't eat this. I can't leave. I remember nothing... almost..."

New quest alert: The Last of the First. Save Kyle.

I had very little time. The mnemonic channel I was using could have been detected and tracked back to me at any moment.

"Do you remember them?" I created a few fully-fledged visual images.

"Her," his servodrives screeched as a biomechanical hand pointed at Kimberly. "She's good."

"Would you like to leave?"

"Yes! Yes! Yes!"

"Then you'll have to help me."

"How can I? They've locked me up here. I don't remember much," he repeated ruefully, then backed off into a dark corner, his outline merging with the gloom.

I shuddered. He'd died on Argus to become part of the research center's equipment. Here they'd developed and tested the new respawn point technology later used on Eurasia. But that hadn't been enough. The number of neuroimplants they needed kept growing and the only way to make them was by using Object Replication.

"Kyle, I'm sorry I can't bring you back to the past," I said. "No one can. But there's always the future. Do you get my point?"

"Out there," his wandering stare fixated on the thick sealed door. "There's nothing but subzero vacuum out there. But they did promise me! They said if I made enough machines they'd let me go!"

My eyes stung. My throat rasped. I focused, straining my mind and using it like a pencil rubber to erase the surrounding room and the frost covering its steely walls. I forced the boundaries of his world apart, sharing the crumbs of my own memories bringing him sensations of warmth, of movement, of freedom.

His ugly face cleared up. His upper lip rose, exposing his teeth. He must have been trying to smile.

"Kyle," I created a mental replica of the devices' diagrams. "Do you think you can build them?"

He knew what I meant. His scary smile expired. His stare focused.

He nodded, shrinking and muttering something. Then he bared his teeth again. "What's the catch?"

"There are none."

My next step was born of desperation. I opened up my mind and let him in. That was the only way to make him trust me.

The creature's eyes lit up. He drew toward me, fingering through my thoughts like a rag-and-bone man. It felt disgusting but I didn't show it. He was welcome to see and to feel them. But if he tried to take anything from me-

He snatched his hand away. "The door isn't

easy to open. It's frozen solid."

"Kyle, but this is only a piece of software! The people who locked you up are all dead. Everything's changed. Here, take this," I forwarded him the scanner file. "Think you can suss out how the research center controls work?"

He wheezed, studying the data. "Will I forever remain like this?"

The fragile ice surrounding the hatch cracked, revealing its outline.

"I'm afraid so. I can't help that. We might try and change your avatar but-"

"Hush!" he pressed a finger to his lips, fear and amazement in his stare. What could have alarmed him so?

His stare alighted on the Founders' navigator on my wrist. "May I?"

"I can't remove it."

"You don't have to."

He touched it. The device sprang to life, its every icon lighting up — even those whose purpose was still a mystery to me.

Kyle mumbled something rueful and stepped back into the corner. Judging by the creaking sound, he must have opened a locker of some kind.

"Here, take it. You might need it," with his withered hand he proffered me a small marble studded with spikes. "Don't lose it. I want to leave. I'll help you. Everything's clear to me now."

I was forced out into the darkness.

* * *

THE NARROW SERVICE TUNNEL was too cramped to move. Next to the hatch that was slightly ajar, Dominic crouched watching the Reapers.

My throat was rasping. My eyes watered. My health had plummeted, quickly and unexpectedly. I couldn't think straight. What could have caused it? Could it have been my in-mode finally packing up? Seeing as the biomonitoring sensors were switched off...

The prickly little marble lay in my hand. What might Kyle have found about me by touching the Founders' navigator on my wrist? Why was his gaze full of compassion?

Your neuromatrix has been temporarily stabilized.

An emergency module connected.

This was all I could understand from the system message written in the strange symbols of the Founders' ancient language.

"So, have you found out anything?" Dominic asked. "Whose voice was it?"

I wanted to reply — but couldn't. My breathing had seized. Everything went momentarily dark.

"Zander?" Dominic swung round, his gear catching on a bundle of cables which rattled.

"I'm okay. Let me get my breath."

You've received an ability: Broken Chains. Your mind-

This was all I had time to read. The noise had attracted the guards. One of them must have noticed the hatch in the ceiling.

"There's someone in there!" he shouted.

"Attention all personnel for an incoming arrival."

This booming voice didn't belong to the cybernetics! This was Kyle's mind breaking free!

"Dominic, don't let anything surprise you," I wheezed a warning.

In a sudden power surge, the lighting panels exploded.

The threads of our lives all led to this respawn point located at the heart of a classified terrestrial research center.

With a flash, the power shield reactivated. In a hiss of compressed air, clouds of green mist filled its interior. I heard Charon's growling and Foggs' exclamation of surprise.

The system was in overload. The rattling speakers crackled with a shaking voice,

Warning... your available nanite stocks are down 99%...

I shoved Dominic aside, pushed the hatch open and jumped down into the room.

The Reapers opened fire. My friends were losing nanites even before they'd had a chance to complete their materialization! The sudden jump had disoriented them. They had no weapons, either.

Kyle — what was taking him so long?

An emerald flash filled the room. Arbido screamed and recoiled at the sight of the ugly squat cyborg.

Quest alert: The Last of the First. Quest completed!

You've received a new level!

The gunfire refused to stop.

Finally I intercepted the deactivation code used by the Reapers. Still, I couldn't use it: I didn't have enough time to decipher it.

I invested all my meager power supply into expanding my personal force shield. I used it to cover Foggs and Kimberly while activating Replication using the cargonite brought in by the Reapers. Clouds of nanites escaped through the vents in the floor.

"Kyle, take control over the nanites!"

Barely visible wisps of mist headed toward him.

Arbido shrank back and stumbled, rolling down the stairs right under a Reaper's feet. Charon grabbed the first thing he saw — a steel stand — and darted to his rescue. He invested all his strength into the blow that sliced harmlessly through the air. You can't harm a nanite creature with that sort of weapon.

"Stop them!" a voice bellowed.

Jurgen was trapped within the power fields. He'd had no chance of ever getting his bearings.

Shots rang out from above. This was Dominic joining in the melee and turning three of the guards into a mass of viscous incandescent jelly. Gunfire rattled back, ripping through the ceiling panels.

Kyle scowled, looking around him. What was taking him so long? Had he lost it?

Finally, the nanites he controlled split into several groups. Dull flashes flickered in the dark.

Object Replication level 30!

Kimberly lunged forward. She picked up the sword he'd made and assaulted the nearest guard with a swinging blow.

An inhuman scream echoed from the walls.

The Reaper exploded in a cascade of neurograms. The gunfire choked in mid-burst. Dropping the gun, the Reaper's body crumbled into nanites.

I activated the Call, pouring the dead enemy's nanites into Kimberly. The girl was having a hard time. She could use an extra layer of armor in battle instead of the rags she had on!

Wheezing, Charon picked up another of Kyle's swords. His fingers entwined with the weapon's servoids. The plasma edges of the blade glowed as it arced through the air.

My mind expander was at its most efficient, allowing me to take in every detail of the fight. I now lived in milliseconds; I could see the energy streams as the liberated neurograms washed over us with their gentle farewell before disappearing for good, fading into our surroundings.

The airlock shuddered. Its sealed doors began to part. The Reapers had received reinforcements!

I managed to replicate nanites one last time, then hit the gap between the slowly parting gates with Plasma Blast. That allowed Foggs and Jurgen some brief respite in order to collect themselves, grab the weapons and enter the dogfight.

Blood rained from the bullet-riddled ceiling.

"Arbido, quit skulking! Go upstairs and check on Dominic!" sparing words, I sent him the Major's mental image. Kimberly, Charon and Foggs struggled to contain the ever-increasing numbers of the enemy.

Kyle, block the airlock and locate the elevator controls!

He stood immobile, frozen. His hesitation might cost us dearly.

Kyle, wake up, man!

He turned round and raised his upper lip in a sinister grin. Limping slightly, he headed for the control stations.

"*Attention all personnel for an incoming arrival,*" the speakers wheezed.

They were trying to get to us from both worlds but they weren't gonna make it! There were no available nanites left here: I'd made sure I'd used up all the available supplies by reinforcing my friends who kept losing nanites to the transmitters built into the Reapers' ammo.

We fought for dear life — a merciless battle that was taking our all, without illusions, at 100% authenticity. Each direct nanite-destroying hit exploded our minds in an agony of pain. Charon had been grazed by a burst of submachine gun fire. Another had passed through Jurgen's arm. Foggs had received two slugs to the head. Kimberly was battling to sustain the enemy alone now.

I hurried to her aid. Foggs was struggling back to his feet without success. A neuromatrix failure, that much was clear. Charon instinctively grabbed at his injured throat, unable to breathe, but he was sure to overcome it soon. Jurgen's right arm hung listlessly.

"Kim, back off!"

She performed a rapid combo and recoiled, putting some distance between herself and her opponents.

The green mist followed her, its bright plumes changing hue as they swirled through the air.

I used several Plasma Blasts to burn a path for myself. Taught by previous experience, I tried to control their outbursts but still the amount of released energy was tremendous. My power shield stayed activated non-stop.

"Kyle, close the airlock! Seal the lab!"

More Reapers continued to arrive. The floor's main tunnel was consumed by smoke. The lighting panels grinned with shards of plastoglass. The walls melted, surrendering to the extreme temperatures.

My supply of nanites dwindled rapidly, each blast taking tens of thousands.

Behind my back, Kimberly was helping Charon while Jurgen dragged Foggs deeper into the room.

"Zander, get out of there! You're in my way!" distorted by interference, Kyle's voice echoed in the earphones.

The lab's massive doors shifted, closing. The hermetic locks began to rotate. Too late! I retreated, spitting out plasma. My shield had expired; the heat singed my face. I could see the Reapers' nanites penetrate the thick bulkheads. This enemy didn't accept defeat.

The Founders' finest technologies, initially destined to create, had been turned into a weapon. We had misinterpreted their legacy and we couldn't do anything to change it anymore. All we could do now was fight. Till the last breath; till our last nanite.

I struck back with Self-Sacrifice. The silent metal shrieked as the Reapers' bodies that were seeping through the walls froze in mid-flow, decorating the bulkheads with a bas-relief of their distorted figures.

The silver dust of deactivated nanites swirled underfoot. Jets of carbon dioxide pelted us from above as the fire extinguishers attempted to put out the ignited wiring. Springing to life, extractors howled.

"Retreat back to the center!" a hoarse voice shouted.

I recoiled. A thin layer of Molecular Mist lined the inner walls. Its incandescent fog swirled, flashing with numerous activations of top-level Object Replication as Kyle created power shield generators, sealing the lab.

* * *

"ZANDER, WHERE ARE WE?" Kimberly looked around herself with curiosity, her eyes still filled with the agitation of the brief but lethal combat.

"Phew," Foggs sank to the floor. "Looks like we've done 'em."

"Help me, someone! He's dying!"

We all turned to Arbido's voice.

I leaned over Dominic. Unlike us (sounds spooky, doesn't it?) he was made of flesh and blood. His armor suit had failed to sustain the hail of pulse gun fire, letting three of the slugs through. The exo's post-effects were the only thing that still supported the weak spark of life within him. Still, his body was too exhausted to keep going. He needed an urgent blood transfusion.

"Look around you, quick! There must be some containers with medical supplies here somewhere!"

Charon didn't understand me but Kimberly

did. She nodded and disappeared into the smoke. Jurgen cast a suspicious glance at Dominic but said nothing and walked back to the control consoles.

Foggs attempted to scramble to his feet but couldn't. Neuromatrix damage was similar to shell shock. He would need some time to recuperate.

Arbido wasn't much good, either. All he could do was groan and fuss around.

Kyle, however, was a different case entirely. For a while he hovered out of my view, waiting for me to look away. Then he lunged at Dominic, his steely fingers closing around his throat.

"Why did you do this to me?"

Dominic wheezed. The fibrillose structure of his armor had caved in. His eyes were now popping out with the strain.

"Stop it!" I forced the cyborg away. "He's not our enemy!"

"They promised me! They promised!"

"Kyle, please! Get a grip! Dominic didn't hurt you! You don't even know him! Do you?"

"No, I don't," Kyle's voice fell, then rose to a shriek again, "It hurt so much! I hurt! I was cold! I had no one to talk to!"

Kimberly defused the situation by coming back with a first-aid kit from the emergency supply she'd discovered. She shoved me a fully charged life support module. "Go help him," she mouthed. "I'll sort this out."

Administering first aid to Dominic was a question of seconds. In this day and age of high technologies — provided you had the right equipment — all it took was locking the clamp on and plugging in a couple of jacks.

"Communications station," he wheezed. "Zander, I beg you..."

No idea why he was so desperate to get there. Not that I minded, really. The in-modes rooms were on the same floor.

"Just lay back and keep quiet. At the moment, we're cut off from the rest of the bunker."

Dominic struggled to sit up. "You need to find a way to get there! It's vital. All the rest is irrelevant..."

He seemed to be rambling. Wasting the last of his energy, he reached for the ammo container built into his armor and produced a small flat box. With quivering fingers he offered it to me. "If I don't survive, all you need to do is connect it to any of the communications consoles."

I fumbled with the unknown device, then tried to scan it, with little result. The thing had no power source. Inside were a few microchips with unfamiliar markings. Nothing to do with the Founders. Just some basic module, as simple as that.

"Jurgen? Take a look at this, will you?"

Jurgen took the device from me and stepped aside without saying a word. He'd clammed up after our battle with the Reapers, speaking little and keeping his own company.

Kimberly, however, seemed to have perked up. Kyle couldn't take his eyes off her. She straddled an upended computer terminal knocked over in the heat of the fight and laid her Sword of a Neuro across her lap, stroking its hilt. The corners of her lips curved in a faint smile.

I walked over to them.

"Don't you remember me?" Kyle kept asking.

"Sorry, kiddo," Kimberly didn't seem to be

taken aback by his grotesque appearance. "I think you used to look different back then, didn't you? How about you get yourself another avatar?" she asked in full seriousness.

"How about me?" Arbido jumped at the chance, his voice rife with hope. "Can I get another avatar?"

She threw her arms around both of them. "Of course you can! Zander, mind sparing a few nanites?"

A reluctant smile touched my lips. This was mind-boggling. We had Reapers conglomerating behind these very walls, trying to squeeze back in and finish us off. And this girl here behaved as if the spine-chilling worst was already over!

I had no nanites to spare: I'd spent every single one in battle. Still, I couldn't say no to all the hope in Kyle and Arbido's eyes.

I was in the process of learning to live. I had to stop being ashamed of the impulses warming my heart. The bored player who'd but a few months ago logged into a new "game of the future" for the first time had long gone.

The finest cargonite dust rose into the air, disturbed by constant flashes of Replication. Still, this wasn't enough. I had to lower the density of my own body 30%.

Kimberly watched my every move closely. Her eyes glowed with approval.

Two murky swirls of nanites enveloped Arbido and Kyle.

Then the mist dispersed.

Kyle glanced at his hands. His face fell. He'd grown taller and more proportionate — but he remained a cyborg. The servomotors implanted into his flesh squeaked softly when he stood up.

"Don't get upset," Kimberly said. "You forgot how you used to look, that's all. It'll be all right. Your memory will come back to you, I promise."

Arbido, however, had changed dramatically. I'd never met him in real life — but the moment I glanced at this aging man, lean and below average height, I knew this was his real self.

Kim snickered, unable to help herself.

"What is it?" Arbido tensed. "What's wrong?"

"Sorry... Please don't mind me. Your feet!"

I too couldn't suppress a smile. Arbido must have recreated his usual clothes: a very expensive tailor-made business suit from some hi-tech weatherproof fabric. On his feet, however, he was wearing a pair of worn-out house slippers so deformed they repeated the shape of his feet. They were comfortable and cozy: a true object of sentimental value.

He didn't look embarrassed. "I'm used to them," he shrugged. Swinging round, he glimpsed his reflection in the depths of a dead monitor and breathed a sigh of relief. "Finally! At least I look like a normal human being. Thanks!"

"Zander," Jurgen had been watching Kyle and Arbido's metamorphosis from a safe distance. Now he motioned me to approach. "Need to talk."

He was still fiddling with the little box Dominic had given him.

"Have you found out what it is?"

"It's a data-destroying device. I've deactivated it."

"Good. Keep it for the time being. I'll look into it. I want you to find the elevator controls," I pointed at its firmly locked doors. "I just hope it'll take the

Reapers some time to breach our power shield. This is a good moment to get to the in-mode room."

"Okay. Just be careful. Dominic doesn't tell us everything. I have a bad feeling about it."

* * *

DOMINIC WAS STILL UNCONSCIOUS when the elevator's doors jingled open.

Together, Jurgen and Kyle unblocked the lab's controls, including power distribution.

"Charon, we need your help!"

Together we carried Dominic into the elevator. Arbido was already there, looking calm and in control. His usual fidgeting was gone. Could the change in his appearance have affected him so much?

Foggs and Kimberly were still keeping their guard outside, covering us from a potential break-in by the Reapers.

I turned to Jurgen. "Did you manage to do something?"

"We've restored a few of the power shields," he replied. "They should hinder the Reapers' advance. But even so we have very little time. We couldn't get to the cargonite stocks. They're stored in special vaults deep underground."

"Listen, I've intercepted an emergency nanite deactivation code but I didn't have the time to decipher it yet. Think you and Kyle could give it a try? What if we broadcast this command via the bunker's data channels?"

"Why not?" Jurgen nodded his approval as I

forwarded him the data. "I'll see what I can do. Only I'm afraid that total nanite deactivation might affect us as well. First we need to get to the in-modes."

"I agree. Where does this elevator come out?"

He shrugged. "It's not a gravity one, is it? It's strictly for emergencies, it only has one route. Although it cuts through all of the bunker's floors, it only stops on three levels. We've managed to get access to them. The good news is, they're 100% free of Reapers."

"How do you know?"

"That's what the security scanners say."

Jurgen seemed to have thawed out a bit after the melee. He was much easier to talk to. "Anyway! Where can it take us?"

"To the alien technologies research center, the long-range space communications station and the exobiology labs."

"The communications station," I decided. "The in-mode rooms are next door to it."

By then, Kyle had already hacked the elevator control panel. "Got it," his voice rang out loud and clear. The avatar's change seemed to have affected it too.

"Kim, Foggs, quick!"

* * *

PHANTOM SERVER awaits you! Sign up now!

This holographic slogan was the first thing we saw at the communications station. How strange. You'd think this wasn't the right place to put up ad modules.

We lay Dominic temporarily on the floor. He was still unconscious and in a bad way. The indicator lights on his breast panel flashed warning signals.

I handed Charon one of the life support cartridges I'd made earlier. "Keep an eye on him, will you? Call me if he comes round."

The room was huge. Rows of workstations towered along the walls. The domed ceiling overhead was a replica of the stellar sky.

"Jurgen, Kyle, I need access to the floor's systems and full control of this level, now! Charon, Kim, Foggs, keep the entryways in your sights."

We'd made it. We had very little left to do. The moment we got access to the global network, we could start recharging the in-modes and moving them. The limited amounts of cargonite gave us hope that the Reapers' expansion into the real world hadn't gone beyond Corporation-owned lands. Our plan was simple. We were going to use military space vehicles to transport the in-modes to a safe location. We would then hack maintenance robots' controls and reprogram them to look after our capsules.

"Zander," Foggs called.

I walked over to him. "You okay?"

"Much better. Listen," he touched his personal navigator. "One question. Why do they keep advertising Phantom Server? There's no such game. We know it already. But what happened to all the other players?"

"The Second Colonial Fleet?" I suggested. "Weren't they sent to storm Darg via the Eurasia station?"

"Nope. Doesn't work. There were millions in the

game. Think about it: The Game of the Future campaign was advertised all over the world. Neuroimplants were issued in their millions. But Eurasia servers can only process a limited number of players."

"You might be right. We'll find out in a moment."

"Zander, take a look," Jurgen sent several data flowcharts onto a holographic monitor. Pictures, stellar maps, blocks of text and video clips — dozens of windows opened simultaneously on the screen.

"Can't we streamline it somehow?" I asked.

"We can organize it chronologically," Kyle agreed. He worked much faster than Jurgen, manipulating files instantly. "There you go. You might find it interesting."

"How about you?"

"I've got lots of work to do."

Very well, why not? We still had a few minutes till all of the floor's machinery surrendered to our control. I just might check and see what the military had been up to here. The way I understood it, the communications station's computers stored the backups of all data ever sent or received.

...

March 12 2210

Confidential

To the Commander of Earth's United Military Space Forces Admiral Jonathan Higgs

Sender: Capt. Malyshev

So! Did that mean that the cartoon NPC running the Eurasia station had a real-life prototype?

Report

The dismantling of the alien starship discovered at the bottom of one of Europa's subglacial oceans is complete. All the available parts have been sent to Earth for further study. I'm commencing search operations.

The recording stopped. Jurgen cussed. "It's blocked my access!"

"It's all right... I'll sort it out..." we heard Dominic's weak voice. He had come round and was trying to scramble to his feet. "Zander, help me... I'll show you..."

"Sorry but we have no time to check out the archives now. They're too big. We get the picture without them. Moving our in-modes is what we should be doing."

"You don't get the picture, that's the problem!" he struggled to say. "You need to see it. Then we must destroy the station. If the Reapers get here, that'll be a new disaster. Give me... more... of that swill."

Was he rambling?

"You want more exo?" Arbido supported his head. "It'll kill you!"

"That's my business," Dominic wheezed. "Let me explain! I'm offering a fair swap. You listen to me. In return, I'll give you full access to the system. To save you time and energy."

"We can still save you if we place you into an in-mode," I said.

"No! Inject me with that stuff! Otherwise you're not getting the access codes!"

I just couldn't understand his fanaticism. What

if whatever he wanted to tell us was indeed important? But I thought we'd sussed it all out already? "Metabolites will kill you. Charon, what do you think you're doing?"

Charon who had the life support cartridges in his safekeeping stepped toward Dominic. In one deft movement he replaced the cartridge in his suit. "That's his right."

Dominic gasped.

The metabolites kicked in fast. He shook his head, then staggered toward the station and slumped into the seat. His hand touched a group of textoglyphs. He blinked several times, then blurted out,

"After the discovery of the alien ship on Europa, we scanned the whole of the Solar system searching for more artifacts. We didn't leave a single rock unturned. It was then that we discovered about a hundred small diamond-shaped objects in the Sun's photosphere. We began monitoring them. Soon we realized that the objects kept growing."

Dominic ran out of breath, then exploded in a torturous bout of coughing. Soon, however, he plucked up enough strength to continue.

"No one could understand the significance of their evolution until one day the segments began to replicate and bind together. Both the data analysis and the situation's prognosis presented us with a shocking development. These segments were building a sphere around our Sun in order to intercept all of its energy!"

No one said a word. Dominic caught his breath and went on, "It didn't take us long to realize that Earth was doomed. Our astronomers discovered nine more Black Suns at various distances from the Solar system."

"Why didn't you destroy them?" Jurgen spat.

"There's no spacecraft capable of entering the photosphere! There's no weapon that could destroy them!"

"And they don't respond to any attempt at contact," Charon growled.

"According to our calculations, our Sun will expire within the next fifteen years," Dominic's voice began to weaken. The repeat metabolite injection hadn't been as effective. "Our last hope lay with the Founders' technologies and their interstellar network. That's when we formed the first group," he hurried to finish, "to test the neuroimplants we'd found on board the alien ship. Still, none of our officers survived the identity transfer."

"So you decided to use gamers," Kyle said darkly.

"And once you got access to alien technologies, they got out of control?" Kimberly snapped. "You managed to kill Earth even before the Sun went out!"

"Wait," Foggs stopped her. "Dominic, I need to know the location of the bunker containing my in-mode. You kept advertising Phantom Server to the last even though there was no such game! You kept luring new players — where to? Why were you giving neuroimplants away, basically for free? What was the real escape plan? How long are those bunkers going to last?"

"There are no bunkers," Dominic replied. "Here, look!"

A spherical 3D screen materialized at the center of the room.

The cold stars glowed in the black sky.

This was real-time streaming using the Founders' communications channels which transmitted signals instantly.

Judging by the exhibited data, this particular monitoring station was located on Eris — a dwarf planet situated in the Kuiper belt just past Neptune's orbit. As if in confirmation, the ashen gray disk of Dysnomia — Eris' only moon — scurried up over the planet's close horizon. And further beyond, huge bulks of interstellar stations ambled unhurriedly through space, accompanied by cruisers and countless interlinked groups of cryogenic platforms.

A shiver ran down my spine.

Dominic's voice barely registered, so great was the shock as reality began to sink in. I was looking at a panorama of deep space unfolding in real time before us. We were watching events happening at this very second billions of miles away from Earth.

The picture changed.

I saw an enormous hall filled with stacked-up rows of translucent capsules. Each was filled with a soft glow outlining the shape of a human being inside.

"Cryo in-modes," Dominic explained. "New-generation ones. All the network users in possession of neuroimplants who expressed their desire to join the Game of the Future were transported on board cryogenic platforms. Their construction was completed about a couple of years ago but it has taken us all this time to move all the users."

"Am I there too?" Foggs exclaimed, disbelieving.

"You are. As are all the players who took part in the Darg landing. Plus millions of other people."

"This fleet, where is it heading?"

"To the Darg system," Dominic replied, then hurried to add as if afraid someone might interrupt him, "You need to understand. Everything was going according to plan. The cryo in-modes are preprogrammed to periodically contact the interstellar network. Groups of users take turns in emerging from stasis for periods of one month. They connect to the network via Eurasia station. The journey is expected to last eight and a half years. During that time, each of the astronauts' identities should have visited Darg several times, gaining the necessary assimilation and survival skills. In the best-case scenario they could have even begun to settle on the system's only habitable planet."

"But then the Outlaws built Avatroid, didn't they?" Jurgen asked. "Argus was destroyed by Phantom Raiders, forcing you to introduce the hybrid?"

"Exactly!" Dominic's voice shook. He was fading fast. "Now the colonial fleet is heading into the unknown. Eurasia station is seriously damaged. Its acceptance rate is at its lowest. Now the future colonists won't be able to acclimatize themselves to their new environment. They won't have enough experience, which means they won't be able to colonize the planet or restore the destroyed stations once the fleet finally arrives at its destination."

"There must be a solution," Kimberly said softly.

"We have eight and a half years to find one," Dominic managed. The metabolites had burned away what meager strength he'd had left. His voice continued to fade, breaking as he spoke.

Suddenly my mind expander began receiving

control codes. "Jurgen, I've got data from Dominic! I'm forwarding it to you. I want you to look into it."

Charon wheezed, staring at the screens. He didn't say a word.

Arbido sat in a heap on the floor, clutching his head. "They are freakin' nuts," he whispered softly. "Darg has been destroyed by their orbital strikes! There's not a single functioning space station! The area is controlled by Avatroid's fleet!"

Dominic's gaze began to cloud as he looked at me. His lips barely moved. "You need to destroy the communications station. If the Reapers get to it, they'll stop the colonial fleet. They'll use remote commands to kill its engines. Millions of people... and their neurograms... sweet, helpless quarry."

"No, Dominic, wait! Don't you die on us!" I tried to help him but failed. His Adam's apple jerked a few times. His head hung to one side. His stare glazed over.

Dead.

I couldn't change that. I didn't know what to do. I couldn't swallow the lump in my throat. I wrapped Dominic's body in Steel Mist and stepped aside. I avoided looking at Charon.

"Zander," a few minutes later, Jurgen walked over to me.

"What is it?"

"I've checked the data he sent us."

"And? Speak up, man!"

"These are the control codes to the Third Colonial Fleet. He gave them to us!"

* * *

THE WORK SPACE of the communications station was formed by three holographic images.

The first screen showed humanity's fleet crossing the Kuiper belt, heading out of the Solar system — basically, going nowhere.

In another nineteen days, the Third Colonial Fleet's on-board systems would relieve the current watch group, sending Vandal, Foggs, Novitsky and all the survivors of the Darg mission back into cryogenic slumber. The fleet's communications stations would then kick back to life and transmit the identities of the next group of half-baked "colonists" to the Darg system via hyperspace.

I could clearly see what was going to happen next.

Badly damaged and drifting the outskirts of the Darg system, Eurasia wouldn't be able to receive all the identity matrices. In which case, Founders' equipment was going to automatically join in, using random respawn points — which more often than not were located in the wreckage.

Thousands of players would have to suffer the consequences of the "alternative start". Believing they were playing a game, they would search for the game developers' prompts in a desperate attempt to survive.

Not many would be lucky enough to live to tell the tale. There were few, if any, safe respawn points left. And neuroimplants knew no mercy.

"We need to deactivate the auto awakening program!" Foggs exclaimed. "Zander, at least my men aren't new to this anymore! You can't send them back into stasis! Who are you going to get instead?"

The mind boggles.

Who are you going to get instead? — the snappy phrase met the others' silent approval, forcing me to take one step forward out of our serried ranks. No one had bothered to ask me if I was ready to accept responsibility for millions of human lives.

"Good idea," Charon added his approval. "Zander, the Haash will join you! Argus is a big station. Surely we'll find some room there for my people too?" he lowered his head, awaiting my answer.

I just loved it! A doomed human fleet and the few remnants of the Haash civilization — and all you needed to do in order to save both from extinction was work out the mystery of interstellar jumps!

Quest alert! New quest available: The Chasm
Skills required: Pioneer, Colonizer
Ability required: Broken Chains
Quest requirements met.
Two civilizations are on the brink of extinction. Their representatives have officially sought your help. Find a way to save humans and the Haash.

You've received 100 AP (Action Points)
Deadline: none

How weird. I couldn't find any further information about those mysterious Action Points. What were they for? Did I really need them?

And I'd thought that the game was over! Why, then, would my interface jump back to life, offering me a new quest? Who'd issued it?

It didn't really matter. I had no need for moral

crutches anymore. "Jurgen, is it really possible to deactivate the awakening protocol?"

"I don't know yet," he answered in all honesty. "But I'm gonna try. The fleet's data exchange channel is stable enough. I have the necessary access codes."

He gave me a funny look. "Zander, may I ask you about something? Could you stop issuing me quests, please? There's no need for this gaming décor anymore."

I stared at him, uncomprehending. "What kind of décor?"

"This!" he sent me the screenshot of a system message he'd just received,

Quest alert! New quest available: Stasis
Contact the Third Colonial Fleet's flagship and abort the awakening protocol, leaving the crew in cryo in-mode capsules in permanent stasis.
Time left until completion: 19 days 2 hrs. 30 min

"Jurgen, just do it!"

"Do you think that the Founders' interface came with a quest generator?" he asked. "But this would mean that-"

"Sorry, man, can we discuss it some other time?" I said, unable to shake off a chilling, unsettling foreboding. Why was I feeling so restless all of a sudden?

"Charon," I asked, "the remaining Haash back on your planet, do they have neuroimplants?"

"*Nowr*," he snapped. "Every single one we had was implanted in the crew members of the reconnaissance ship."

"And cargonite stores, did you find any?"

"*Nowr.* Our second ship was equipped with the Founders' communications device. We had to find the planet and report its coordinates," he lowered his head in sorrow.

"How long can your people last?"

"Three full orbits."

"What, only three years?!"

"By now, the second ship should be completed," I'd never seen Charon so agitated. "Everyone should have already boarded it. We don't have a stasis technology," he explained. "But we're naturally capable of hibernating. By lowering on-board temperature, everyone should have already fallen asleep. The ship is located on the planet's surface and protected by a force shield which is powered by the on-board reactor. The reactor will last three full orbits!"

It's all right. We'll sort this out, I told myself. Still, a chill ran down the back of my head. Not a pleasant feeling. Charon was only a wing leader. He wasn't privy to the "sacred mystery", as he'd put it. I still needed to make level 70 in Mnemotechnics to unlock my Global Network ability. Then I'd be able to scan the Haash system, contact their colonial transport and send them Argus' coordinates.

I was too restless to think straight. Then again, all these funny sensations were part of me now. I'd better learn to live with them.

My gaze paused on the second holographic screen.

Within it, the light of our Sun was diffused, obstructed by numerous diamond-shaped objects. Very soon this cradle of humanity would sink into pitch darkness, just as had happened to the Haash' planet as well as dozens of other worlds — once densely populated and now deserted.

We had no idea what kind of technology we were dealing with. Who made these star-trapping machines and why? What was the purpose of all the stellar energy they harvested?

They couldn't have belonged to the Founders. Their nanites were too feeble — they would have crumbled in the heat of the photosphere. I had a funny feeling these weren't machines at all. More like a cosmic non-organic life form — not necessarily sentient but highly prolific and power-hungry. If you maxed out the zoom, you could see tiny particles constantly leaving the large diamond-shaped segments. They dove into the ocean of solar plasma where they grew and replicated, then soared back up into the photosphere to form yet another segment.

THE THIRD 3D MONITOR showed identical panoramas of deserted cities, their tiered mile-long towers still consumed by the thick emissions. Our planet's technosphere kept doing its job — and so it should, considering its extreme robotization levels.

I looked at the towers. A few of their windows were still glowing. Life still lingered behind those façades. "Kyle, I'll need to have the Earth's technosphere analyzed."

"What exactly are you interested in?"

"How long will the cities' reactors last? Is it possible to redistribute the existing resources? Can we organize robots into groups that would search for survivors' in-modes and recharge them?"

"Aren't we going to deactivate the game's servers?" Arbido asked. "Wouldn't it be better to kill phantom worlds instead? This way, NPCs will disappear and all the players will be subjected to emergency logouts."

"To do what? To croak in the dying cities? To realize they've been left behind?" Kimberly snapped.

"But cyberspace is even worse!" Arbido offered.

Kyle sniffed his indignation. He kept casting adoring glances at Kimberly, his gaze naïve in its childlike eloquence. "We can't switch off all the game worlds!"

"Why not?" Foggs asked.

"Because that's millions of servers, safely protected and scattered all over the world!" Kyle exclaimed. "Some of them are located on orbital stations even. And most of them perform functions other than gaming! If we mess with them, the entire global network will collapse!"

"What about the Crystal Sphere?" Arbido insisted.

"Are you completely stupid? Don't you understand?" Kyle was about to lose it. "Gaming worlds have merged! Reapers are everywhere! If we switch off the Crystal Sphere, they'll survive anyway!"

"So you're suggesting leaving it all as it is?" Arbido too got hot under the collar. "Let all those smart enough not to have bought into Phantom Server's advertisement die slowly inside their in-modes?"

He was right. This was another problem we were facing, one impossible to ignore. I just didn't see a solution. A forced logout would lead to death, chaos and disaster. I knew this better than anyone else. The kind of people we were speaking of had long denounced the real world. All they'd do, they'd log back in.

"Please don't argue," Kimberly touched her sword strewn with microchips. "No need to complicate things. I'm staying behind. Nobody touches the Crystal Sphere! Leave the servers on."

"You nuts?" Arbido demanded. "What do you mean, you're staying behind? Why would you do that?"

"Gameplay is still king. It evens the odds," her fingers brushed the weapon's blood groove. The Founders' runic script obediently glowed under her touch. The dull purple of the cargonite blade shimmered in waves. "This is our world," she concluded in a soft but firm voice.

"But Kim," Jurgen tried to reason with her, "the virtual worlds are merging! This process is irreversible — and unpredictable!"

"I know. This in my decision. I'm going back to the Crystal Sphere. I'll see if I can find other survivors. I'll give them weapons against the Reapers. We are Neuros. This is our world."

The adoration in Kyle's eyes spoke for itself. No need to ask this one about his immediate plans.

"We're Neuros," he echoed.

Kimberly smiled back to him.

I knew what she was thinking of. I knew the extent of her dreams. Whatever happened to virtual reality, there would always be a secret little location deep there somewhere. She'd be happy there.

But her path toward it would be rife with danger.

"Here, take this," the translucent copy of the Founders' navigator left my hand. "You can use it to locate your in-modes," I added just in case. "I'm pretty sure Kyle should be capable of occasionally venturing into the real world to recharge them?"

"Thanks," she gratefully accepted the copy. "I promise you we'll find a safe place and reinstall all the in-modes there."

Each of us was making our own choice.

Our lives had momentarily met only to diverge again, each path made of one's own feats and desires.

* * *

"GOT IT!" Kyle exclaimed. "I've got access to the combat vehicle hangar!"

"Show me," I said. "What have you got there?"

"Not much, but enough for what we're about to do," he switched the picture to the monitors, showing hangar after hangar of military assault and landing vehicles awaiting orders.

"Excellent. I'm sure you will need them. At the moment, we need a military flybot with a large cargo hold and a group of on-board *serves*."

"I've got one just like that! Take a look," Kyle switched to another camera view.

The vehicle looked very respectable. The latest military space model. Fully automatic. The data Dominic had sent us allowed us to enable remote task assignment — which I immediately put to good use.

Somewhere in the bunker's depths cargo belts sprang to life. The sealed gate opened, revealing a separate in-mode storage room. A hundred and five capsules in total. Twenty of them were arranged in a circle in the middle of the room. The other ones — apparently installed later — formed separate sections divided by wide passages.

Everybody was there. Jurgen, Frieda, Ralph, the children. Plus a few other survivors — whatever had happened to their identity matrices, I'd no idea yet. Their names said nothing to us.

"Let's load them all up."

Serves had already received access to the in-modes' personal life support modules and replaced them. What a relief. Jurgen seemed to have perked up too. Back in the Darg system, our friends had escaped death.

Twelve of the in-modes began their brief journey. Soon *serves* were already loading them on board the flybot. We uploaded a new course to its autopilot. First it would pick up Arbido's capsule, followed by a brief stop at my house. Then it would begin a thousand-mile flight to the military space reserve base.

It looked like Arbido's plan had worked, after all. Another couple of hours, then we'd be able to breathe freely.

"Zander," Jurgen walked over to me. The nanites forming his body momentarily flashed a soft golden light as he'd received a new level. "I've managed to deactivate the auto awakening program on board Eurasia. Which means that we can keep the Daugoth clan members. I've also canceled the uploading of new identity matrices until further notice."

"Have you found the Colonial Fleet databases?"

"I have, and I've already downloaded everything

we need. Now we can build a remotely-controlled communications station on board the Relic."

"Great job! Thanks! What's your Technologist level now?"

"A hundred and two. But that's thanks to their special learning modules. I downloaded them too!"

"Do you think they might have something for me?" I asked.

"You might be able to raise Alien Technologies 20 points at least. But Mnemotechnics is a problem, sorry. All we have is way below your level."

"Never mind. I can always level it up with Liori and the Daugoths. We'll use the new technologies to restore the Relic. Anything else?"

"You asked me about the military's secret files," Jurgen said. "I've got them. Why do you need the reports on the first twenty subjects?"

"I'll tell you later. I need to sort it out myself first. There're lots of things we might need to reconsider. Can we do it later?"

"As you wish. The data's in my mind expander. Would you like me to copy it for you?"

"Absolutely," I said. "Think you can upload it to my Synaps?"

"I'd rather we waited till your in-mode is recharged. That's one hell of an information overload."

"No. Do it now."

Jurgen lingered. "I don't think it's a good idea."

"Why? Do you know something?"

"I've stopped receiving feedback from your in-mode's biomonitoring sensors."

"Normal. You've disconnected them, haven't you?"

"Not really. I just decreased the feedback. But

now they're completely dead."

"When did that happen?"

"About an hour after your disappearance. We didn't know it was possible to cross into the real world, did we? We just thought you got caught in some deformation or other. Kimberly did warn us that some of the testing areas weren't stable."

"All right, so the sensors are dead, big deal. Can't see your problem. I feel okay. No need to overcomplicate things. Didn't they have to hack my in-mode? The biomonitoring system must have packed up."

"So you want me to send you the data? That's your final word?"

"Yes. Enough about that. Just send it."

By then, the in-modes had already been loaded on board the flybot. The loading bay closed. The craft reversed. The antigravity engines kicked in, lifting the flybot into the air. A diaphragm shutter opened up in the hangar's domed roof.

Oh. The altitude was impressive. We'd left the technopark way below. Its structures looked like toy blocks.

Kyle and Kimberly walked over to us. "The Reapers are stirring. They're trying to get to the reactor," Kyle said, continuously monitoring the situation. "They might try to de-energize the bunker in order to bring down the force fields."

"They wouldn't dare," I said. "The testing grounds are their only habitat."

"Oh yes, they would," Kyle said confidently. "The servers can last forty-eight hours on emergency power no problem. But the force fields will go down straight away."

"So what do you suggest?"

"We need to leave. If they break through, we can't sustain them. There're only six of us. Not enough nanites."

"Okay. Then I suggest you go to the communications station and get the data destruction under way. Once it's done we're leaving for the Crystal Sphere."

"But what about our in-modes?" Arbido demanded, anxious.

"Yours will be picked up in a few minutes. There shouldn't be any problems. The flybot has already cleared the Corporation's grounds. The cities are deserted so I don't think it will get into any trouble. We control the backup bunker's systems. It's ready to receive the capsules. The automatics will do the rest. That's it! Let's do it!"

* * *

CHARON STOOD by the screen looking at the stars. "Zander?" he turned round at the sound of my footsteps.

"You shouldn't have given him more exo."

"I'm not going to justify my actions. Dominic was dying. The in-mode couldn't have helped him. But every sentient being has the right to a noble gesture. Dominic is a hero amongst humans."

"We could have sorted it out without this sacrifice."

"*Nowr.* You'd have wasted a lot of time arguing. His life was dwindling away. Things might have taken a different turn."

I could see this conversation was difficult for Charon. The Haash never questioned a person's right to gallantry. "Next time you want to apply your race's values to humans, you'd better ask me first," I said.

"Arbido's in-mode has been collected!" Kyle reported. "The flybot is moving on to its next destination."

I walked over to the control panels. Like any human being, I needed some time to embrace the circumstances.

I glanced over the communications consoles as Jurgen began uploading the data into my mind expander. The upload went remarkably fast and didn't seem to stress out my body. Never had my Synaps been so stable nor functioned so well.

By now, Kyle was almost done with the data destruction. This was a load off my mind. The Reapers weren't going to get to the Colonial Fleet!

Besides, I had a very nasty surprise in store for them. Several groups of nanites were now moving deep into the bunker toward the cargonite stores: cargonite that had been made from the wreckage of the Founders' ship.

We had to stop the NPCs' expansion into the real world. We'd already stripped them of their ability to infiltrate it. Now was the time to destroy the strategic stocks of the unreplenishable metal.

My new ability — Self-Replication — suited my purpose just fine. Once the Reapers finally got to the lower floors, the cargonite depots would be empty. The nanites would have used it all up and left Earth heading for the Sun, destined to burn away in its photosphere.

The screens began to go blank.

That was it. Time to go.

Zander, the flybot's systems can't contact your in-mode! Jurgen PM'd me, anxious.

I switched over to the flybot's channel.

Its scanners were focused on the façade of my tower block, barely visible behind the slowly growing cloud of swirling emissions. The flybot banked smoothly, getting closer.

Still no answer from my in-mode. The building's systems were de-energized. The signatures of the emergency power supplies barely glowed. I could see a few power imprints of maintenance robots within the effective scanning zone. It looked like they'd just disconnected the building from the grid!

That wasn't possible. The *serves* couldn't shut a building down as long as a single in-mode capsule inside was still functioning! This was against their programming!

I sent a mental command to the flybot. Its gun ports opened, showering the building's façade with a barrage of laser fire. A perfectly round fragment of the wall crumbled, disappearing into the gloom below.

The wind rushed into my apartment, upending the old office chair and ripping off a couple of loose wall panels.

A maintenance ramp slid out of the flybot, letting out a few agile serves which scrambled down it into my room.

The tinted plastic of my in-mode capsule was blank. Not a single indicator light showed through.

My throat clenched. I couldn't believe my eyes. What could have happened here? Had Reapers done this?

No. They couldn't have. They had no idea who I

was. They had no information that could have allowed them to connect me to a real-world location.

Another important detail: shutting down a building wasn't a one-minute job. The robots would have needed both time and the clearance to do so.

Which meant that my in-mode had only packed up a couple of hours ago.

What was going on?

I felt fine! My head was clear. I didn't feel sick or anything. Considering my neuroimplant's borderline lethal authenticity levels, it was hard to believe that I might have missed the moment of my in-mode's failure.

Yes, but-

Hadn't I deactivated biomonitoring?

I sent the *serves* a command to open my in-mode.

Nobody said anything but I could hear them holding their breath. The servodrives screeched back to life. Raising clouds of dust, the capsule's teardrop lid rose and slid aside.

My face inside the capsule was gaunt. Or should I say shriveled? My body had burned itself away. I struggled to focus, staring at myself as the serves took my body temperature.

Their verdict was definite and unambiguous. Death had occurred an hour and a half ago.

The details made me nauseous. I broke the connection and turned away, gasping for air.

Now I remembered the sudden bout of weakness I'd struggled with back in the maintenance corridor, just as the Reapers had noticed the opened ceiling hatch.

What was the name of that ability I'd received?

I hadn't even had the time to check it out!

I opened the interface tab. The letters swam and blurred before my eyes.

Broken Chains. Your mind has shaken off the bounds of your fragile temporal body. Now your identity matrix can travel between worlds.

Warning! Always double-check availability of nanites in your destination point before departure. Make sure you've saved a back-up copy of your identity at the central node of the hyperspace network. Alternatively, you can do so at any available network point.

I slumped down and clutched my head.

"Zander," Kimberly touched my shoulder. "I know how it feels. It's scary. But you'll get used to it. It won't take long."

I didn't say anything. I needed at least a couple of minutes to realize what had just happened.

"And now you and Liori can-"

"Kim, please. Give me a minute."

"I can't. We don't have a minute. The Reapers have shut the bunker down. We need to go!"

THE CRYSTAL SPHERE

THE WARBLER'S BANKS had changed dramatically.

The location was bathed in sunlight. A breeze touched our faces, bringing the scent of the forest. You wouldn't have thought this place was all scorched when we'd passed through it just recently.

Game worlds kept merging. The testing grounds' programs were doing their best to restore what had been lost and fill in the blanks, assisting the merge. Still, the Earth's cyberspace was enormous — and in many of its other parts, things might have not gone as smoothly as here.

Where the ford used to be, a sturdy log bridge now stood. When we cleared the reed banks, we faced a chain of shallow hills interspersed with areas of wasteland and occasional patches of greenery.

Something creaked under the bridge.

"Zander!" Forrest the Forest Sprite scrambled out of his hiding place. "You're back! I can't believe it!"

"Do you remember him?" I asked Kimberly.

She nodded, then reached out to give me a hug. "Tell Liori," she whispered, "that I'll never forget her. And one other thing. We'll always be here. I want you to know that. As long as our planet's technosphere holds. As long as a single reactor still glows."

She held my stare, then swung round and stepped onto the bridge. She didn't say goodbye.

The curves of her armor gleamed purple in the sun.

The fiery runes along her sword's blade began to glow.

Kyle caught up with her and strode by her side. Forrest hung behind them, creaking, "Wait for me! What am I supposed to do here alone? All the marshes have run dry!"

As long as a single reactor still glows.

* * *

JURGEN WATCHED Kimberly leave. "We should be going too," he turned to me. "Are you ready?"

"No," I admitted.

"We'd better be off, then!" he touched his navigator and disappeared.

Foggs dematerialized next. Arbido's outline faded too.

Charon touched my hand. "Together?" hot breath escaped his jaws.

"Come on, then!"

His three-digit hand clutched my wrist.

Darkness.

CHAPTER NINE

DARG SYSTEM
ON BOARD THE FOUNDERS' FRIGATE
TWO MONTHS LATER

ACCORDING TO our on-board time, it was early morning.

Our cabin was bathed in soft shadows. The holographic screens began to glow with the faint strip of sunrise.

Liori was still asleep. This was our first day off in the two months of working against time.

You'd be surprised but identity matrices need to sleep too. This is purely psychological.

I watched the woman I loved, racking my brains for something to make her happy.

I remembered the artificial pond I'd seen in that building back on Earth, framed with real greenery. For some reason, real-life memories stood apart from all the other experiences, no matter how vivid.

Our cabin was big enough but a pond would definitely be out of place here. How about a plant? A flower? At the time, I'd caught a whiff of it — it had seemed familiar. Admittedly I didn't know the plant's name and I didn't feel like searching through the databases. I might just make one.

"Hush, be quiet!" I told the nanites mentally. They obeyed, creeping slowly and soundlessly to form a new object.

It didn't look that bad. Not bad at all. And the smell was similar: a pleasant scent, not at all overpowering.

"It's beautiful!" Liori stretched, rolled onto her stomach and pressed her body close to mine.

"Morning, sweetheart."

Yes, we were made of nanites, both of us. It had changed a lot of things — but not our feelings for each other.

Liori sniffed the flower. A shadow crossed her face.

"Don't you like its scent?"

"This flower... it's beautiful. Think you can make a vase for it?" she gave me a kiss, ignoring my question.

I looked her in the eye.

"I'll be right back," Liori said. She seemed to be ill at ease, alarmed even. She rose and disappeared inside the shower module.

How strange.

I got dressed and made coffee for both of us. The flower caught my eye. Whatever might be wrong with it?

Automatically I built a vase and slumped into a

seat, waiting for Liori to reappear. Gradually my thoughts turned to our current problems.

It had been two months since we'd come back from Earth. The situation in the Darg system was unsettling. Avatroid kept increasing his fleet's potential. The hybrid was conspicuous by his absence. Our recon groups had tried to locate him. They'd gone through Oasis with a fine-tooth comb but the station hadn't betrayed its secret.

Talking about Oasis, its upgrade had outlived itself, gradually fading to nothing. It's true that there'd been sightings of new mobs on some of its decks as well as traces of low-level AIs' activity, but that was nothing in the grand scale of things.

The Daugoth clan — each and every one of them — had joined the Relic's crew. Now we had two hundred fifteen people on board, counting the Manticore members. Their leader Aquilon had turned out to be quite an uncompromising bastard. Even though I'd clued him into the real state of affairs he'd refused to join us point blank — followed by thirty more of his players.

We needed to have a talk with him again. The Manticore's corvettes activity attracted unwanted attention to Argus. We weren't yet ready to openly challenge the ancient AIs so we were busy leveling up before one decisive battle for Darg. And I'd never for one moment forgotten about the Third Colonial Fleet whose future depended solely upon us.

In these two months, we'd managed to restore the Relic and develop new command sequences for combat nanite control. I'd opened the Mnemotechnics skill for seventy volunteers. Thirty more were now acquiring a second specialization — Technologist —

under Jurgen's guidance. Add to this the same number of Mechanics coached by Danezerath. Ralph, Charon and Maurugael were busy training twenty pilots. A group led by Foggs and Vandal practiced the combat boarding of enemy ships, learning to fight against AIs as well as partially embodied enemies. In short, we were all busy. Between all this daily practice, combat landings on other stations, repairing the Relic and studying new technologies, our levels kept growing very nicely.

Even Arbido began learning new skills. He had no one to trade with and he'd already finished straightening up our warehouses. So now he'd discovered a penchant for technology. These days I could often see him in the company of Jurgen and Danezerath.

If we looked at the past two months from the point of new interesting discoveries, we'd had few. It had all been about the daily grind: leveling up, repairing the frigate, more training, studying artifacts and adding file after scanner file to our database.

The main thing we'd realized was that we couldn't ignore the Founders' interface. Its unique development branches alone might help us solve the mystery of interstellar jumps and master the Founders' technological legacy. Which in turn would allow us to save billions of lives.

I made a mental plan for the day. I might try to approach Aquilon again, then follow up with a new round of negotiations with Roakhmar who didn't make it easy for anyone. The Dargian Disciples worshipped the Founders as part of their religion — which meant they weren't going to help us in our struggle against the ancient AIs. Neither did they want to discuss the very possibility of a human colony on their planet.

"Your coffee's cold," toweling her hair, Liori walked out of the shower module. She donned a shirt and smiled. A warm, happy smile.

"Sweetheart," I admired her, my heart filled with warmth.

She climbed into the seat opposite and pulled her legs up, making herself comfortable. She cast a furtive glance at the vase. Again a shadow crossed her face.

"What's up? What's wrong with the flower? You don't like the smell, do you?"

"I couldn't smell it," she admitted, taking a sip of her coffee.

"Would you like my neurogram?" I stopped in mid-sentence, realizing I'd just put my foot in it.

She hadn't taken offence. Still, she'd grown subdued.

"Zander," she said, fingering a strand of her blonde hair, "I've been thinking. About neurochips. So once we level up to 100, we'll be able to build them — and then what? Many of our experiences come from the past anyway. Some of them were generated by in-modes as we went along. Like smells, for instance. Does that mean that a neuroimplant can't create something new — something that none of us has ever experienced?"

"There's no proof of that," I pointed out. "But it's true that at the early stages of the crew's digitization we'll have to make do with each person's own range of experiences."

"Excuse me," she interrupted. "Without new feelings we'll age really quickly. Mental ageing is just another form of death. I start to understand a lot now. Take this coffee, for instance: had I never tasted it before, what would it have tasted like now? Just like some warm water?"

"All right, all right. But what if we do share our neurograms?"

"That's not a solution! All we'll do, we'll turn into versions of each other. We'll become a unified gray mass. And how about the children? How are they supposed to develop if their neuroimplants can't generate new experiences? You don't think this might be why the network's creators are not around?"

"What, do you want to say they've become extinct? Or that they downsized?"

"Yes, sort of."

What a predicament. I'd never have thought that immortality-generating technologies could come with so many strings attached.

"Sorry," Liori said. "I didn't mean to upset you. I just can't stop thinking about it. What will become of us?"

I took her in my arms. "Can we talk about it later?"

She draped herself around my neck, answering my kiss.

* * *

JURGEN TRIED to contact us several times, but I didn't give a damn. Not today. Business could wait.

We lay in bed looking at the stars. It was Liori who'd changed the picture to the telescopic view.

"I used to be frightened of outer space," she

whispered. "But now it fascinates me."

A sly smile crossed her lips. Now she looked like a mischievous little girl taking her first steps into the world. Clinging to me, staring fearlessly into the abyss.

The new incoming call wasn't exactly welcome.

Liori breathed a sigh. "You'd better answer it. Jurgen would have never called you if it wasn't something important."

Reluctantly I switched to mnemonic communications. "Yes?"

"Where are you two now?!" Jurgen sounded seriously alarmed.

"In my room. Why?"

"Oasis is updating!" he sent me a screenshot.

I didn't recognize the ancient station. Most of its structures were glowing with heat. Someone was using its cargonite: I could clearly see thick clouds of Molecular Mist. The station's reactors were unstable. What the hell? Was someone trying to *melt* the station?

"Avatroid?" I suggested.

"Worse."

"What can be worse than a mad ancient AI?"

"I'm afraid it's the Reapers."

"The what?! We destroyed the interstellar communications! They can't escape Earth!"

"Then you'd better tell me what this is," he forwarded me a scan taken by the recon probe. On it, about a hundred heavy Raptors were falling into combat formations. I'd only seen this type of craft back on Earth, and even then only in blueprint.

"Do we know their target?"

"Not yet."

"Keep an eye on them. We're coming."

"Please do."

* * *

A TECHNOGENIC Inferno.

I'd never thought I'd see it. True, we'd adapted some of the Founders' obviously peaceful inventions for combat purposes in the past, but not so blatantly. Nor on this scale.

"We did destroy the communications!" Arbido exclaimed, perplexed. "Dominic never told us they had backups!"

"He might not have known," Jurgen snapped. "They used Oasis as a point of access. The hybrid may have been equipped with a communications channel of his own. We should have thought about it!"

"So that's his work, then?" Charon asked.

"I don't think so," I said. "The hybrid is gone. He'd started playing up already before we left for Earth. I'm afraid, the Reapers got to his neurograms."

"Ripping him apart?" Foggs asked in disbelief. "You mean they got access to his skills? And used them to restore the communications?"

Vandal cringed. "As if you can't see."

Outer space was seething. The gigantic station resembled a cooling star surrounded by a newborn nebula. Its center kept disgorging more matter. The station's outer structures were melting, their outlines growing porous and unstable. The Reapers must have removed reactor shields, causing reactor blocks to heat uncontrollably, melting the cargonite.

New combat craft kept forming within the clouds of incandescent matter. The process, though, didn't go as fast as Avatroid's once had. Nor did their choice of craft impress us with variety. They were all Raptors and Condors, but they kept materializing in their hundreds. Reapers aimed for volume over quality. They had no experience or abilities of their own, so they were using military space programs which we didn't even know existed.

"Mnemotechs on duty, merge your abilities," I commanded. "We need a scanner file — now!"

Reapers kept arriving.

What were they going to select as their next target? Or were their armadas prepared to sweep through space, indiscriminately devouring everything in their path?

If there was such a thing in the Universe as Fate, today it wasn't on our side. It was pretty clear that the Reapers weren't going to stop at Oasis. Their synthetic intellects would continue to build up their military presence uncontrollably. Their mode of thinking was similar to that of the first primitive AIs. The neurograms they'd looted hadn't breathed life into them, only confused them, plunging them into dismay and uncontrollable urges. Some of the Raptors kept breaking out of formation attacking each other, making the mass of ships resemble packs of fighting dogs.

Surely someone had to control these hordes? While smaller dogfights remained unnoticed, any attempts at more serious conflicts were being nipped in the bud. Our tracking systems had identified several groups of modified Raptors whose job seemed to be to maintain order by sending the more quarrelsome of the sentient mechanisms back into the incandescent Inferno to be remelted.

That's exactly how it was. I'm not exaggerating.

Finally, the scanner file arrived. I skimmed it and breathed a sigh of relief. "These are all made by Object Replication. It's just some nanites forming permanent molecular bonds."

"Does that mean they can be destroyed with regular weapons?" Foggs asked.

"It does. With the exception of a few Raptors," I said.

"This is scary," Jurgen whispered. "Once they form a network and join their processing capacities, nothing or no one can stand in their way."

"We need to attack them first! Now!" Vandal tensed, watching a group of about fifteen hundred Condors break off from the formation and accelerate toward Darg.

"Send some probes to follow them!" I snapped. "All mnemotechs to their positions! Remember the drill! Activate the multi-level shields! Level one: power field generators! Level two: Active Shield! Level three, external: Steel Mist! Use low thrust to clear the dock!"

I laid the course. Once the Relic moved close to Argus, it would be very hard to detect on a low orbit. That would give us considerable freedom to maneuver.

"Jurgen, give me the Manticore and the Disciples!"

"Zander, we can't stop them!" Arbido butted in. "They're tens of thousands!"

"I see. What do you suggest? Should we wait until they begin to recycle Argus?"

"But they're invincible! Even Avatroid wouldn't do much against them!"

"We'll see."

"What do you want? To kill us all? We need to drive the Relic away! We still have time to lie low!"

"We can't lie low forever," I snapped.

Charon growled his agreement. Jurgen nodded. The argument died before it even started.

"I have Aquilon on the line!"

The Manticore leader didn't look alarmed but rather puzzled. "Zander, I thought we had an agreement? What's up?"

The Relic had already entered its Argus orbit. I forwarded Aquilon the data from our tracking systems.

"The Reapers? An invasion?" Aquilon was looking for a catch, refusing to believe me. He was still angry with me, blaming me for losing the half of his men who'd chosen to join the Daugoths.

"Aha, you're so stuck in your Corporation sector you can't see past your own nose," I said. "Send out a few scouts if you don't believe me. Just make it quick. How many functioning corvettes have you got?"

"Two out of five. Why?"

"Don't even think of flying them now. Wait until I have some mnemotechs for you. They'll take care of your shields and camouflage."

"Is this some sick way of getting to my ships? You just don't stop, do you?"

"I don't need your ships! But if you want to save lives, you'd better think fast! Argus is right in the path of the Reapers' fleet. The station will be either captured or recycled. Take your pick."

"Give me some time! I need to check it!"

"Be my guest. Just keep in mind we deorbit soon."

* * *

THE RELIC slid along Argus' hull.

All the primary hull modules had been depressurized. The crew were in position. We'd been preparing for more unavoidable clashes with Avatroid — but now life had banked into a new turn!

"A compound group target, seventy Raptors and thirty Condors, in seven light seconds, heading on a course for Argus!"

The Oasis station now resembled a melted candle enveloped in clouds of crimson, its incandescent depths constantly sparkling with new ship signatures.

"Three of Avatroid's fleets have left the asteroid belt!"

It looked like the ancient AIs didn't want to be left out. They must have assessed the danger and decided to attack.

"Zander?" Liori turned to me. We were separated by personal force shields and the translucent holographic tablets that we'd used to divide the cockpit into work stations. "What do we do?"

The Manticore hadn't replied yet. We'd also failed to establish contact with Darg.

Avatroid was our enemy. We'd tried hard to conceal our studies of the Founders' technology from him. We'd been doing our best not to betray our presence at the station. All Relic repairs had been conducted under the protection of Steel Mist.

"Set a course for Dock Two. Prepare tractor beams. Action stations, continue target surveillance. Maintain communications with the Manticore using a secure channel."

Aquilon came back online. Clad in a heavy armor suit, he was dragging some crates toward an open hatch of a corvette.

"Hey man, what you're doing?"

"Evacuating the equipment," he snapped back.

"Drop it and get on board! Where's everyone?"

"They're dismantling life support modules in the living quarters."

"Aquilon, leave it! We'll share our supplies with you! You have two minutes before the Relic picks up the corvettes. Two minutes!" I repeated. "We won't be able to come back and rescue whoever's left behind!"

"He won't do it," Charon said darkly. "He'll try to drag it out. He doesn't care about his people."

I made the only possible decision. "We stay on orbit. Jurgen, contact the Manticore players directly. Put them in the picture. Tell them to drop everything and board the corvettes. We'll give them another five minutes."

You have an incoming call from Darg

Finally!

The holographic avatar of the Disciples' leader materialized at the center of the cockpit. "Zander?" he sounded surprised. "I didn't expect to see you. Our meeting is scheduled for tomorrow. Are you in the mood for a chat?"

"Roakhmar, I have no time! Listen carefully," I gave him a brief run-down on the situation. "Why did you stop monitoring deep space?"

"We don't have the resources. The Raiders keep downing our probes. Thanks for the warning. We'll meet them head on."

"Good luck!"

The Dargian shrunk his head into his shoulders. Now the Reapers were in for a nasty surprise. True, the Dargian space defense systems were geared up against large ships, but I was sure Roakhmar would come up with something. The Disciples knew the ancient technologies like the palms of their hands. And they were excellent warriors.

"Jurgen, what's with the Eurasia?"

"She doesn't respond."

"But what about our probes?"

"Neither. I'm afraid they've been shot down."

"Is the Colonial Fleet in any danger?"

"Certainly. The Eurasia has a communications station too. We've changed the flagship's access codes but it's only a question of time until the Reapers hack them."

"Pick up the corvettes and adopt an attack course!"

"Target?"

"Eurasia!"

* * *

THE RELIC was ready for battle.

We had enough cargonite in its holds to sustain a prolonged combat. Most of the areas closest to the airlocks had been turned into replicated nanites storage. There they swirled in vacuum, awaiting our commands.

Avatroid's fleets were heading for Oasis. I kept a watchful eye on them. The outer space between the two stations was littered with drifting debris —

evidence of millennia-old battles. I'd often wondered who they might have been and why they'd turned this place into a battlefield.

Now, as I looked at the Reapers' hordes, I thought I knew the answer.

The Founders had created the interstellar network but they'd done little to protect it. Once they'd vanished into history, many other civilizations had gotten the chance to use their technologies.

The Darg system harbored unique cargonite deposits in its asteroid belt. That made it a strategic location for any potential Universe pioneer.

"We aren't going to help Avatroid, are we?" Arbido asked grimly.

"Zander, the corvettes are out," Foggs interrupted him.

Two ships sporting Manticore logos showed above Argus' curving horizon. They had no camouflage at all! Was Aquilon out of his mind?!

"Enemy Raptors have defined their goals and are zoning in."

"Continue on this course! Mnemotechs on Deck 10, release the nanites! Replicate on command!"

"Let's go!"

At a safe distance from our ship, one of Argus' hull structures began to melt, losing shape. We tried to use exterior sources of nanites whenever possible, saving our precious on-board cargonite stocks for an absolute emergency.

The enemy Raptors activated their shields and dispersed, acting in twos and hugging the station's hull.

The Manticore's corvettes fired their heavy lasers but without much success: they'd only just cleared the dock and Argus' outline prevented them from laying down effective fire.

My mind entered the Relic's on-board network. Liori was busy controlling groups of replicated nanites, ready to send them to protect the corvettes as soon as she had the opportunity.

Our main objective now was to stop the heavy assault craft. We'd developed this tactic in case of a mass attack of Phantom Raiders but hadn't yet had a chance to test it under combat conditions.

I turned the frigate around, accelerating smoothly. The station shifted in the screens, dropping below while falling behind us. Now I could clearly see the assault ships maneuvering amid the hull structures and a group of enemy Condors covering them.

The Raptors' powerful force fields didn't allow us to use nanites against them. The simultaneous tracking of a hundred targets was the absolute limit for my mind expander. Each of the corvettes had already had numerous breaches trailing gas. Their engines were struggling. They wouldn't last long.

Obeying my mental command, the Founders' navigation module began to rotate in the Relic's hull radars. We'd adapted it, making it battle-worthy. Yes, we'd meddled with the ancient technologies, adding a few upgrades in order to create a dual-purpose device.

A communications burst left the ship. The device's range in combat mode was limited to one light second.

Resonance frequency of the force fields established. Ready to transmit data.

The load on my mind kept growing. This was the drawback of this particular technology: the device couldn't be controlled by automatics. We'd done so on purpose, creating an artifact beyond the AIs' control.

Our numerous experiments had shown that whenever we used Object Replication, there was always a small number of unutilized nanites left over. Now these redundant nanites were entrusted with the task of transmitting the combat control code.

The mnemonic hit reached the enemy.

The targets' markers changed their color from red to momentary green, immediately turning gray.

The communications station switched off. Gradually I returned to my senses. Jurgen, Charon and Maurugael had taken over the frigate's controls.

Darkness receded, releasing my mind. I could make out Argus' outline and the two corvettes sheltering alongside its hull. The Raptors had almost caught up with them.

My heart was fluttering.

"Zander, you've done it!" Charon's voice shook with exhaustion.

I watched the nearest Raptor. It didn't fire. Instead, it was careening toward the nearest hull structure head-on, not attempting to change course.

A bleak picture appeared in my mind's view. I could see the Raptor's cockpit and its pilot still in his seat. A plume of smoke escaped his visor.

A burst of fire. The screech of deformed metal. A deafening pop of decompression.

We'd won the first battle. More and more explosions came, followed by collisions. A group of enemy Condors passed Argus head-on at full speed and left on a blind course.

The two helpless Manticore corvettes drifted dangerously close to the station, one moving sideways, the other spinning uncontrollably.

"Grab the corvettes and let's go! Set a course for Eurasia!"

* * *

TALK ABOUT the irony of fate.

We'd thought we'd have to confront the AIs, mop up the stations, then bring the Earth's Colonial Fleet to the Darg system.

This plan had now collapsed.

Once again our future was unknown. The Reapers' invasion had thwarted our plans.

The enemy numbers continued to grow.

The avant-garde of Avatroid's Phantom Raiders had already engaged with the Reapers. Outer space in our path was seething.

I switched over to the common channel.

My throat was dry. Still, I had to say it.

"Listen, guys," I addressed the crew. "You've a difficult choice to make. We need to destroy Eurasia's servers and communications. This is the only guarantee against the Reapers getting to the Colonial Fleet. At the moment, it's Eurasia that provides your identities' presence in the Darg system. Considering this, I offer you the choice to leave the Relic. You can do so via the personal navigation modules on your wrists. Your in-modes will be automatically switched to stasis mode."

I caught my breath and went on, "Those who are willing to stay should be prepared for their transformation. At the moment of communications shutdown, your identities and your appearance will be nanite-replicated. You have five minutes to make up your minds. The clock starts now."

"Zander?" immediately I received a call from Frieda. "How's this all going to happen?"

"It won't take long. We have plenty of nanites. Once the connection is broken, your personal navigation device will self-destruct. The nanites it's made of will stabilize your identity matrix," I told her what I'd already experienced myself. "More nanites will join in the process, forming your appearance almost instantaneously. If you don't know the symptoms, you might not even notice anything."

"I'd like Liori to come to our room and conduct the initiation in person."

"Initiation?"

"That's what I told the children. That we were going to initiate them as astronauts."

"Very well."

"Let's do it now. Before the attack starts."

"Liori, did you hear that? Can you do it? Or do you want me to go?"

"Zander, you'd better stay on the bridge. I'll do it."

You have an incoming call from Darg.

Roakhmar's avatar appeared in my mental view. Never before had I seen the Disciples' leader looking so lost.

"Speak up," I said.

"Zander, we're suffering incredible losses. Our space defenses are useless against thousands of small ships," he blurted out, afraid of a break in communications. The hissing and tweeting sounds of his speech merged into rapid trills. My semantic processor's auto translate struggled to keep up. "I know I wasn't too forthcoming! I know I tried to sabotage the negotiations! But they're annihilating us! Help us, please!"

"I can't turn the Relic round at the moment. Think you can last twenty-four hours?"

"If we retreat to our clan's citadel, we'll last longer! Will you help us?"

"Yes," I had to think on my feet. The situation unfolded too fast to allow me the luxury of pondering. "We'll try to battle through to you and evacuate the survivors."

"Word of a Human?"

"Word of a Human."

Quest update alert: The Chasm!

A representative of a third civilization nearing extinction has sought your help.

You need to evacuate Dargian survivors.

Your Colonizer skill has been confirmed. You've received 50 Action Points.

"Jurgen, report!"

I hadn't had time to find out what those "action points" were and how I could spend them while saving civilizations.

"The crew's numbers have dropped by fifty-four men," he reported.

"How many mnemotechs have we lost?"

"None."

"Excellent. I'm going to switch to the common

channel now. Be prepared. The command staff will set an example to the crew by using their navigator modules first."

"Zander, I still need to issue navigators to the ten corvette survivors!"

"Do it now but be quick! Time's an issue!"

Liori returned to the bridge and walked over to me.

"And?" my heart froze, awaiting her answer.

"The boys liked it. The girls were a bit frightened. Arbido helped them by joining in their transformation. Frieda is fine. She asked me to tell you that someone's trying to listen in to our mnemonic frequencies."

"Who's that?"

"She thinks it's Avatroid. Still, her empathic skills aren't enough for a definite answer."

"Nothing concrete, then?"

"Nothing. She thought she saw a mental image of someone. It could be just stress."

"But what makes her think it's Avatroid?"

"'*We won't attack the Colonizer*'," Liori quoted. "Did you tell Frieda about the quest you'd received back on Earth?"

"No. I didn't tell anyone apart from you. Actually, the quest has just been updated," I told her about my conversation with Roakhmar.

Liori didn't look impressed with my decision. "Let's see how the AIs react to it. Evacuating the Dargians isn't going to be easy. I don't think they'll let us through," she pointed at the screens dotted with thousands of specks streaking toward the planet.

The situation grew more complicated by the minute. After the Reapers had scorched Oasis, they were now attempting to recycle Argus — but were met by the barrage of our drones and traps: all the practice objects that our mnemotechs had built in the two months of rushed leveling.

* * *

SPACE IN THE RELIC'S PATH glowed and sparkled with every color of the rainbow. Where Oasis had been, a cloud of incandescent gas now floated. Avatroid's fleet was busy fighting. His cruisers and frigates looked invincible, their shields repelling blows with remarkable ease. Their return fire and frequent flashes of Disintegrations burned holes in the enemy ranks.

The Reapers were definitely losing. Their main forces had already departed for Darg, leaving less than a couple of thousand craft behind — a mere trifle for Avatroid's AIs.

Away from the seething battle, the ancient cemetery of combat craft drifted through space against a backdrop of the gas giant Wearong. Now it had begun flashing with new signatures.

I focused on them but couldn't yet work out what was going on in the thick of all the clustered debris.

We kept accelerating toward Eurasia. The vicinity of the station too was awash with flashes of light, but at least the Reapers attacked it selectively, trying to spare the station's vital systems. Which was another proof of their intentions.

"Boost the engines!"

Jurgen had just reported that the crew's

transformation was complete. We were now a hundred and sixty. Ten of the Manticore members had chosen to log out. Their in-modes had switched to stasis mode.

Avatroid's ships had passed within one light second from us but none of them had opened fire. His cruisers turned around and headed back into the thick of battle. Their shields had lost a lot of power. The ships' hulls glowed crimson from numerous direct hits.

"Eurasia's in the killing zone!"

A silent plume of incandescent gas and dust spewed out in front of Wearong. Considering the distance, its tail had to be millions of miles long! The drifting debris, including the entire hulks of large ships, were being sucked into the vortex of disintegration. The Reapers must have used some incredibly powerful artificial gravity source. They didn't waste time harvesting and recycling the cargonite; I could already see the first flashes of Object Replication.

These unexpected reinforcements plunged into battle head-on. My Synaps kept counting new targets. Nine hundred Raptors! The heavy assault ships quickly fell into formation and fired a simultaneous volley, targeting Avatroid's nearest cruiser.

Its shields flared up and expired, exposing the behemoth ship's hull to a barrage of fire which pierced the cargonite like butter, creating the already familiar signature deformations.

Those modified Raptors were using the ammo developed by the Earth's military space forces. What a leap in the Reapers' evolution! In just two months, they'd managed to restore the interstellar communications channel initially created for the hybrid, learned to build primitive battleships and equipped them with nanite-effective weapons!

"Eurasia's under fire! Enemy's targeting her reactor units!"

Another cruiser had lost its shields and was torn apart by the chain reaction of decompression explosions within.

"Eurasia's reactors hit! The station is self-destructing!"

"Turn the Relic round and set a course to Wearong!"

"Zander, what the hell are you-"

"Just do it! Jurgen, report to your station! Everyone, follow your orders!"

About a hundred Raptors turned toward us and regrouped, taking up a combat course.

Instinctively Arbido squeezed his eyes shut. Charon and Danezerath stared calmly at the approaching death. Liori touched my mind with a warm vibration, then turned her attention back to the controls.

"Attention all mnemotechs on combat decks! Distribute the targets and report!"

The Relic's shields were rapidly going down under the barrage of fire.

"Nanite groups released!" a voice rang out. "Wave one!"

The mnemotechs' hits reached their targets, exploding like hundreds of blinding suns in the thick of the enemy formation, bringing down shields and disabling enemy sensors.

"Wave two! Target Disintegration!"

The Relic was now moving through a sea of fire.

Our force fields were dead, our emitters in overload, our accumulators busy recharging. An Active Shield unfolded around the ship, protecting the Relic's hull from the flow of radiation.

"Group target at ten degrees starboard!"

Two hundred and eighteen Raptors! They were coming from the direction of Wearong, almost head-on, slightly above the ecliptic. Their shields were barely glowing: they must have second-guessed our tactics and were going easy on power in order to be able to restore their defenses ASAP.

"Resonance frequency established! Now transmitting extermination codes!"

Hundreds of enemy craft lost control in a chaos of exploding collisions. The Reapers left Avatroid's battered fleet alone and converged on us from every direction. The ships' cemetery they were using to replenish their resources was slowly growing straight ahead of us.

"The Active Shield maxed out! Not enough nanites!"

"Electromagnetic batteries, rapid fire! Maintain course!"

The incandescent cloud was drawing close. Our coil guns spat incessantly.

Flashes of Object Replication released more and more Raptors. Our hull was finally being breached but we didn't suffer any decompression. We'd learned from our past experience and had decompressed all the primary hull modules.

Almost there.

My mind reached out into the cloud of Molecular Mist created by the Reapers.

I released my nanites into it, then used the

skill only available to those in possession of the Colonizer ability.

Self-Replication!

About a hundred Raptors and Condors burned away before they had the chance to complete their materialization. Continuing to self-replicate, billions of nanites rushed back toward the Relic, recycling everything in their path.

Until I aborted the process, nothing could stop it. The Reapers weren't going to get a single nanite. The entire giant Molecular Mist they'd created was now working for us!

We'd done our homework preparing to fight for this star system. Now the nanites were falling into dense groups which spread through space, ready to self-destruct in Plasma Blasts the moment their targets entered the killing zones.

This wasn't victory yet. Three of Avatroid's fleets had been reduced to clouds of debris swirling through space. By using the mass attack technique, the Reapers had suffered considerable damage but the bulk of their force was out storming Darg. It would soon be back to finish us off.

Oasis had burned out. Eurasia was no more.

I had no idea how long we'd last. Our enemies were bound to change their tactics, assaulting us in small groups to gradually tire us out and exhaust our ship's resources.

Incoming call. Source: Avatroid's flagship
Body of the message:
Human, we need to talk. Come round. This isn't

a trap.

Barely twenty minutes had elapsed since the Relic had left the docks.

In those twenty minutes, two space stations had been destroyed, three AI-controlled fleets defeated and thousands of Reapers' ships burned out.

Under such conditions, you had to think on your feet.

"Check the ship and report all damage. Mechanics, commence repairs. Defense group, activate Steel Mist. Navigators, calculate a course to Avatroid's flagship!"

* * *

AVATROID — this materialized avatar of an ancient AI — was fused with a bulkhead. He could still move some of his servodrives but was unable to wrestle himself free or move without help.

"Zander?" he watched me painfully, aware that I might have accepted his invitation with the sole intention of finishing him off.

Considering the scope of death and destruction he'd brought upon this star system, his assumption wasn't exactly ungrounded.

"Why did you call me up? That's not a state to entertain guests in! Don't you have a backup copy?"

"No," he screeched.

"Sorry, I don't believe you."

His mechanical arm twitched a few times, then began jerking toward the casing that covered his central systems.

A fire-damaged piece of cargonite clanged to the floor. "Look."

Droplets of red liquid hovered in mid-air. Avatroid's spinal slots housed a great many neurochips, connected to the rest of his body by some pale threads encased in watertight transparent tubes. In place of a human chest he had a multitude of armor-plated cylinders.

"Open one," Avatroid said.

Dozens of sensors lit up on his body's mysterious components. Such a degree of trust in me meant he was utterly desperate.

What was wrong with him?

I touched one of the cylinders. With a click of magnetic locks, its front part swung aside and began to slide away.

Below it sat a transparent test jar filled with yellowish liquid. Inside it bobbed a wrinkled mass of gray matter.

An organic neuronet module?

"Why?" I asked, flabbergasted. "What prompted you to create a weak link in your impregnable system?"

"I wanted to be like you," Avatroid croaked. "I've outlived my technical purpose. I wanted... to be free. To travel."

Quest alert: The Nature of Avatroid. Quest completed!
You've received a new level!

At moments like these, system messages felt totally inappropriate.

The souls of humans, xenomorphs and AIs —

they were all burning in a technogenic Inferno. We walked the edge of this chasm, barely keeping our balance. "And that's what made you kill and ravage?"

"Don't you do the same? I was growing. Those were birthing pains. This is something you'll never understand, Human. But then it was over. Others came."

"We call them Reapers."

"I don't care what you call them. Names don't change anything. They're synthetic digitized identities of organic creatures!"

"Why, is that bad?"

"Only an identity matrix of an organically born being is capable of traveling the worlds. That's one of the network's settings."

"Does that mean you can't leave the Darg system?"

"No. I can't. That's why I wanted to *change*. But it's not about me anymore. My fleet is defeated. My mind is failing. But these creatures... they absorb neurograms. Nothing like this has ever happened before. We need to stop them... while it's still possible. Give me a chance... to fulfill my purpose."

"Sounds a bit haughty, doesn't it?"

"It sounds scary," Avatroid's eyes were locked on mine.

"What can you do?"

"Nothing... almost. You do it."

"You're joking? I'm just a player. Less than six months ago I was smoking mobs and didn't give a damn!"

"You're a Colonizer. I'll give you all the codes."

"Which codes?"

"The jump codes. The defense codes. The rest

you'll have to work out yourself. We have no time left. Say yes."

Zander, Liori's voice added to my thoughts, *They're back. Five thousand ships.*

"What's the significance of this Colonizer skill?" I demanded. "How can I stop the Reapers? What's the nature of interstellar jumps?"

He only answered my last question. "Physical bodies can't travel through hyperspace. What's transmitted is the information about them. To perform a jump, you need to transmit a full scanner file of an object. It'll be used to create a new object at the point of arrival."

"So this is the Founders' big secret?"

"It's never been a secret. The transmission code is."

"You want to say you're going to give it to me? What do you want in return?"

"Stop them. That's enough."

"How do you want me to stop them?"

His glare singed my face. "Go," he screeched. "Go, or you'll die pointlessly in a pointless battle."

New command code received.

New star system coordinates received.

A full scanner file of the Relic frigate received.

A wormhole has been opened. You have thirty minutes to issue jump orders.

Chapter Ten

An unknown location in deep space

The wormhole has been closed.
Materialization complete.
You've arrived at-

My semantic processor faltered, searching for the right translation.

You've arrived at the... Central system.

Observation screens lit up, revealing a mind-blowing panorama.

Hundreds of chiseled cargonite structures encircled an incredible space station, forming a complex albeit faded and partially damaged technogenic necklace around it.

Phantom Server.

Its hull's outline was formed by a multitude of spired structures, their configuration repeating the pattern of the unfamiliar constellations.

These were hyperspace communications modules. I could see some of them surge with occasional charges of energy. Still, most of them were dark, covered in digs and dents.

The ancient network's central node must have been millions of years old. Both time and outer space had changed its initial layout. The light of the system's far-off sun curdled on the molten bodies of starships scorched in the fiery inferno of age-old battles.

That didn't surprise me. The Founders' legacy had been misinterpreted by young civilizations that had adapted it for their own expansion needs. They had partaken of the ancient mysteries while still too young to appreciate their true power. They'd broken loose into the Universe, damaging the ancient network in their desperate struggle for sole possession of its central node.

"Raiders!" Arbido exclaimed.

The veil of metallized dust shifted around the station. External cameras zoomed in, revealing tens of thousands of AI-piloted combat craft coming for the Relic.

Our communications station kicked in, transmitting Avatroid's codes.

This was make or break. We'd just performed a hyper jump preceded by a desperate battle. Our ship's shields were barely glowing at 5 megs. They needed time to restore.

Friendly Contact!

The targets' markers changed color, their advance through space changing its course, then reversing. Only a small group of Raiders, a hundred at the most, swept past us, exposing themselves to our screens in all their awesome technogenic omnipotence, then headed toward the system's edge.

The Relic's stern lit up with the glow of its plasma engines as the frigate accelerated, approaching the nearest of the three docking terminals which hung in a semicircle over the hull like an open-work crescent moon.

As we approached, more details hove into view: countless clusters of vacuum docks, the honeycombs of launch pods and vast landing pads which could accommodate behemoth starships.

The kingdom of cold dead metal.

The station would have indeed been a phantom, had it not been for the blurred signatures of some still functioning devices within.

I took over the controls. Slowly I turned the ship round to level up its speed with the station's slow rotation.

Emergency docking mechanisms kicked in. Softly the Relic touched the landing pad. A dozen drones promptly made by our mnemotechs appeared in the dull flashes of Object Replication, then headed toward the nearest hull structures, scanning and streaming data back.

* * *

THE STATION'S holographic model rotated slowly at

the center of our ship's informatorium.

"Now," Jurgen paced along it, "Avatroid was wrong. Our visit is a few million years late. There's no one here capable of listening to our problems, let alone solving them."

"I'm not surprised," Arbido crossed his legs, casting skeptical glances at the picture. "Avatroid remembers Phantom Server from the times of the Founders' heyday. Which isn't helping. Still, the long-range communications are still functional. They're de-energized, but look at this," he pointed at a weak signature that flashed across the screen. "Besides, our jump has been successful which raises another question: who or what is responsible for the ship's materialization on this side? If I remember rightly, it has to be the station's AI, no less. Zander, am I right?"

"You are. At least that's what the system notes on the Colonizer ability say."

"The station's AI? Then we need to get out and find it!" Vandal said.

"And where are you going to look for it?" Foggs zoomed in on the station's model. Any potential power imprints were lost in the maze of countless rooms. Only a few blurred spots glowed weakly within the depths of the gargantuan structure. The nanites hadn't yet got that far, busy inspecting the primary hull decks.

"Let's start with those," Vandal pointed at the blurred signals.

Phantom Server was eighty-seven miles in diameter. That was doable for the Relic's scanners which had actually provided the data for creating the holographic model. Still, the transport hubs had been destroyed, blocked in many places by emergency bulkheads. I'd have hated to barge into the station using brute force but there didn't seem to be any other way to get past all the obstacles. We'd already made several fruitless attempts to lay a potential course.

"I got the impression someone's barricaded deep inside the station," Ralph offered. "In which case we should expect traps in our way."

At that moment the station's communications systems kicked back in. Their activations seemed to be random and lasted but a few seconds, creating the same kind of power surges over the hull structures as those we'd already witnessed.

"Now that's interesting," Liori highlighted a weak power trail. "Take a look at this! This is definitely a data transmission!"

"So what?" Foggs raised a quizzical eyebrow.

"Why did it have to deviate toward the station's center? What prevented two communications modules within direct line of vision from reaching each other directly?"

Ralph shrugged. "How do we know? Maybe that's just the way they do these things."

The next time the communications sprang back to life, I was prepared. I connected my Synaps to the Relic's systems and was able to track the data exchange channel.

"Zander?" Charon craned his neck.

"Same thing. It passes through the center. And look, here's another signature," I added another power imprint to our plans of Phantom Server.

Jurgen peered at the faint imprint. "A respawn point? Compare it with this," he opened a similar image in the operative window.

"It looks identical," Charon agreed.

"This might actually solve the problem," Arbido decided to show off his new knowledge. "Two respawn points can be connected to make a transport channel, am I correct?"

"You are indeed," Jurgen nodded his approval. "Changing the settings might take some time but I think I can do it."

An emergency alarm echoed through my mind.

"A wormhole's opened!" Charon exclaimed.

A fiery dot appeared within one of the openwork structures, followed by the vague outlines of five gigantic spaceships.

We anticipated their materialization, expecting the Phantom Raiders patrolling the station to jump into action. They didn't.

The cruiser, the frigate and three cargo ships remained semi-transparent. We were looking at the real ships' optical phantoms. They drifted through the debris and disappeared.

* * *

IT TOOK US almost twenty-four hours to reset the respawn point and connect a transport module to the Founders' navigator (which incidentally was how the hybrid had beamed me up on board Eurasia). Doing so proved to be a job and a half. Mnemotechs, engineers and technologists — in the end we all had to join in.

In the meantime, we counted ninety-seven individual jumps plus five more incidents of wormholes opening. We witnessed the arrival of three more groups of miscellaneous spacecraft and two fleets: one military, the other commercial.

The designs of most of them were totally unfamiliar to us. None of them had ultimately materialized: all we'd seen were their optical phantoms.

We stopped paying attention to new hyperspace jumps. The Relic's systems continued to register new instances of interstellar communications all the time.

I wasn't surprised that this central node of the interstellar network had long become a myth. Phantom Server! — the name fit perfectly. The star system was supposed to be a point of transit but something was preventing ships from entering our 3D continuum. Their crews were bound to see the station's phantom image on their screens complete with all the hull structures and fleets of Raiders surrounding it.

Why had it allowed the Relic through, then?

Liori and I had a theory but we still needed to check it out. And the truth lay deep inside Phantom Server.

"All done," Jurgen finally reported. He'd run the test three times to check the system for any glitches.

"Good," I nodded my encouragement to Liori, then clicked my helmet on. Here, realism was key which was why all of us were clad in pressurized combat armor.

The transport pad could only fit five people so we had to split into groups. Jurgen had to stay behind to keep an eye on the Server's performance. Vandal's men were to go first. Their job was to mop up the arrival zone and ensure its safety. Liori, Charon,

Foggs, Danezerath and myself were to go next. The third group was comprised of five engineers and mnemotechs: I was pretty sure the depths of the station were chock full of all sorts of obscure devices. They all had to be scanned and studied.

If everything went well, more backup groups would arrive. But at the moment, we were impatiently waiting to see how the first group would fare.

We're ready, Vandal reported.

"Off you go," Jurgen touched the sensor.

A green aura surrounded Vandal and his men, swallowing them.

One second... two... three...

"It's dark in here," Vandal's voice came, distorted by interference. "No enemy resistance."

"Let's go!" I stepped onto the platform.

My mind shifted. It felt like falling from an enormous height, followed by a leg-shattering jolt. My armor's servomotors rustled in the midst of a dull fading glow.

Our helmets' flashlights sliced through the dark. You didn't really need lighting with mind expanders, but our Synapses were down, forcing us to use backup devices.

Our implants' sensors were still working but their range was minimal — three feet at the most.

"This is a large closed space," Vandal reported. "No doors, hatches or airlocks observed."

We stepped aside to vacate a space for the next group.

Darkness surged with flashes of green which looked just like a regular respawn. Transfer successful.

"Jurgen, do you read me?"

After a second's delay, his voice came back. "The line is very bad. Can you stream the data to me?"

I did.

"You're slightly off," he reported back. "You're supposed to be about a hundred and fifty feet from where you're now."

"But this place has a respawn device!" Liori exclaimed.

"It's probably the backup," Jurgen replied. "It must have kicked in and taken over the transfer channel."

"Never mind," I said. "We shouldn't jump to conclusions. We need to have a good look around first. There's something that stops our mind expanders from working. Don't send anybody else quite yet. Stay posted."

"Roger that. Be careful."

* * *

THE ROOM WAS HUGE but empty, with the respawn point at its center. This place looked eerily reminiscent of Founders Square back on Argus.

"Come over here," Vandal's voice sounded in the earphones. He flashed his light a few times to direct us.

The place had an atmosphere. Our sensors had already analyzed it. The insides of our visors flashed a biological hazard warning.

"Someone's beaten us to it," Charon said.

The floor was strewn with the remains of some creatures. Pieces of gear glistened under the flashlights.

"Jurgen, can you see this?" I pointed the light under my feet.

"The picture isn't good but I can. Should I send in Novitsky?"

"No. We'll do some scanning now and I want him to receive and process the data."

I turned, motioning Ralph to come over. "Go and check if we can get back."

"I don't understand," Liori studied the remains. "They came here and died. But Zander, this is organic matter! Whoever they were, they didn't use nanite matrix replication."

"Foggs, take your men and study the perimeter."

"What are we looking for?"

"An entry point."

A popping sound came from the center of the room.

"The transfer system works," Ralph reported. "I'm back on board the Relic."

Good news.

"Right! Join your mind expanders to make a network," I ordered.

The darkness shrank back. The sensors of our Synapses and Neurons now worked in synch, consolidating the data. Still, the results weren't exactly optimistic. The room held no hidden devices. All the bulkheads were safely shielded.

"I observe traces of fire damage! A couple of large patches exceeding human height," Foggs reported.

"Stay where you are," I said. "Jurgen, I want you to guide me. Where do you see the signatures?

Aha, right... I can see them," I headed toward a new marker glowing in the gloom.

Another patch on the wall! Its shape didn't suggest a breach hole. Most likely, this was where a corridor had once been, leading to the part of the station we needed.

"Zander, watch out!" Liori exclaimed.

I froze. What now?

"Do you see the deformations?"

I took a better look. Indeed, the structure of the wall around the patch seemed blurred, rippling vaguely. "Release a probe."

Vandal obeyed. Slowly the probe floated off at about three feet high, its spherical surface studded with sensors.

With a flash, it touched the wall. The scorched probe dropped to the floor and rolled aside.

"This is a hologram protected by a force field," Jurgen said. "I'll now search for the resonance frequency. You'll need to wait. I'll send you new scanner settings."

I stepped toward the wall.

"Zander, don't!" Foggs shouted. "It's too dangerous!"

The threads of energy reached out toward me. The signature of the force field changed.

Liori's voice was the last thing I heard,

"Step back, everyone! Zander can do it, not you! He has the right!"

I hope so, my love.

* * *

THE PLACE was well lit. No signs of damage here. My Synaps had finally kicked in, allowing me to see tons of equipment lying around. These were the signatures that had been registered by the Relic's sensors.

The place was flooded with streams of energy coursing around me, changing their signatures. They didn't extinguish as I approached.

No one would ever have battled through here by brute force. Pointless trying to hack the codes or destroy the defenses of what was Phantom Server's heart. Created millions of years ago, it would probably last the same again. Powered by the energies of hyperspace, its components didn't depend on external conditions.

I stood within infospace.

* * *

A BLACK SUN slowly rose over the dull horizon of a dying planet.

I was looking at the Founders' world. They had created an artificial casing for their own star and very nearly fallen victim to their own scientific progress.

Why, might you ask?

Now that I stood within infospace I knew the answer.

They wanted to travel the Universe, free from its laws and boundaries — but creating space metrics by trial and error had proven too difficult. None of their spaceships could accommodate a reactor powerful enough to do so. That's why they'd thought that utilizing the energy of stars might be a solution. In theory, a single diamond-shaped accumulator segment orbiting their sun could produce the desired impulse without hurting their planet's environment. The segment's surface was too negligible compared to that of the star's photosphere!

Still, the road to the stars is paved with thorns. The accumulator segments kept breaking down, failing under the star's extreme conditions. Repairing them didn't seem worth the time: it was much easier to create a new one, sturdier and better than the last.

That's how the Founders had come up with the concept of the "protomineral life form". Now these segments could self-replicate to replace the broken elements when necessary.

This had become the Founders' undoing. The replication process took on a life of its own. Very soon a second segment was born in the star's photosphere, followed by another. And another. And yet another.

The Founders had been on the brink of an ecological disaster. Desperate for a solution, they'd discovered cargonite's properties which had allowed them to create the first nanites. Still, by then it had been too late.

The artificial mantle around the sun had closed. Obeying their initial programs, the protomineral segments diligently channeled the accumulated energy into forming the first wormholes. But it wasn't the Founders' spaceships that had performed the first jumps but samples of this protomineral life form.

I paused, unable to take in the entire scope of those ancient developments and their consequences for the Universe.

These almighty beings had fallen victim to their own technology. Many of them had died — but those who'd survived, persevered with their research. They went underground where, warm in the heat of their reactors, they continued experimenting with nanites until they'd learned to build artificial neuronets and digitize their identities.

The periodical release of energy which had resulted in creation of new wormholes had allowed them to study hyperspace — but how were they supposed to enjoy life after centuries of digitized existence when new emotions weren't available and old ones had long faded, forgotten?

Too late had they realized that there was another way of instantly traveling the Universe. Hyperspace was capable of transmitting information, wasn't it? And the process didn't take too much power.

Had this discovery liberated them?

I didn't think so.

Now I knew exactly why the Founders had formed their AI fleets, sending them on millennia-long voyages between the stars.

The Founders had come up with a new system allowing them to interact with the Universe. Still, in order for it to work, all its destination points had to have the technological foundation necessary for the travelers' complete replication, otherwise they risked remaining ethereal phantoms capable of perceiving but not interacting with new environments.

The Founders sent countless nanites to thousands of planets, hoping to respawn and rectify their past mistakes by stopping the expansion of Black Suns. But once again they couldn't contain their urges.

They were so few, so desperate to live and enjoy life that they couldn't fight off a new temptation, disappearing in the midst of other civilizations, changing worlds, eras and guises as they pleased.

Only few had remained loyal to their initial goal. It was they who, in their foresight, had created the universal nanite control interface, hoping that young space races might one day study their legacy and follow its unique development branches — and hopefully go one step further than they had.

But what if we hadn't?

In such a case, we still had a secure survival tool that would work even if all the stars in our Galaxy died of old age.

As long as a single reactor still glows, I couldn't stop thinking of Kimberly's farewell.

* * *

PAST YET ANOTHER wall of energy, I was confronted by rows of devices that looked marginally like our in-modes.

These were the cameras of biological reconstruction. This was where the ancient beings had built new organic bodies for themselves whenever they wished to re-experience real life after long periods of phantom existence.

Information streams washed over my mind. My skills kept growing impressively. I kept scanning, saving new scanner files in the knowledge that I wasn't likely to ever come back here.

You know why?

The quest I'd accepted, that's what had granted me access to the heart of Phantom Server.

I wasn't here to ask for anything for myself. I had the right to be here. I had come as a Colonizer responsible for the fates of three civilizations.

* * *

You have crossed over into the System's Heart.

Use the celestial map to switch to the Colonizer interface.

Spend the available Action Points wisely. You can:

- Lay a new route;

- Open a new wormhole;

- Establish contact with a star system of your choice;

- Transport identity matrices and other objects within the limits of the interstellar network.

Warning! The number of available Action Points is limited!

Here in the heart of Phantom Server they had the same force escalators as in the Temple of Light back on Darg. Its vast space was similarly split into rooms by force fields.

As the elevator brought me up to the next level, I had some time to pull myself together and prepare to face the awesome future.

A stream of energy brought me into a gigantic spherical hall.

I found myself on the inside of a 3D celestial map with the star system housing Phantom Server at its center. Fiery stars crowded me in the dark.

A bit further on I noticed a communications station and a respawn point. They seemed to be connected to all of the station's still functioning systems.

Sheets of green light flashed at irregular intervals. I watched as translucent avatars materialized only to disappear again. I'd never seen such a variety of xenomorph beings.

The depths of the map around me twinkled occasional lights marking their departure and destination points.

The interstellar network.

Every system the Founders had ever visited was marked on it.

I saw Black Suns, oozing their dull heat — there were over a hundred of them already as protomineral life forms continued their expansion.

Known cargonite deposits were marked with a special sign, as were its stores built by the Founders.

The fine lines of still-active routes curved through the dark, intertwining and parting in every direction. I could see thousands of inhabited worlds bustling with activity — civilizations using the Founders' ancient technologies in their daily life.

Phantom Server's AI remained impartial and silent, as if condoning my right to be here, not forcing me to make up my mind. Still I discovered a few prompts as yellow markers had appeared next to a few planets suitable for colonization.

I searched the map for Earth.

There it was. A tiny dot at the very frontier of inhabited space. Our Sun was already enveloped in a dark aura. We couldn't change that anymore.

The two systems nearest to it were Darg and Haash.

Obeying my mental effort, part of the map zoomed in.

I was facing a difficult task. There were no planets suitable for colonization nearby. And I had a very limited number of Action Points available.

I tried to lay a new route. My hand traced it among the stars as my Action Points dwindled, barely enough to take the Third Colonial Fleet to the nearest system containing an uninhabited planet with an oxygen-based atmosphere.

This was a hard choice.

At a certain point, I felt angry. This was still a game, played all over the interstellar network. The way the Founders had seen it, players had to pay for every step of their expansion.

For those awesome beings who'd developed the game's rules and its interface, this was only an impersonal resource allowing a player to invest some of his or her AP. In order to activate this entire *Summa Technologiae* and open a new wormhole for the Third Colonial Fleet, I'd have to ignore the survival of both the Haash and the Dargians. There just didn't seem to be any other solution!

But what were we going to encounter on the other side of the chasm?

The fact that the planet's atmosphere contained some oxygen said nothing. Its biosphere could still be aggressive or incompatible.

Abort!

Desperate hopes of three dying civilizations

were braided into the lifeless numbers.

I had to find another way.

Besides, there were also the Reapers invading the Darg system to consider.

I zoomed in some more. Pointless getting angry. I couldn't change the rules. I had to follow them.

But did the problem even have an optimal solution?

I studied the zoomed-in area long and hard, reading every marker, considering the consequences of every possible step.

Three fine lines connected Darg to three other systems.

A system message popped up,

You're about to block the selected routes.
Are you sure?
This step will sever all ties with a star system rich in natural resources. No one will be able to use the advantages offered by hyperspace technologies to either enter or exit it.

Yes! Confirm! This was a negligible price to pay compared to the dangers posed by the Reapers. They were a new plague capable of spreading to all inhabited worlds.

My next step prompted another system warning,

You're about to use your resources to transport a single identity matrix. This will diminish the number of your available Action Points 10%.

Accept!

You're about to send one packet of data to the Darg system prior to blocking it permanently. This will diminish the number of your available Action Points 10%.

Accept!

I played by the rules and within my remit. The Phantom Server's AI couldn't prevent me from doing what I was doing. All it could do was keep the score of all the "unadvisable actions" I was making, reporting,

Warning! You don't have enough available Action Points to colonize the nearest world with a suitable biosphere.

Abort colonization: Yes/No

No!

Choose a planet for colonization

My gaze alighted on a star system within reach of the Third Colonial Fleet. Tagged with a question mark, the system was currently off line. The AI which had been sent there to research the potential cargonite resources, had reported its arrival, sent the information back and had never been heard of again.

That was it, then. My gaze shifted, drawing a new route. Breathlessly I awaited the answer, knowing that the communications stations had just kicked in, sending a request that had cost me every remaining Action Point I still had.

Reply received.
Enter the new planet's name:_____

Rubicon.

Accepted. The databases have been updated with the new name.
Would you like to lay a route between the Central system and the Rubicon system?

Yes!

New navigational marker set up. Route laid and confirmed.

You've received a new ability: The Follower
The navigational route laid by you has been added to the hyperspace network. Every time it is used to transport a spaceship or a single traveler, you will receive a small number of Action Points for you to use in the future, allowing you to keep your Colonizer skill.

Quest alert: The Chasm. Quest completed!
You seem to have wasted the resources available to you. At this point, you cannot rescue three civilizations. Come back when you have enough available Action Points necessary to perform colonization.

Now transporting you and the other crew members back on board the Relic.

* * *

Respawn.

The green glow streamed through the air, dissolving slowly.

Reality was still blurring. Charon's far-off growl was drowned out by the hissing and tweeting of the Dargian language.

Roakhmar was beyond himself, furious, disoriented. He lashed out at me, "Zander, I was in the midst of a battle! Give me a good reason or send me back *now*! Otherwise, I swear by the Founders-"

"Cool down. The Darg system has been blocked. I can't send you back. No one can leave it from now on."

"My people!" Roakhmar exclaimed, desperate. "We're struggling to keep the last citadel of our Clan, and you-"

"I've pulled you out of battle to save all three of our civilizations! Get a grip! Then we'll talk."

Roakhmar stared at me insanely, unable to grasp my actions just like the Phantom Server AI had been.

"Jurgen, I'm sending you the jump settings. We're leaving the Central system ASAP."

"And where, may I ask you," Jurgen raised an eyebrow, "are we going? What kind of planet is it?" he checked against his databases. "Rubicon? Never heard about it!"

"It's our new home," I said wearily.

You've received a new level!
+5 to Charisma!
Three civilizations have accepted you as their

leader.

Now calculating jump settings.

Warning! The AI located in the Rubicon system is not responding. We cannot guarantee the materialization of the ship and its crew at this destination point.

Are you sure you want to continue?

Unhesitantly I uploaded Avatroid's scanner file to the communications station and pressed *Send.*

"Yes," I said. "I'm sure."

Jump coordinates confirmed. Dematerialization in 10... 9... 8...

* * *

THE SECOND PLANET OF THE RUBICON SYSTEM.

THE AIRLOCK of our Raptor hissed open.

A thick blanket of crimson-tinted clouds hung low, heavy with lightning.

We looked around us, speechless.

The planet was primeval. Groups of volcanoes erupted on the horizon. The air temperature was 160 F. To our right, an ocean boiled against a ragged coastline, spewing geysers of steam into the air.

The heavy rain evaporated before it could touch the cracked surface of this lava valley.

Our scanners detected cargonite deposits everywhere, its veins and nuggets small but numerous.

Liori and I approached the edge of the boiling water. The yellow-tinged cliffs oozed a toxic haze. Our sensors were deep in the red.

Roakhmar walked over to us, looking resolute. "Shall we start?"

"Wait a bit. Danezerath is downloading the databases."

"Have you managed to contact the Haash system?" he asked in surprise.

"I have. Since I visited Phantom Server, all my skills and abilities have grown quite a lot."

"But still not enough, have they?" Roakhmar asked haughtily. He was having a hard time coming to grips with his new position, which resulted in occasional bouts of temper.

"None of us can do it alone," Liori replied.

The Dargian shrank his head into his shoulders — a funny habit pointing at his extreme impatience. Never mind. It wasn't the first time we had to work as a team. We'd gel.

"All done!" Jurgen and Danezerath scrambled out of the Raptor. "We've got the databases. We really should keep a safe distance. The ocean might flood the shore."

"That's irrelevant," Roakhmar dug in his heels.

* * *

AFTER A BRIEF DISCUSSION we decided to withdraw further into the valley.

Charon, Vandal and Foggs watched us from afar.

"Make a group," I told the others, "and join your abilities."

Jurgen tilted his head back and froze: a level 120 Technologist.

Liori and I held hands. We were both Mnemotechs, levels 90 and 95 respectively.

Roakhmar stepped back. He was the most advanced of us all. Back on Darg, I'd never had the chance to glean his true power.

Danezerath: a level 80 Mechanic.

Novitsky: a level 57 Exobiologist.

Our minds touched. Slowly our inner estrangement faded as our skills and abilities began to fuse together.

I opened the scanner file I'd made back in the Dargian Temple of Light and uploaded it to the network. "Commence replication."

The ground shuddered. The valley surged with flames. Newborn nanites swirled at a distance, forming a cloud that kept growing, attracting bolts of lightning.

Clouds thickened overhead. The wind grew. A roaring noise came from the ocean.

Jurgen and Danezerath were busy getting the model ready while we created new nanite colonies.

Novitsky was but an observer for the time being. His turn was yet to come.

Billions of nanites spiraled into a vortex. I activated Self-Replication, sending more and more incandescent threads of nanites to feed the swirling twister.

My interface flashed nine-digit numbers. I'd

never have been able to control this number of nanites without Liori and Roakhmar's help.

"The model's completed," Danezerath reported. "No deviations from the scanner file found."

"Databases ready for uploading," Jurgen chipped in.

"Confirm," Novitsky's voice faltered with anxiety.

The level-100 replication matrix — the result of our combined effort — took some time to materialize.

A clap of thunder came first. A few square miles of the valley began to cave in, as if pounded in by an enormous punching fist.

The swirling nanite tornado began to separate into layers. The sky showered earth with lightning bolts.

The earth ran with cracks, releasing subterranean fire.

The area of our manmade disaster spread rapidly, its fiery blister swelling.

The new technogenic environment swallowed us. Our mental images began to structure the nanites. The fire and smoke parted, revealing the yet unstable rippling outline of a device that resembled a giant organic molecule.

Genesis.

The ancient machine, an early child of the Founders' power, capable of transfiguring whole planets.

It had been lost for good, apart from its scanner file I'd copied into my mind expander. Our joint efforts had allowed us to build it anew!

Novitsky, Roakhmar and Danezerath were now uploading their own databases to it — all the information about the biospheres of three different planets.

Their co-existence on one planet was impossible, which was why our colonization zones would have to be separated from each other by force fields.

"All done," Roakhmar's voice was barely audible, exhausted. He was the only one with the skill necessary to program the device.

The planetary transformation machine switched to automatic mode.

It was already busy working. Its antigravs kicked in. The barrage of lightning began to subside. The wind began to abate. The clouds alone hung low over the valley.

* * *

"THIS IS RELIC. Ready for activation," a report came from the orbit.

This was the moment of truth. Rebuilding Genesis and commencing the planet's transformation was only a small part of our plan.

The frigate's long-range communications sprang to life, sending us a very good clear picture.

A black sun hung low over an alien horizon. Its mineral segments emitted radiation invisible to the human eye. Still, I could see it thanks to the Founders' artifact that the Haash had built into the grounded spaceship which now housed the last of them.

The planet's frozen surface shuddered as our

command, transmitted via hyperspace, activated their starship's engines.

The ship settled into the planet's orbit. Obeying my orders, its navigational systems accepted Rubicon's coordinates.

The ship's cruise engines kicked in.

Charon, your turn.

The Haash astronaut quickly found his way around the ship's systems. The temperature in one of its modules began to rise.

Good. We can disconnect now. We'll contact the ship's commander once he awakes from his stasis. At the moment, we've done everything we could.

A mental reply touched my mind,

You're The Friend of the Haash. And so you will remain.

Next.

This time I had Roakhmar working with me.

I'd blocked the Darg system. But later we'd discovered a probe outside its limits. It contained a brief message addressed to us.

We saw the Disciples' last citadel besieged by the Reapers.

The walls of this mountain fortress still held. Its force field emitters continued to work. Nevertheless, its defenders were doomed. The enemy was too numerous, contained solely by plasma blasts that scorched the planet's surface for miles around.

Then the fortress shuddered and began to collapse. Its walls and its towers crumbled, revealing a gigantic spaceship enveloped in a dazzling halo of force shields. A Founders' spaceship.

Its antimatter engines fired up while still within the planet's atmosphere.

Flames enveloped Darg and poured forth into space, momentarily deactivating its orbital blockade.

A few Dargian symbols flashed through my mental view and broke off.

Coordinates accepted. We've made it. Wait for us. We're coming in peace...

Next.

Liori's thoughts emanated warmth, supporting me.

We were on board Wayfarer, flagship of the Third Colonial Fleet.

The complex pattern of stars moved slowly across enormous observation screens.

Destination accepted. Rubicon system coordinates received.

The cluster of combat craft, interstellar stations and link after countless link of cryogenic platforms changed their courses. They carried billions of people, their minds irresponsive in their cryogenic sleep.

* * *

I OPENED MY EYES and met Liori's gaze.

She smiled.

Shall we go on?

Nanites swirled up.

Navigational marker: created
Destination point: created
You've received a new level!
Your Colonizer skill has grown 1 pt.
New nanite control codes available.

Epilogue

Rubicon planet
A year later

THE BUNKER was located deep underground. Every object within, every part of its highly sophisticated equipment was comprised of nanites: the product of a top-level Mnemotechnics skill.

Row after row of identical capsules glowed from the inside. The jagged lines of vital graphs meandered across bio monitor screens.

I opened my eyes.

The inside of the capsule stank of medication. The transparent lid hissed, rising and sliding behind the headrest.

Manipulator arms promptly removed countless sensors from my body.

My vision blurred. Still, I soon regained some energy.

I sat up and looked around me, recognizing the

room. The neighboring capsules were empty. Had I been the last one to wake up?

I wanted to get up, find some clothes and get out onto the surface but an invisible force held me gently back.

Mind expander Synaps Z+: installed
Semantic processor: installed
Reflex enhancer: installed
Metabolic corrector: installed

You can get dressed. The elevator to the surface is located down the corridor.

A couple of minutes later, the elevator whooshed me up into the sunlight.

A road went downhill. I walked unhurriedly, taking in chestfuls of the breeze pregnant with strange smells. The sun stood high in the clear skies.

The air blurred to my right where a force shield protected the human colonization zone.

A new group of colonists had just arrived. They looked around themselves without noticing me: the force shield was opaque from their side.

These were the colonists' avatars. Their hosts were dozens of light years away, on board the Colonial Fleet's cryogenic platforms. They had no idea of survival in an alien environment but their unfailing belief in the safety of respawn would fearlessly confront any potential threat.

They had a lot to learn.

They still had the Founders' interface to master. But first and foremost, they would have to learn how to love and enjoy life.

The road turned again, revealing the ocean.

The beach was filled with the happy screaming of children.

From where I stood, I could already see Frieda and Jurgen.

And Arbido! Didn't he look younger! He must have drained the biological reconstruction chamber dry!

Vandal, Foggs, Novitsky and Ralph stood knee-deep in the water, taking measurements and passionately arguing over something.

Liori sat on the shore. The breeze ruffled her cropped hair. She smiled, watching Charon and five-year-old Inge drawing something in the wet sand.

This was our home for many years to come. We were meant to stay here, waiting for those who were now traversing the depths of space.

Once our colony had grown strong, we could go back to where we'd come from. One day we'd switch our cryo in-modes back on and enter a network address. Earth's address.

The planet that was still breathing its reactors' heat.

But that would be a totally different story.

- End of Book Three -

ANNEX

The MC's final stats:

Zander. Level 162. Colonizer

Main characteristics:

Intellect, 42 (+1 as a semantic processor bonus)
Strength, 30
Willpower, 50
Agility, 20 (+2 as a reflex enhancer bonus)
Perception, 50 (+2 as a mind expander bonus)
Stamina, 55 (+5 as a metabolic corrector bonus)
Learning Skills, 30
Charisma, 5

Skills:

Traveler 1
Assigned upon the first independent interstellar identity matrix transfer.

Pioneer 1
Assigned upon the landing on a planet which

has either been unexplored or whose information has been lost.

Interaction
Allows the player to interact with real-life objects

Colonizer 1
Assigns Action Points allowing the player to transport spaceships via hyperspace, lay new routes and create new colonies. May also allow access to the heart of Phantom Server (requires a certain minimum number of AP)

Broken Chains 1
Self-stabilizes your identity matrix (requires a personal navigator)
Allows the player to visit any star system, provided he or she is in possession of its coordinates.

Piloting of Small Spacecraft, 30
Allows the player to fly fighter, assault and small cargo craft

Piloting of Medium and Large Spacecraft, 20
Allows the player to fly corvettes, frigates, cruisers and their formations

Combat Maneuvering, 45
Also allows the player's ship to enter a planet's atmosphere

Navigation, 39
Allows the player to lay courses and calculate

optimal routes

Mechanic, 5:
Repairs
Allows the player to repair any equipment he or she is familiar with
Equipment building
Allows a player to build new devices by combining parts of any equipment he or she is familiar with

Science, 98
Allows the player to create scanner files, read power imprints, modify existing devices and create replication matrices from known samples (requires Mnemotechnics skill)

Alien Technologies, 55 (allows the player to study alien equipment)

Mnemotechnics, 95 (Each Mnemotechnics point gives a player two points for developing his or her Mnemotechnic skill)
Allows the player to use his or her Mnemonic abilities and receive nanite control codes

Technologist, 30 (allows the player to connect to technology databases)

Exobiologist, 1 (allows the player to connect to exobiology databases)

Combat skills, 49:
Light weapons

Heavy weapons
Energy weapons
Accuracy
Critical hits, 4 (+40% to the possibility of dealing critical damage to the enemy)
Defense, 3 (lowers all incoming damage 30%)

Mnemotechnic skills:

Replication, 25 (on your command, a small group of nanites uses a selected source material to self-reproduce until the total number of nanites reaches 100,000)

Self-Replication, 1 (nanites are preset to seek new source materials and create new colonies)

Steel Mist, 10 (protects you from enemy scanners)

Active Shield, 10 (requires a Founders' neuronet module)
Allows nanites to automatically react to any threat by forming a protective cover. Expends both energy and nanites quickly.

The Call, 20 (brings available nanite groups under your control, including small numbers of enemy nanites)

Differential Nanite Control, 1 (requires a Founders' neuronet module).
Allows simultaneous control of up to 10 nanite groups which have been assigned different tasks.

Object Replication, 19 (allows the use of available nanites and power to build working copies of various devices)

Piercing Vision, 15 (allows the dispatch of nanite groups on reconnaissance missions with further reception of data from them in real time)

Global Network, 1 (allows the scanning of star systems using the hyperspace network)

Disintegration, 15 (destroys molecular bonds in a selected object)

Plasma Blast, 15 (allows a selected nanite group to self-destruct, forming a cloud of ionized gas)

Plasma Lash, 9 (requires a generator built by Object Replication)

Self-Sacrifice 10 (allows your nanites to self-destruct in order to exterminate enemy nanites)

Integration, 5 (allows you to upgrade your weapons and gear)

Advanced Integration, 14 (allows you to upgrade complex equipment, including spaceships' subsystems)

Nanite Deactivation, 1 (requires an emergency control code to deactivate enemy nanite groups)

System failure, 5 (temporarily disables cybernetic parts of a selected device)

Breakdown, 5 (temporarily disables moving parts of a selected device)

Critical Damage, 9 (permanently disables moving parts of a selected device)

ALSO BY ANDREI LIVADNY:

Edge of Reality (Phantom Server Book #1)

He is a cyber dweller. A gamer who's grown up in the web of virtual illusion woven from hundreds of phantom worlds. His biggest dream is to dump the real world for good.

His desperate hunger of new experiences forces him to take a risk and become one of the first proud owners of a neuronet implant. The new gadget becomes part of him — but soon it's not enough. If only he could finally burn all his bridges and make a step beyond the real world!

He soon gets this opportunity. A new universe, overflowing with mystery and unimaginable, mind-blowing authenticity, opens up before him.

This is Phantom Server. The game of the future where your pursuit of an adrenaline rush soon turns into a battle for survival. But the most terrifying mystery lies ahead when you gradually start to realize: this is a road of no return. Your every decision may become your last. Your every step leads you further along the abyss between life and death.

The Eurasia fleet has entered the Darg star system. The unsuspecting players look forward to the adventure of their lifetimes. Zander alone is now facing a harsh and unpredictable "alternative storyline".

The girl he loved is gone. His nervous system is impregnated with artificial neurons that contain fragments of ancient AIs and their identities. Zander's body is implanted with alien artifacts that allow him to survive in the deadly cyberspace of Phantom Server. But his unique development branch pushes him toward the edge of the precipice where his every step may become his last; where future itself is vague and uncertain.

The Island of Hope

An intergalactic war has scorched dozens of planets and destroyed millions of lives, leaving in its wake dead carcasses of drifting spacecraft where desperate battles used to unfold. These are perilous places unfit for habitation... or are they?

About the Author

Andrei Livadny is a popular Russian science fiction author. Born on May 27 1969 in the city of Pskov, he was an avid reader from an early age. But it was the Russian translation of Robert A. Heinlein's *The Orphans of the Sky* that decided his choice of future occupation. The story has become a pivotal moment in the boy's life, leaving a lasting impression on him.

Andrei wrote his first book at the age of eight. Since then, he's never stopped working on new books. His passion for science fiction has gradually become his career.

In 1998, Andrei debuted in Russia's leading publishing house EKSMO with his novella *The Island of Hope*. Since then, he has penned over 90 books that have enjoyed a total of 153 editions.

Andrei has created several unique worlds, each unlike the previous. He wrote *A History of Our Galaxy* with humanity itself as a protagonist. This sixty-book series creates a history of our future civilization and its contacts with alien races, forming a convincing and logical picture of humanity's development for two millennia from now.

Besides hard science fiction, Andrei Livadny also works in cyberpunk genres which allow him to focus on human relationships and raise questions about artificial intelligence and identity uploading, describing cyberspace as humanity's future environment.

The English translation of *A History of Our Galaxy* will be available shortly.

Want to be the first to know about our latest LitRPG, sci fi and fantasy titles from your favorite authors?

Subscribe to our NEW RELEASES newsletter:
http://eepurl.com/b7niIL

Thank you for reading *Black Sun!*
If you like what you've read, check out other LitRPG
novels published by Magic Dome Books:

Dark Paladin LitRPG series by Vasily Mahanenko:
The Beginning
The Quest

**The Dark Herbalist LitRPG series
by Michael Atamanov:**
Video Game Plotline Tester
Stay on the Wing

The Neuro LitRPG series by Andrei Livadny:
The Crystal Sphere
The Curse of Rion Castle

**The Way of the Shaman LitRPG series
by Vasily Mahanenko:**
Survival Quest
The Kartoss Gambit
The Secret of the Dark Forest
The Phantom Castle
The Karmadont Chess Set
The Hour of Pain (a bonus short story)

Galactogon LitRPG series by Vasily Mahanenko:
Start the Game!

Phantom Server LitRPG series by Andrei Livadny:
Edge of Reality
The Outlaw
Black Sun

**Perimeter Defense LitRPG series by Michael
Atamanov:**
Sector Eight
Beyond Death
New Contract

Mirror World LitRPG series by Alexey Osadchuk:
Project Daily Grind
The Citadel
The Way of the Outcast

AlterGame LitRPG series by Andrew Novak:
The First Player

The Expansion (The History of the Galaxy) series
by A. Livadny:
Blind Punch

Citadel World series by Kir Lukovkin:
The URANUS Code

The Game Master series by A. Bobl and A.
Levitsky:
The Lag

The Sublime Electricity series by Pavel Kornev
The Illustrious
The Heartless
Leopold Orso and the Case of the Bloody Tree

Moskau *(a dystopian thriller)* by **G. Zotov**

Memoria. A Corporation of Lies
(an action-packed dystopian technothriller)
by Alex Bobl

Point Apocalypse
(a near-future action thriller)
by Alex Bobl

You're in Game!
(LitRPG Stories from Bestselling Authors)

The Naked Demon (a paranormal romance)
by Sherrie L.

In order to have new books of the series translated faster, we need your help and support! Please consider leaving a review or spread the word by recommending *Black Sun* to your friends and posting the link on social media. The more people buy the book, the sooner we'll be able to make new translations available.

Thank you!

Till next time!